THE RUNNING DIARIES
BY JOHN TRAINOR

PART I

Chapter One

John Trainor, July 2019

I'm a pretty quiet guy by nature. Typically, I'll sit back in a group of new people, listen and react. But for whatever reason, when the situation presents itself, I love to make speeches. I guess it's because I think of myself as a writer and as a story teller. Frankly, those are two of my only skills. So if I have the chance to use them to make someone smile or to help fight for a worthy cause, I do it. And I'm excited about it.

That's how I ended up here: shuffling nervously with my papers, preparing to present my defense for the Bloomsburg Men's Cross Country and Track and Field teams. We were set to be dissolved, cut from the budget, and we were doing everything we could to try and keep our squads on the books. Our protesting to date hadn't made much impact and, considering the slashes happening around us, things didn't look particularly promising for us Huskies.

I suppose using the term "us" is a little misleading. I'm actually no longer a part of Bloomsburg's team. Or a member of its student body in general. I graduated in May and, in all technical senses of the word, became an independent individual. But, in this wacky sport, the line between team and individual is usually a little blurry. I mean don't get me wrong, I'm mortal enemies with all the other schools in the PSAC and will hate them until the day I die. But if I see one of them out on a run, I'll give them a cordial nod rather than a punch in the face. Unless it's Ryan Phillips. He's the exception.

What I'm trying to say is that, ultimately, runners are all a community. We are each working toward the same goal: to be the best version of ourselves we can be. Even if there's animosity, there's at least respect. Except, of course, Ryan Phillips. Never Ryan Phillips.

So even though this budget cut doesn't affect me directly, I felt compelled to do something for my future runners who would be following in my all too literal footsteps. And so I spoke.

"Track certainly has intrinsic value. It's a really fun sport-most of the time anyway. You go out every race and try to push your body to its absolute limits. There's no loop holes or short cuts. It's just run fast. Jump high. Throw far. That's competition in its purest form.

"But track's greatest value is in the life lessons it teaches to its athletes. You need to be dedicated. You need to be disciplined. You need to make sacrifices. When someone offers you the chance to make a bad decision-anything from staying out all night to taking illicit substances-it can give you another reason to say no. It takes balance, time management and work ethic to achieve success. Therefore, it's not a surprise that our Cross Country and Track teams have the highest GPAs in the entire school."

I felt like this was a good line to really hammer my point home. Grades are supposed to be important in school, right? I took a moment to let that sentence sit. One of the older members of my audience picked his nose. I may have overestimated the line's value.

"A lot of people complain that our generation is too entitled and expects everything to just be handed to them without any work. Well, there's no better way to teach people about hard work than the sport of track and field. It takes constant training-tireless labor-to excel. If you slack off, you will get beat. Plain and simple.

"Socially it can be critical as well. Again, what people say our generation is missing can be found within cross country. When you go on a run with your teammates, it's just you guys out there. We can't run with lap tops. There's no texting each other. It's just you and your friends having a conversation. Learning. Growing. Communication in its most simplistic and cherished form."

Appealing to the good old days. That was sure to get at least a nod of approval from these baby boomers on the committee. I looked over at the nose-picker. He flicked his booger across the room. It could have been worse. At least he was awake, unlike the guy it landed on.

"Anyone who has ever competed on a track or cross country team understands the unique attitude of these runners. The sport naturally allows you to enjoy everyone's successes. Sure, there is a competitive fire to win and score points for your team, but there is also a joy that comes from watching hard working teammates set big personal bests. Or fighting with a rival and pushing each other under a big time barrier for the first time.

"When another team or athlete does well, we are happy for them. And the converse is certainly true as well."

So there were the pillars. It seemed like maybe a few people were buying what I was selling. But, overall, I suspect people's minds were generally made up. I suppose I shouldn't have been surprised. Oh well, might as well bring it home.

"Just to be clear, I'm not lobbying for other sports to be cut instead. All sports have their place. My track is someone else's tennis. Or golf. Or football. And why would I want to take away their passion? But I do hope that fans of other sports can see that my passion is the same as theirs. Even if my sport is more boring or less mainstream, it doesn't mean my love of the game is any less important. That the lessons and skills that come out of my sport are any less significant. Right now, athletes are fighting an uphill battle and we need *everyone's* support.

"I hope that we can all remember the pillars of track and field. Competition in its purest form. Communication in its purest form. Humanity in its purest form. And if that's not worth saving, I'm not really sure what is."

***

"So it turns out nothing's worth saving." The boy to my left took a long swig of his beer. We each had our own coping mechanisms. While he drank quickly from his glass, I sat staring absentmindedly into my own, as if I could somehow find a couple thousand dollars to solve my problem if I searched diligently enough. Surprisingly, that's not where they're hiding the money.

Just a few hours after my fervent defense of our cross country program, I posted up at a local bar with my best friend and Co-captain Gary Fox, mourning its demise. Yes, I know it's hard to believe, but a well-crafted think piece wasn't enough to change the hard line facts of an increasingly bankrupt state government or a consistently underappreciated sport. Ok, so the word "underappreciated" may have some bias to it, but if you thought I was going to play this perfectly neutral, I haven't sufficiently introduced myself.

"If it makes you feel any better, I thought your speech was really good," Gary said comfortingly. The statement itself didn't make me feel any better, but the intent behind it helped a little bit. "Can you print me out a copy?" His direct question forced me to speak for the first time since we sat down.

"Yeah."

But he was going to have to work harder than that to get a full sentence.

"Cool," he polished off his beverage and stood up from the table. "And you might as well drink it, Train. Can't get drunk with your eyes." Nothing about my behavior changed. He stared to walk away, but added "When I get back, I'm buying you another one."

I hate it when he buys me another one. Something about the principle of not letting things go to waste makes me feel obligated to finish it-even when I don't want or need it. That's why my 21st birthday ended with a sobbing phone call to my mother from the dormitory bathroom floor. No, I won't be elaborating. I've already divulged too much.

After a few short moments, someone slid back on the seat beside me. Figuring it was Gary, I decided not to look up from my relatively untouched beverage.

"You lose something in there?" It was a female voice, so I was pretty sure it wasn't Gary. Unless he had gotten way better at impersonations. I raised my head, looking into the face of a pretty girl with brunette hair. By now I was at least 99 percent sure this wasn't Gary.

"No … uh … I know it's just beer in there," I replied, my voice cracking slightly from lack of use. I think it's my clever wit that helped me win over so many women during my collegiate years.

"Is everything alright? I'm just guessing here, but something seems wrong."

"Yeah … it's a long story." I looked back over toward the bathroom, wondering how quickly Gary might re-emerge. "I should probably tell you that my friend-"

"Oh, I know," she replied. "He's over there talking to my friend." She pointed to another girl, about the same age, with red hair and freckles. She was indeed talking to Gary. Her story checked out. "To be perfectly honest, I'm just here to hold down the fort until he gives her his number." She added bluntly. Looking a little closer, her friend did look a bit more recognizable. I think she was in my calculus class or something. "So, you might as well tell me your long story."

"Well, if you're gonna be stuck listening to me talk, I should probably buy you a drink." I caught the eye of the bartender. This was about as smooth as I could possibly hope to be.

"That's OK, I'll pay for my own. I don't want to lead you on or make it seem like I'm interested in you."

Super. I took my first big swig from my cup. I needed it. She ordered a drink of her own and then turned back to me. "So, let's hear it." I looked across the room at Gary. He was smiling and laughing. I'm not super well versed in the bro code, but I'd wager breaking that pair apart would violate it.

"Today I spoke in front of some of Bloomsburg's board members, trying to get them to reconsider cutting the Men's Cross Country and Track and Field teams. But they didn't."

In retrospect, it really wasn't that long of a story.

"We had a cross country skiing team here?" My new drinking mate asked, looking astonished. "No wonder they decided to defund it. There's been like no snow."

"No, Cross Country *running*." I tried my best to be civil, but it felt like her words had been a personal attack on my family. "You've never heard of it?"

"Nope. What is it?"

"Have you ever done, like, a local 5k road race?" She nodded. "Well, it's a lot like that. Except instead of running on streets, you run across terrain. Hills, grass, mud, things like that."

"Oooh, so it's like a Spartan-"

"No, it's not a Spartan race. There's no obstacles to climb or anything. It's strictly running based."

"Do they still spray you with colors?"

"No," I was becoming increasingly agitated, now starting to fidget in my chair. "It's not some gimmick driven event. It's about racing head to head against the guy next to you. Whoever is stronger and faster is gonna win. Simple as that."

"Sounds boring. But I don't really like sports much." She shrugged. I smiled weakly before looking back over toward Gary. I was grateful to see he was heading back this way. She noticed it too and, I'm sure equally relieved, prepared for her exit. "Well, nice meeting you, uh …"

"John," I filled in for her.

"Stacy." She lingered for another second before standing, "Good luck with your-well-your not a Spartan race."

"Thanks." I looked down to take another drink of my beer. When I looked back up, Gary had filled her vacated space, causing me to double take in confusion.

"She seemed kinda cute. Did you get her-what's got you in such a huff?" He changed tone, noticing my disgruntled tearing at the paper on the outside of my bottle.

"Nothing," I replied, tossing a moist scrap onto the counter. "So, who were you talking to?"

"This girl Elizabeth. I tutored her last semester in like Calculus class or something … She kept trying to get me to give her my number." He finished sourly.

"What's wrong with that? You like her, don't you?"

"Not really."

"But I saw you! You were smiling and laughing."

"Nah dude, I was giving you the signal! You couldn't tell that was the fake laugh with the 'save me' eyes?"

"No. Because that's not a thing."

"It's a thing."

I sighed and went back to picking apart my label. "So what did you do?"

"I gave her my number." Gary said flatly. "Not like I had much of a choice. She had me cornered" He looked at me carefully. "I'm guessing your experience didn't go much better?"

"We didn't have a lot in common."

"So she hates running?"

"I didn't say that."

"Well it's the only interest you have, so I figured it out." I opened my mouth to respond, but, admittedly, he had made a good point. "At least she got you to drink half of your beer. That's a positive."

"Why do people not get Cross Country?" I blurted out in frustration the question I had been deliberating the whole night. "Like … nobody cares."

"You're just figuring this out?"

"No, I guess not … But I just thought maybe, if I could teach people more about the sport, get them to really understand what it's about-"

"You're going about it the wrong way. The sport in and of itself, it's fine, but what makes it truly great is the people. The journey. The struggle. You can't just *make* people understand that. They have to experience it." Gary reached over and grabbed the beer from my hands. "And people aren't exactly going to line up for that." He tipped the bottle back and chugged the rest of the drink before placing it back on the counter. "Now, c'mon let's get out of here."

Walking away from the bar and toward the exit, we went past the two girls we had interacted with earlier that night. I gave a polite wave, but Gary ushered me forward to make sure we didn't get caught in another conversation. While we pushed ahead, I noticed Gary's ex-tutee's shirt for the first time. Printed across the front in orange text were the words "Vikings Field Hockey". Seeing them flash in front of me as I was dwelling on Gary's last monologue made something click in my mind.

"Gary," I reached out and grabbed his arm. "Did Elizabeth go to Union Valley High School?"

"I don't know," He said, continuing forward unperturbed, "Maybe. That does sounds vaguely familiar." We exited the building and trudged back up the road toward our apartment, conveniently located just a few minutes away.

"I'm gonna need you to call her." I said decisively.

"You're kidding right? Didn't we just over this?" Gary shook his head. "We move out next month and then my goal is to never see her again."

"This is important. I've got an idea."

"Unless it's as good as our DadHat YouTube series, I don't care."

We continued our journey down the road before turning east onto a darker side road. Although Gary said he didn't care, I knew him better than that. His curiosity would eventually cause him to break down and ask about my idea. It'd probably take a couple days, maybe even a week, but in the end he'd-

"OK, fine. What do you want?" Gary asked sounding defeated. Wow, he broke even quicker than expected. With a rush of excitement, I turned to him and firmly relayed my request.

"I need you to help me get in contact with Jimmy Springer."

Jimmy Springer, November 5th 2016

Anticipation and nervousness. He was anxious more so than eager. At some level, he was excited about the opportunity to race again. He had always been a fierce competitor. But certainly this was different than how he had felt when he first trekked to Hershey as a freshman. He was so much freer back then. There was no pressure. No weight of expectation.

As Jimmy walked along the course, he was followed by the usual stares and whispers. Trying to ignore it, he made his way toward the finish line. Although there was a crowd, he was tall enough to see over top. It was a decent enough view of the small school competitors sprinting their way down the straightaway. Grimaces of pain were etched across their faces as waves of athletes raced to the line. He watched as a skinny, brown-haired boy in a purple jersey powered his way past a pack, his head rolling wildly and spit flying from his lips. As he hit the finishing mat, his legs buckled and he went flying off to the left. There, he crawled on all fours to the side of the course and vomited. He looked at him curiously.

"Jimmy c'mon, let's go!"

He snapped his gaze away from the post-race carnage and turned his back on the scene. Then, he gracefully broke into stride.

Chapter Two

John Trainor, July 2019

I know you may not believe me considering the first story I told you, but I really don't get angry about much. For the most part, I'm an easy going guy. But the phone call that I received two days after the official death sentence of our cross country team really got me pissed off. Allow me to elaborate.

"Who was that?" Gary asked as he watched my phone fly across the room and into the couch.

"It was Bloomsburg," I replied, angrily stalking into the room behind the airborne communication device. "Asking me to make a donation to the school."

"Please tell me you're kidding."

"I wish," I slouched down on the couch, wincing slightly as I realized my phone lay in a, well, *inconvenient* location beneath me. "Has it even been two months? I still don't have a full-time job yet."

"They're desperate," Gary responded calmly. "You of all people should understand that." His reasonableness really bothered me. Why couldn't he jump onboard with my irrational rage like a true friend?

"Well, I'll tell you one thing, if I ever do have the money to donate, I'm not giving it blindly to the school," I said, repositioning myself into a more comfortable position, "Otherwise, instead of it going to something important, they'll just use it to build some science building or something."

"Yeah, that would be terrible," Gary said sarcastically. He clicked away at his phone, typing out a message.

"Who are you texting?" I asked, pulling out my laptop from my backpack.

"That girl Elizabeth from the bar," Gary replied.

"Still? Dude, you know you're off the hook right? You already got me Springer's number. I'm all set. I'm meeting up with him in a couple weeks."

"Yeah I know." He shifted uncomfortably in his chair. "We just, uh, hit it off when we went out the other night. So I think we're going to do it again."

"That's great dude!" I resisted the urge to ask the questions on the tip of my tongue and instead just be positive. I could see Gary felt awkward about his change of heart so rather than press, I changed the subject. "Do you know how to easily search on the LetsRace forums?" I said, clicking around on my laptop.

"I just usually google whatever it is I'm looking for and then add 'LetsRace' on the end of it." He got up and joined me on the couch. "What is it you're looking for?"

"I'm just doing some research for the interview. I feel like there must be a ton of discussion topics about Jimmy Springer. Especially from high school. You can't avoid landing on some spirited debate between anonymous trolls."

"Ah, sounds like LetsRace," Gary said, pocketing his phone and leaning back on the couch. "Should we be concerned that the most popular website for discussing our sport is crawling with some of the sketchiest internet users in the world?"

"I don't think it's all bad. I've learned some interesting stuff … Plus you remember the 100 lions vs. 20 snakes thread?"

"Yeah," Gary replied reminiscently, "How'd that ever get up to 20 pages? Everyone knows the lions would win."

"You're kidding, right?" I replied, sitting up in outrage. As I did so, I sat back on top of my phone, causing a brief spark of pain. But it didn't depress my passion. "The snakes are easily the choice."

"No way, dude. These are lions we are talking about. They are the *kings* of the animal kingdom, they can't be taken down by some stupid snakes."

"Um, excuse me, but these aren't 'stupid snakes'. This is a group of the most bad-ass venomous reptiles in the world. Lions aren't gonna just roll over these guys. You're perception of snakes is too limited."

"There's only 20 of them!" Gary was now standing up, unable to stay seated in the midst of this important philosophical debate between a pair of recent college graduates. Your tuition dollars at work. "They've got the snakes outnumbered five to one!"

"Well I'm glad you can at least do basic math seeing as your other calculations have been way off base."

"Have you watched The Lion King recently?"

"Have you watched Anaconda recently?"

Gary paused, distracted from the fervor of battle. "Have you?"

"No, you know that I scare easily," I replied defensively, "I deduced all I need to know from those trailers. Ice Cube was no match for that monster!"

"I'm beginning to fear we may have strayed from the point."

"I'm going to be honest, I completely forgot what we were talking about." I had become quite invested in this whole lions vs. snakes thing. "Oh, right! Jimmy Springer." Typing out on the computer I yielded some search results. I clicked through the links as Gary watched from over my shoulder.

"My goodness, you'd think this guy was some major celebrity the way people talk about him." Gary remarked, reading some of the thread titles, "It goes from *Springer Wins State Title #5: Greatest Ever?* to a year later

Jimmy Springer: Most Overrated Runner of All-Time. Hard to believe all this craziness for just a high school track and field runner."

"Yeah, he really went through the gauntlet on there." I clicked into a topic labeled *Time for Springer to Hang Up Spikes?* and began to recite some of the more distinctive comments. "*Jimmy was a great runner, but his time at the apex of our sport is over. Time to make way for the new guys in PA. Maybe he can retool and have success in college.*"

"*Springer is solid, but he doesn't make guys better,*" Gary read, "*There aren't even five guys on his cross country team while King and Miller have squads that are competing for state championships.* Yikes. Or wait, how about this one: *I've heard he's very cocky. Probably bought into his own hype. Now the rumor is he's going to transfer to Coatesville and make some kind of super team.* What is this guy-Kyrie Irving? Why does everyone care?"

"You've got to understand, us PA high schoolers, we take our distance running very seriously. I mean some people get pretty obsessive about this stuff." I closed the internet browsers, finished looking through the ringer of material on this teenage prodigy. Instead, I opened up a word document.

"I guess that makes sense. How many views does your blog get again?"

"When the postseason comes around it's usually a couple thousand hits a day." I replied. He was referring to my distance running blog, TrainHard, which I had started in high school as a passion project to cover the Pennsylvania High School scene. Now, even years removed from school myself, people still flocked to the site and I kind of felt obligated to keep it around. It gave me something of a purpose.

Of course, now I had something new to give me a sense of purpose. I considered my computer screen for a moment. As of now all I had was a title across the first page. That purpose thing's still a work in progress.

Jimmy Springer, August 2013

"Are you excited for today?" James Springer asked his son. Jimmy nodded enthusiastically from the passenger seat next to his father.

"A little nervous though," he said smiling sheepishly. It was briefly silent. He turned away from his father to stare out the window, letting his thoughts wander. "What if ... What if I'm the worst one?" He felt silly asking, but he felt it was necessary to stop the squirming in his stomach. After a moment, he took a quick glance back at his father, who was smiling.

"In every race, somebody has to finish last. Even the Olympics."

His son frowned. "When I become a dad, am I only going to be able to speak in cliché?" They laughed as James made the turn into the high school. A few other students were already standing at the edge of the parking lot, one looking small and nervous: exactly as Jimmy felt on the inside. He must have been another freshman.

"Do you have your physical form?"

"Yeah, it's in my shorts pocket." He removed it as proof while his father pulled into a parking spot. With the car in park, James could finally take a moment to look down at his son. He fidgeted slightly under his father's gaze. "Alright ... Well I'll see you after practice?" Jimmy turned to open the door.

"Jim, don't be scared of being the slowest. The real pressure is on whoever is the fastest." He grinned and gave his son a wink.

"Haha ... Well luckily I don't think I'm going to have to worry about that." And with a quick wave goodbye, he shut the door, leaving to walk nervously toward the growing group of runners gathering by the grass.

"We'll see."

John Trainor, August 2019

When you see somebody online or on TV, they never look quite the same as they do in person. Meeting Jimmy Springer was no exception. He was taller than I expected, his hair a bit more unwieldy, but what really struck me was his body composition. He was incredibly skinny, but also quite toned and muscular. Maybe skinny isn't the right word, perhaps more lean? There was essentially no fat on his body. No unnecessary bulk. He was built for speed.

Things were a bit awkward when I first started the interview. Not because of him. He was cool. I, on the other hand, was a little star struck. I get nervous. The same thing happened to me at the Millrose Games when I was waiting right behind Bernard Lagat in the snack bar line. I wanted to say something, even if it was just a "big fan" or an "I love you", but I lost the words in my throat. I didn't say anything. I think I was breathing pretty loudly though. If that counts for something.

The good news is, unlike that snack bar line, it was a bit harder for Jimmy to escape and a bit more difficult for me to stand idly by without saying anything. And so we eventually got comfortable with one another and the interview could begin with my personal favorite opening question.

"So how did you get your start in running?" I asked, flipping on the record button and placing the device between us. He pondered for a brief second before launching in to a surprisingly well-polished response. I suppose I wasn't the only one who liked to use this question.

"When I was like six or seven, I started playing organized sports. I remember I was in this soccer league with my buddy Riley Joseph ... The first game we scored so many goals, we made half the opposing team cry. The parents tried to separate us after that actually, but Riley's dad protected us. He knew we liked playing together and said this league was supposed to be about having fun. Why split us up in a league where we weren't even supposed to keep score?

"It made sense, but a lot of times people aren't reasonable. They hated us after that. They targeted us during games, slide tackling at our legs, checking us when the refs weren't paying attention. When you're on top, there's only one place for you to go. And literally, everybody else wants to move up and take your spot."

Jimmy gave me a lot of gems for quotes. If I felt like he had more to say, I tried to just listen quietly and let him talk. It was fascinating and every sentence helped to paint a slightly better picture of this kid's life.

"I played soccer for a while with good success. In middle school, our local club team made it to the regional finals. We went up against these kids from this town called Coatesville. At this point, I'd gotten a bit of a reputation. I scored a hat trick in the semis and so a few coaches in the area came out to the finals just to see what I could do. It got me pretty fired up, seeing the big crowd, competing on this special field. Both my parents came.

"It quickly became apparent Coatesville had prepared for me specifically. They picked me out of the line-up right away. Every time I touched the ball, they sent multiple guys at me. It was miserable. Early in the game, I would pass out of it and try to get my teammates going since they were so wide open. But that didn't work. After that I became increasingly frustrated to the point where I was forcing the issue, trying to do too much. We ended up losing 1-0. I can still remember crying the whole ride home to Union Valley."

We had some similar traits. I think a lot of runners have that competitive drive, that deep rooted hatred of losing. But we were different as well. He wasn't quite as laid back and easy going as a lot of guys I knew. When we are racing, most runners are obviously serious and focused, but when you step back there's typically a lot of joking and laughing. I couldn't say for sure at this point, but Jimmy seemed a bit more stoic. It was hard to imagine him joining in on some of the pranks we pulled on one another at Bloomsburg.

"I learned to be self-sufficient at a young age. Whenever I wanted to go somewhere that wasn't too far away, I would just run there. Once, I was out jogging over to Riley's house and I ran by this guy gardening in the front lawn. When he saw me go by, he snapped up and called out to try and get my attention. I didn't hear him, so I just kept going." Jimmy smiled at the memory, a brief window into his lighter side. "Then, the guy starts chasing after me on foot, trying to get me to stop. It was one of the creepiest things." He laughed.

"I guess he did some research on me or something because the next day he showed up at the middle school. He was hanging out with one of my science teachers when I walked into Chem class. At the time it was actually really scary because I thought he was this stalker or something. But turns out this was all part of the charm of Coach Ames." He shook his head, still continuing to grin.

"He was the high school track coach and so he urged me to go out for the middle school team in the spring. He said it would be a great way to stay in shape and develop speed for my first high school soccer season. I liked that idea a lot. I knew I had to get a lot better if I was going to come back and beat those Coatesville kids."

"So what changed your mind?" I asked, "Did track just come more naturally to you?"

"Hell no," Jimmy responded with a chuckle. "My first race was this 800 against our neighboring school Spring Ford. The coaches told me I had to run two laps around the track. Seemed easy enough. I went out the first lap and just sprinted right to the front. I mean why not? It was only two laps. I opened up this big lead over the next guy. When I went through the first lap, I remember everybody was watching me in awe. It felt good.

"And then on that second lap, I tied up *so* badly. I remember I just stopped being able to lift my legs. It was so painful. But I needed to get across that line first. I fought as hard as I could to hold it together, until, with maybe 50 meters to go, some other kid went passed me. I got second. Right then, I vowed that was never going to happen again. And, the rest of the season, it didn't."

"So after that, no more soccer?"

"Yeah, once that track season ended I was hooked. What I liked most was the fact that, no matter how good I got, nobody could double team me. They couldn't use trick plays or gimmicks. If they were going to beat me, there was only one way to do it: running faster."

"Well, it seems like you made the right decision. Considering your freshman success, I'd assume it was smooth sailing from there?"

"Eh, not exactly. I had a lot of regrets at first. With the older guys, I had trouble fitting in, especially considering how fast I was. Generally, people don't like the idea of getting smoked by the freshman."

"Really? Did they bully you?"

"I guess technically, yeah. There was some name calling and stuff, but what hurt most was the fact that I wasn't included. I got left out of pre-meet events and weekend hang outs. Things didn't turn for me until I had that first real friend. So eventually, I did start to feel comfortable.

"But things that first year were always … complicated."

"3:01 … 3:02 … 3:03 …"

"What the heck, Springer?" the boy spat between gasps for breath.

"I knew you were an idiot, but I didn't think you were deaf, too."

"Don't be bitter because you can't hang at five minute pace …"

"Oh wow Glenn, I thought Coach was the only one on Boy Wonder's d-"

"C'mon let's jog, we don't have a lot of recovery left," Glenn cut across his teammate as the group began a labored jog back towards the opposite end of the track. Jimmy trotted along in awkward silence. He had yet to say a word all practice.

High School is a unique time. It's a mix of 18-year-old, legal man-children and 14-year-old barely teenage boys who are still fascinated by facial hair. Most of the time these entities are separated by the boundaries of grade level, but on the cross country team there was no such distinction. When you get on the course, it's one race and the fastest man wins. No matter what your birth certificate says.

"It's about how big they are, not how much hair you got on 'em" Glenn Fisher said in between breathes as he and his younger teammate slowly jogged around lane six of the track. Jimmy managed to squeeze a laugh in between his panting. "We are a good team. You make us better. Anyone who can't accept that should get out of the way." They reached the 200 start line and stopped, turning to wait for a trio of other runners. None of whom looked particularly happy.

"30 more seconds boys." Coach Ames was checking his watch, looking up at the incoming stragglers. The newcomers reluctantly lined up alongside Glenn and Jimmy. "Not you, Springer," Coach Ames pulled his freshman stand out by the back of his t-shirt. One of the older runners looked back and smirked. Jimmy looked sullen.

"Coach I'm fine, just let me-" He tried to argue, but Ames cut across him.

"Three ... Two ... One ... Hit it boys!" The quartet set off without their youngest member, leaving coach and athlete alone in tense silence. Once the runners rounded the first curve, clearing themselves from earshot, Coach Ames turned to Jimmy and gave him an understanding look. Speaking softly he said, "Jimmy, has anybody ever told you running is 90% mental?"

"Yeah, I've heard."

"Well that's a myth. It's something people who aren't particularly talented made up so that they will believe they can beat somebody they really can't. People who say that are either overly optimistic dreamers or untrustworthy liars."

"But ... You told me that Coach," Jimmy responded sheepishly. To his surprise, his Coach smiled widely.

"So which one do you think I am?" He left Jimmy blinking and confused as he shouted a lap split to the passing runners. Then he turned back to his youngest pupil. "So?"

"Um ... the dreamer?" He mumbled awkwardly. "I -well I don't think you're a lair ..."

"So have a little faith in the plan, Jimmy! You can trust me. I've got big optimistic dreams for your future."

With marginally more patience, he waited.

***

Jimmy rode his bike down the street, moving slowly due to heavy legs. The day's workout was beginning to set in and he was now regretting not taking Fisher's stretching speech more seriously. The sun had already disappeared from the sky before he changed course to circle back toward his home.

He pedaled casually, alternating between the left and right side of the empty road. It was blissful. Alone with his thoughts, enjoying the peaceful silence. He continued down a side street, passing a dog chained to a tree. A man smoking a cigar. A teenager getting out of his car.

"Jimmy! Hey, Jimmy!" The yelling broke his serenity. He let out a deep sigh as he rotated his bike and hit the brakes. He knew the voice and he did not have much interest in talking to the man it belonged to.

"Hey Matt, what's going on," he said emotionlessly as the teenager approached him. The boy strode cautiously yet determinedly forward, making a concerted effort not to look away from Jimmy's eyes.

"Hey ... Um ... What are you doing out this late? Extra cross training?" Matt said awkwardly.

"No, I needed to get out of the house. My parents were fighting and I ..." He didn't feel the need to continue. He had already shared much more than he would have liked.

"Look," Matt pressed on determinedly, disregarding the complaint. "I'm sorry about the way I've been acting toward you. I didn't mean to be such a jerk ... I just ... Well I don't like to lose ... Especially to a freshman ..." He was rambling a bit, but Jimmy could tell his intentions were genuine. "But that's my issue not yours. We need you." He finished confidently.

"Um-thanks. It's not a big deal, really. I'm sure if it was the other way-"

"No, it is a big deal." He reaffirmed. "I don't want you blaming yourself for something that's not your fault." Together they stood in near silence, the sound of a barking dog the only reminder of their location.

"We're going to have a little party at my house for the Eagles game next week. You should come by. All the guys will be there. It can give you a chance to get to know everybody a little better."

Jimmy gave his teammate a searching look. *Am I ready to be friendly with this guy?*

"Um ... I'll try to come. Assuming I don't have too much work."

Matt smiled and took the non-committal response in stride. "Alright, great!"

"Cool, I'll talk to you then. I gotta get back home or my parents will freak." And Jimmy turned his bike to pedal home, his legs a bit lighter than they had been moments before.

Chapter Three

Jimmy Springer, September 2013

"Spikes … uniform … um … what am I forgetting?" He pulled open the top drawer of his bedside table and frantically flipped through a stack of underwear and socks.

"Jimmy, your friend is outside!"

With a final spin around his bedroom, he rushed through the door and down the stairs to his mother.

"Mom, what I am forgetting?" he asked, slightly panicked, as he transferred a rain jacket from his closet into his backpack. She grinned and patted his arm gently.

"Do you have your spikes and your uniform?"

"Yeah, but-"

"Then you're fine," she cut in reassuringly. "Take it from me, the worst thing you can do is overthink things." She ended with another smile and encouraging pat. Jimmy looked into her eyes and managed to weakly return her beam. He swung his pack over his shoulders, gave his mother a hug and turned to make his way outside.

"You guys are coming later, right?" he asked, looking back over his shoulder.

"I wouldn't miss your first invitational!" She paused and checked her watch. "Of course I might have to leave without your father," her tone had become darker, "he's always busy working. You would think maybe for *this-*"

"I get it Mom," Jimmy replied in solemn anger. "I'll see you at 11."

"I'm not feeling too great about this Eagles season man, that Kansas City game was brutal."

Jimmy sat in the front passenger seat alongside teammate Matt Burke as he drove through the neighborhoods towards the high school. The freshman fiddled with his bag nervously while the senior spoke.

"Maybe we need to just put in Foles and see what happens, you know?" Matt looked across at Springer who gave a non-committal shrug.

"Yeah … I'd be willing to train with some baby horses, I guess …"

"Baby horses? What the-no not foals! I'm talking about Nick *Foles.*" Matt pulled his car into the parking lot for the school library, across the street from where the cross country team would catch their bus. "What's up with you, man? Everything ok?"

"Yeah, everything's cool." Jimmy gathered up his backpack and moved to open his door, but Matt locked it. Jimmy flashed him an angry look that was returned with a caring smile.

"C'mon man, just talk to me." He stared at him with his finger hovering over the lock button, "Then I'll let you out."

Jimmy gave a frustrated sigh. "Look man, just open the door." He went to unlock it again, but Matt clicked it shut. "How old are you like 12?!" He whined. Waiting for an unlikely answer to his rhetorical question, he stared at his teammate, but received no response. "What are you waiting for me to say? There's nothing …" he trailed off exasperated. Again he went for the door, but again was denied. "Fine!" he yelled, "You want to know what's wrong?! I'm scared, alright? I'm scared I'm gonna suck or … embarrass myself. Everybody's counting on me and … and I don't want to let everybody down …" he trailed off at the end, his screaming fading into a soft whisper. "Can I get out of the *goddam* car now?"

Matt considered him briefly. "Jimmy, do you think you can run faster being chased by a rabbit or being chased by a black bear?"

"Don't patronize me right now, I'm not-"

"Right, the bear," he pressed on unperturbed, "And you know why? Because you'd be *scared*. Fear doesn't have to be a bad thing; you just have to know how to use it." He unlocked the doors and opened his own, while Jimmy gratefully followed his lead. Matt gathered his drawstring bag and, together, they carefully crossed the street.

"You steal that one from Coach?" Jimmy asked, slightly bemused. He was now beginning to calm down after his initial outburst.

"Hey, come on now. I'm a clever enough guy to come up with something like that on my own." Matt smirked, eyebrows raised. The pair walked together up the sidewalk, carrying their racing gear. The rest of the team had already assembled.

"What took you so long, Burke? You guys doing your nails and gossiping?"

"Yeah we tried out that salon you usually go to. It was pretty good," Matt responded with a grin. He and Jimmy moved to the back of the crowd, which was now arranging themselves into a line for the bus. Coach Ames stood at the front, checking off each runner's names as they stepped on board the vehicle.

"… Fisher … Armstrong … Burke … and Springer …" he made a mark on clipboard after each name. "That's all seven, then. Driver, we are good to go."

Matt took a seat in the back of the bus with a few other runners, while Jimmy took a closer seat behind Glenn Fisher.

"Everything going alright, Jimmy?" Glenn asked as he sat down.

"Yeah, no complaints," he responded, sticking his backpack into the corner of his seat and leaning up against it.

"Excellent news … Great day for a race!" The senior chirped excitedly. His enthusiasm was infectious to the nervous freshman.

Jimmy thought very highly of Glenn. Although he was a bit quirky and awkward at times, he had always encouraged Jimmy to persevere through the harassment he had sometimes faced, becoming a valued and supportive friend. Glenn was also the fastest runner on the team, having finished 23rd at the previous year's state championships. He had a strong work ethic and disciplined approach to the sport that Jimmy particularly admired.

"Hey, so what makes this course so great, Glenn?" Jimmy asked, now ready to discuss the challenge ahead. After a moments silence, he peered over the seat in front of him, looking for an answer. There was a faint sound of music.

"Did you say something?" Glenn pulled out his left ear bud. "Sorry, I kinda have a pre-race music routine …"

"Oh yeah, I was just-nevermind," Jimmy said shrinking back into his seat. *Music. That's what I was forgetting.* He looked around the bus and noticed all his teammates were wired in to a song, some loud, others softer and more relaxing. Feeling suddenly lonely, he withdrew back into his thoughts. As much as he tried to shake it, fear of failure dominated his emotions. *What am I even doing … I don't belong here …*

"What's up, superstar?"

Jimmy was shaken from his revere by the arrival of one of his teammates in the seat next to him.

"Hey Matt … um … what are you-"

"You looked pretty bored over here by yourself. Thought you could use a little company." Jimmy looked at him skeptically. "I promise I won't lock you in the bus."

Jimmy smiled despite himself. "You don't need to, like, listen to music or whatever? Glenn said he has a 'pre-race music routine'."

Burke laughed, "Did he? Classic Fish. You know it is possible to take running *too* seriously." He pulled a granola bar from his pocket. "Personally, I try to have as little in my 'routine' as possible. That way I don't freak out if everything doesn't go 'according to plan'." He added air quotations to the end of the sentence, before unwrapping his snack. "So is Ames going to actually let you race today?"

"Dunno." After being held out of the first two invitationals, Jimmy had raced a pair of dual meets for Union Valley, but both times, he had been instructed to run within a pack. "I hope so."

"I'd bet he does," Matt said confidently. He bit off a piece of his granola bar. "Juzt becayful," he added while finishing chewing. "If you go out too fast on this course, you'll really regret it."

"So what exactly is this course like? Glenn says it's awesome-"

"Hershey? No way dude. This course sucks. It's brutally hilly right at the worst part of the race. Most of the second mile. You have to save something for that stretch. But if you don't get out fast, it narrows super quickly and you'll be wasting energy trying to pass chumps like Armstrong all race." He pointed over his shoulder at one of his teammates, fast asleep in his bus seat.

"Personally, I think it takes a couple tries to get it right." Seeing the intimidated look on Jimmy's face, he added, "But hey, maybe you'll be a natural!"

A few hours later, the Union Valley Cross Country team jogged as a pack of seven along the grass, headed for a bright orange tent. Glenn Fisher and Jimmy Springer were running side by side at the front with a group of five no more than two steps behind.

"… and coming into the final hill, I just thought 'I need three more guys to get on the medal stand' and that's when I found that extra gear. I just think I had a mental edge on the other guys," Glenn was saying to his younger teammate who was listening intently. Meanwhile, a shorter brown haired boy behind them rolled his eyes. The group came to a stop just in front of their coach, who was flipping through notes on a clipboard. His hair stood up at a variety of angles and his glasses were askew, but he was either unaware or unconcerned.

"Take them through drills please, Glenn," he said without looking up from his papers.

"Let's line up guys!" They moved a bit to the right of the tent, giving themselves some room to stretch out. Glenn positioned himself in the middle of the group, with Jimmy to his right. Together they cycled through a set of plyometric drills, with Glenn periodically pausing to comment on someone's technique. Occasionally, Coach Ames would call one of his runners away from the group to privately discuss some last minute tactics. He saved his youngest runner for last.

"Springer!" he called as the boys broke formation to put on their racing spikes. Jimmy wandered nervously over to his Coach, who was standing just out of earshot from the tent. "How you feeling today, Springer? Nervous?"

"A little bit," he said honestly. Coach Ames smiled.

"A little pre-race butterflies never hurt anybody." He looked down briefly at his clipboard. "I've got you and the pack scheduled to try and hit the mile in five minutes. It's a bit quick, but I'd like us to get out over our heads today. It should better prepare us for states."

Jimmy nodded in understanding.

"I told Burke, Armstrong and Dooney the same thing so you should be able to work together." He paused to look up from his notes and meet Jimmy's eyes. "But I'm unleashing you today, Springer. Don't let anybody hold you back the second half of the race." Then, switching from his serious tone, "I've got some money riding on you."

Jimmy smiled as Ames ushered him back to his teammates.

"Spikes and uniforms, gentlemen-we've got ten minutes until the start."

Dropping to the ground, Jimmy quickly switched over his shoes. Most of his teammates were already finished. Matt pulled his jersey from his drawstring bag and placed it around his neck so it hung like a cape down his back.

"You look ridiculous, Burke," the shorter, brown-haired boy said, smiling as he admired Matt's attire. "Or should I say Superman?"

"*Batman*," Matt replied in a deep voice, striking a dramatic pose. "Batman doesn't have super powers, but he's still a hero. It's a metaphor for how I race." The Union Valley boys laughed.

With Jimmy now at the tail end of the group, the Vikings slowly trickled towards the start line, a few runners taking a stride in that direction. Many of the other teams were already in their starting boxes. Race officials were checking them in.

"Union Valley, how many runners?" a shorter mustached man asked as the team filed into box number eleven.

"Seven runners, sir," Glenn answered. The official double-checked the number with a quick head count and then moved on to box ten. Once he had passed, Glenn took a final, loping stride, which Jimmy mirrored. All around him, runners were striding through the grass, some sprinting at full speed, others in a controlled glide. Fans and parents were sprinkled along the sides of the start line, outlining the opening straightaway. Scanning the group, Jimmy located his mother and father holding hands about 100 meters down the straightaway. When they made eye contact, his mother waved vigorously while his father flashed him a thumbs up. Their son beamed back at them.

A whistle sounded from the official, signaling the runners to return to their starting positions. The scatter of Union Valley athletes reassembled within box eleven. Preparing to leave, Coach Ames gave each of his athletes a high five and wished them luck. "I'll see you boys at the mile … Use that fear, gentlemen. Remember, it's easier to run fast when you're being chased by a grizzly bear!" And he dashed away from the pack, sprinting off to his first checkpoint on the course.

Matt and Jimmy made eye contact from within the pack and shared a grin.

"I thought you said you didn't steal that from Coach?"

"I didn't," Matt replied coyly, "I said black bear." He gave Jimmy a wink, before both turned their attention to the starter in the middle of the field.

"Runners …. Take your mark!"

Union Valley had squeezed three runners at the top of their box. Fisher was positioned at the front right, with Burke in the center and Dooney on the left. Springer was tucked in behind Fisher and Burke with Armstrong to his left. The combination of Fisher and Burke made for an intimidating front line; both runners stood well over six feet tall. Although Jimmy had nearly crested six foot himself, he was easily obscured by his longer teammates. Armstrong and Dooney were both quite a bit shorter, but also more muscular and compact. Each leaned forward, one leg in front of the other.

Bang!

At the sound of the gun, the line of runners erupted into a sprint, flowing together on top of one another. Fisher was off the line quickly and had already positioned himself near the lead. Dooney made himself as wide as possible to protect his space as Armstrong followed just behind. Burke and Springer were a bit more jostled, neither able to fully open their long stride amidst the scrum. Moving into the first turn, Burke consciously swung out to the far left, giving himself room to extend. Jimmy did not follow, sitting almost dead center of the thundering herd.

The stampede of harriers continued, rolling through the opening stretch at a quick clip. Union Valley was struggling to form its usual tight pack among the crowd. Jimmy was racing alongside a pair of runners in green and white jerseys and, while going around a slight turn, he could see there were two more from the same team just behind. Ahead of him, he could see the tall figure of Glenn Fisher bobbing at the front of the field. Glenn was only five or ten seconds in front of Jimmy, but to the freshman it seemed like an endless mass of bodies were wedged between them.

Slowly but surely, Jimmy navigated the crowd so that he, Dooney and Armstrong were packed together and able to react to each other's moves. Leading them by a few steps, still running on the outside edge of the course, was Matt Burke, towering over his closest competitors in much the same way that Fisher did. From his position, he had a much easier running lane, but he was forced to take a few turns quite wide. If he felt this was an ineffective strategy, he showed no signs of it. Matt made no attempt to change course as the field approached the first mile mark and the race's first set of hills.

It was a crowded pack heading into this first climb and many of the runners who had set out at a fast early pace were slowing drastically within the wave of athletes. Conversely, Jimmy still felt strong, pumping along through the incline. However, he found few running lanes within the mass of struggling bodies. Meanwhile, Matt floated away on the outside, gliding past the slowing runners and keeping his eyes up toward the next group. Jimmy looked over his shoulder to see Dooney and Armstrong, each grimacing a bit but keeping strong. Up ahead, he noticed a clock cycling through dark red numbers.

5:00 ... 5:01 ... 5:02 ...

Matt was well clear of his three teammates as the pack of runners crested the hill and turned their attention to an upcoming descent. There were still a slew of bodies ahead of both men, but as the gap between Jimmy and Matt grew, the former feared the implications for Union Valley's team scoring. He knew from his early invitationals that the places for each of a team's first five runners were added together to create a final score. The lowest set of cumulative places would win. Based on a quick check, Jimmy could see a few of those same green and white jerseys were peppering his path ahead. Another team, wearing red and blue, also looked like they had four or five men ahead of him. As things were currently organized, Union Valley would surely be no better than third in the standings.

The pack turned hard into the downhill and, within the bunch, runners were clipping and pushing to get a free shot through the group. Springer longed for an escape from the madness. He couldn't find any sort of rhythm within the horde. Glancing to his outside, he stepped around a pair of runners and extended just ahead of them. Once on flat ground, he continued with three hard steps and surged beyond another pack, bringing him to the shoulder of one of the runner's from the team wearing blue.

Checking behind him, he noticed that Dooney and Armstrong had not matched his surge. Unsure of himself, Jimmy pulled back slightly, hoping his teammates would catch up to him. The blue runner inched further in front. *Come on, we've got to go.*

Meanwhile, Burke was steadily moving through the field, looking strong and confident. Although he had run some extra distance, it had been smooth and unperturbed. Based on his current position, it had been a worthwhile decision. As Matt continued to move through the field, he kept his eyes ahead, either unaware or unconcerned that he had left his teammates in his wake.

Frustrated, Jimmy drifted a bit towards the outside, taking his next turn extra wide. He checked behind him once more, updating himself on the progress of the Viking's fourth and fifth runners. Springer had been expecting that his group of four would run together the whole race, working as a pack just as they had been taught in practice. Matt's rogue behavior had left his freshman teammate angry and disordered.

As they approached the next set of hills, a viscous middle section of the course, Jimmy was brought back to reality when he spotted his coach along the left side, waving furiously.

"Alright Matt, keep picking guys off! Bonner still has three in front of you!"

Doesn't sound like Coach is upset with him for breaking ranks, Jimmy thought, further addling his increasingly tired mind. He was on the opposite side of the course from his coach, so Ames did not spot him immediately. It was not until Jimmy was already half-way into his ascent that he heard instruction.

"DON'T HOLD BACK SPRINGER!!" He added an emphatic swear for good measure.

OK, now *he sounds upset* ...

Fear and adrenaline kicked in and Jimmy went to work on the hill. He pumped his arms furiously as he drove through, tearing past his previously stalked prey in blue and keeping eyes up on a pack of about six runners rapidly approaching. As he leaned into another turn, he refused to check behind him and instead scanned hungrily in front for the tall, orange figure of Matt Burke. A switch had flipped within him. He wasn't supposed to be waiting or pacing. For the first time in his high school career, he was *racing*. And his competitive energies were now locked in on catching his teammate.

Storming through the course, he gained steam with every runner he paced. Numbers floated to his ears, only half-comprehended as he zoomed onward. *23! 18!* But nothing changed his strategy. Nothing swayed his focus. He pressed on ferociously, refusing to take his eyes from the towering figure in orange and blue.

Jimmy flew down a steep descent and, barely maintaining his balance, careened around a sharp turn. He was within two or three seconds of Matt. One final surge would bring him to his shoulder. But as Jimmy completed the turn, he looked up in horror at a large, intimidating hill that the runners ahead of him were beginning to climb. All of a sudden, he realized his legs were burning and his breathing was rough and strained. Running to the base of the mountain, he let his head droop to look at his feet.

"Come on, Jimmy! Attack the hill!"

"You're doing great Jim-bo! Keep fighting!"

He recognized the voices. They floated clearly to him amidst the frenzied screaming of fans and coaches. Both of his parents cheered loudly from their position next to the course and transferred through their voices, a little burst of momentum flooded to him. His fight was renewed as he picked up his eyes, his knees, and his pace. He locked back in on Matt's jersey. As the pair crested the hill and prepared for yet another sharp downhill, they were finally running side by side.

Matt peered sideways as his teammate came to his shoulder. Burke had previously been struggling, but the fear of losing to one of his training partners had reinvigorated him. Coming back down the hill, the duo opened up their strides, each sprinting furiously, nearly out of control, hoping to drop the other. As they approached 800 meters to go, they passed a few more opposing runners, but their attention was only on one another.

Jimmy's body ached as he crested yet another incline, driving his arms to try and aid his failing legs. He wanted to simply quit or relax and coast to the finish, but to his right, Matt was unrelenting. So he followed. *Almost there. You have to be almost there. Turn your brain off and race.*

But as the young freshman wrapped around a tree he realized, to his dismay, that he was facing one final, perilous climb. He had completely forgotten what his teammates had talked about all week in practice. It was the course's most difficult hill, a cruel prank at the end of a gut-wrenching journey: "Cardiac Hill". *You've got to be kidding me ...*

Defeated, Jimmy's shoulders drooped and his head fell, as he slowed dramatically into the ascent. He had taken a hard punch to the stomach and it had allowed his previous fears to resurface. Conversely, Matt powered through the incline, beginning to reopen a gap. Burke looked ridiculous, his arms flying wildly in all directions, trying to will his body through the climb. But there was no doubt he was pushing his body to its limits.

As he hit the top, Matt looked back for a split second to check for Jimmy. Their eyes met for a fleeting moment before he turned to break into his sprint. *He thinks he's got me.* For some reason, in that instant, the last remains of Jimmy's competitive fire reignited. *I don't want to lose to this guy. I* can't *lose to this guy.*

Jimmy hit the top of the hill with an extra shot of enthusiasm. His legs were like rubber, but he focused his energies on efficiently turning over, trying to hold form despite the overwhelming physical pressure to let it fall to pieces. He could see the clock just ahead of him, see the point where he needed to cross the line, and this heightened his confidence.

It's right there. Don't hold back. Just sprint. He tried furiously to convince himself it was a good idea. *Come on, just sprint. Go. GO!* And he blasted from his spot, breaking as best he could into a furious finishing kick. It was easier, now that he had hit this final gear, to hold this upgraded intensity. He was flying down the straightaway, chasing his senior teammate, embracing the dull roar of the crowd. His surroundings were essentially a blur; nothing was clear besides the single towering figure in orange just ahead of him. There were other runners nearby, but he ignored them. Nothing seemed to motivate him the same way his fellow Viking did. And with a concerted effort, steps before the line, Jimmy charged ahead of his rival. *I got him.* With great pride, he eased his way through the finish line, finally allowing himself to relax his strained mind and aching physique.

Suddenly a body came soaring along his left side, falling wildly to the ground and tumbling forward through the finish shoot. It was Matt, throwing down one last ditch sprint for the lead, never giving up until the race was completely over. And he had been rewarded.

Walking through the finish area in a haze of shock and anger, Jimmy bypassed the water station and immediately sought out the Union Valley tent. Inwardly, he screamed a string of curses as he walked along in silence. He kicked a tree branch out of his path in frustration, but his legs were not recovered enough to support his efforts. Stumbling and losing balance, he tripped over himself and landed painfully on the cold ground. For a moment, he lay there, sprawled on his back and watching his stomach rise and fall with each breath. *I had him … How I could let him beat me?*

Somewhere in the distance, Jimmy could hear Glenn Fisher's voice talking excitedly to someone, recounting the race.

"Once I got to the bottom of the hill, I knew it was go time and it was just all about guts. I don't have the natural gifts that those guys have, but I just thought, 'I've worked so much harder than all these guys, I deserve this' and that's when I made my move."

A variety of other stories were floating to him as more and more runners cleared the finish line and flowed out among the spectators, finding parents and teammates to recount their journey. The Union Valley squad appeared to be assembling around Fisher and Coach Ames near their tent. Jimmy had no desire to rise and join them. He simply laid on his back, eyes closed, gently tapping the back of his hands into his head again and again. *I had him … I effing had him …*

"You good, superstar?" Jimmy felt a gentle kick to his right lat muscle and opened his eyes. Matt stood over him, looking mentally and physically drained. Exactly how Jimmy felt. He extended a hand and helped pull Springer to his feet.

"Yeah, em fan." Jimmy mumbled, finding his balance as he prepared to walk alongside his teammate. "Good race, man." It pierced him as he said it. It made the loss feel more real.

"Yeah, you too …" Matt sounded equally despondent. "Just sucks, I think I missed my one chance to beat you today. You'll only get better from here."

Jimmy stopped dead in his tracks. "What the heck are you talking about?"

Matt rubbed his forehead and grimaced, coping with his exhaustion. "You know … this is your first race, you're going to get the hang of it-"

"No, that's not what I meant. *You* beat *me*. I saw you … I saw you pass me, right there at the end."

"Nah, pretty sure I just missed you." He put his arm around Jimmy's shoulder and encouraged him to keep walking back in the direction of the tent. "It's chip timing anyway, so they will go off foot rather than torso. They won't review that sort of thing unless it's like states or something."

"Well then it doesn't really count does it?" Jimmy said, "I'm not counting a win like that." All of a sudden, he was having an easier time accepting and embracing the defeat. He was proud to have fought this battle with his teammate and proud of his opponent's accomplishment, refusing to denigrate it.

Matt smiled, bemused by Springer's denials. "Fine, I guess we can call it a tie." They were back at the tent now and they split from one another to change their clothes. "For the sake of team scoring it all counts the same anyway. I think we both might have cracked the top ten individuals."

"Wait, really?" Jimmy had completely forgotten the team competition. He had been so absorbed in his individual struggle. "So how'd we finish?"

"Well I took second," Glenn said proudly, joining in on the conversation. "Dooney and Armstrong both think they were top 30 or so,"

"Coach said 29th and 35th," Reggie called from his position on the ground as he changed into his training shoes. "We are looking at a score somewhere in the low 80s."

"Might be enough to win, how many Bonner guys were out front? They had a big pack down by us …"

Jimmy turned his attention away from discussion of the team championship and instead searched outside the tent for his parents. He spotted them a short distance away, talking to an older, taller man he recognized as Mr. Burke.

"Dad will be happy," Matt said, hopping up to join Jimmy as he walked toward his parents, "I missed his PR again this week. But I think I can get him on a faster course."

"What did we run?"

"I thought it was like 16:40-16:45,"

"Ah, yeah I've got some work to do to get my Mom's time then," Jimmy muttered casually.

"Are you serious?" It was Matt's turn now to stop dead, "What's her best time?"

Jimmy smiled, "15:10." And he walked on, leaving Matt struggling to return his jaw to its normal position.

John Trainor, August 2019

"15:10?!" I could relate to Matt Burke. I nearly fell out of my interview chair once I heard the time. But like in a professional way.

"Where did you think I got my talent from?" Jimmy responded, grinning. "My mom was a really strong runner in college. Second place at NCAAs for Cross Country her senior year at Georgetown. I'd have thought the infamous 'jtrain' would already know that."

"I'm slacking," I replied, "I don't remember any Springers from my past skimming through the archives."

"Well, she never raced under Springer. What do you got on Langley? Mary Langley."

The name seemed to have a reminiscent ring as it bounced around my ears, but I couldn't pinpoint why. "It sounds familiar. I've definitely heard it somewhere before." I scratched my head absentmindedly staring, before admitting defeat and moving on. "So what happened? Did she make it to the Olympics?"

"Her goal was the Sydney Games in 2000, but it wasn't meant to be. She retired from running less than a year after that 15:10."

"Injury?"

"Baby." He pointed at himself with his two thumbs. "James Austin Springer. February 16th, 1999." He stretched his long limbs above his head as he adjusted himself in his seat. "It's funny, she didn't know it at the time, but she was already pregnant with me when she ran her personal best. She always tells me I've been fast since before I was even born."

We laughed. Looking at the lanky champion from Union Valley, I was reminded just how naturally gifted this man was. Sometimes it's easy to overlook that key ingredient in success. As they say, you can't teach talent.

Chapter Four

John Trainor, August 2019

"Ever since I found distance running, I've been in love with it. No need to take my word for it, ask any of the girls I've dated and they will tell you. I have a bit of an obsessive personality. And by 'a bit' I mean 'incredibly'. And by 'girls' I mean 'girl'. So, naturally, once I fell in love with distance running, it took over my life. I spent countless afternoons researching times on VaniaRunning, posting on LetsRace's message board and, eventually, starting my own full-fledged distance running blog.

I stuck mainly to what I knew best, the Pennsylvania High School landscape, trying to use my particular expertise to grab views in an underdeveloped market. It worked out surprisingly well, as I established a small following of stat nerds like myself. The track community is well stocked with these types. Something to do with all the numbers involved I'd guess.

But in the fall of 2016, I left my high school in the suburbs outside Philadelphia and took my show on the road at Bloomsburg. Given my pseudo-adult status, I decided to hang up the keyboard and transition away from the high school scene. And that was it. Well, that *would* have been it if Gary and I didn't volunteer to help out at Bloomsburg's high school invite in September.

It was here, on my new campus, that I discovered Ben Havleck, a five foot five combination of heart and grit who set the course on fire. And just like that, the spark was back, the blog was alive and I had a front row seat for the events that would eventually populate the pages of my book.

I reflected on that moment as I drove away from my alma mater and into one of the neighboring developments. Also on my mind was the fact I had just used the internet to investigate a man I barely know in order to find his home address. It's kind of scary how little effort it took honestly. I've developed a real knack for online research over the years. Not that I'm proud of it or anything. That would be weird to be proud of stalking skills.

Brrng! Brrng!

The car echoed as my phone's ring took over the radio. I tapped an icon on the steering wheel and Gary's voice filled the car.

"What's up Zat?" I asked over the gentle hum of the car. Oh, that's right, I should probably mention that "Zat" is Gary's nickname. It's short for "Zatopek". Which is short for "Emil Zatopek". No time to explain now, just understand that if I say "Zat" I mean "Gary" and you'll get through this section fine.

"Hey man-Woah. Where are you? I should all echo-ey."

"I'm in the car. Driving to Ben Havleck's house."

"*Are you serious? You found his address?*" He said it in a "you're crazy" kind of way, but I chose to hear it in an "I'm impressed" kind of way. We can argue about his actual intention later.

"Yeah dude, it was easy. All it took was some careful googling. I'm a master at this stalking thing." Alright, so I was a *little* proud of it.

"*OK, well have fun, creep. You still cool to give me a lift to the bus station later?*"

"Yeah, no problem. I've gotta check the schedules there for next week anyway."

"*Sweet. Talk to you in a bit.*"

He had near perfect timing as a few moments after Gary hung up, I was pulling up to the curb on the corner of Park and Garber Street. With a few butterflies in my stomach, I exited the car and walked up through the front yard. I could hear the muffled sound of a doorbell as I pressed and released the small button in front of me. Then, after a short waiting period, a young girl, maybe about ten years old, answered the door.

"Hi, how can I help you?" She asked politely.

"Hi, I-um-I'm looking for Ben Havleck … is this the right house?" I double checked the number prominently displayed over the mailbox.

"This is his house, but he's not here," Anticipating my follow up, she added, "He's in Flagstaff, Arizona for the next couple weeks."

If you're wondering, they don't have buses that travel that far. I checked.

Ben Havleck, November 5th 2016

"*Next stop Hershey, Pennsylvania. Next stop Hershey.*" The announcement was barely decipherable over the bus speakers. But it didn't matter. The bus was essentially empty and the only noise Ben could hear was the music coming from his headphones.

… *Whatever tomorrow brings, I'll be there ... With open arms and open eyes yeaah …*

As the bus rolled into motion again, Ben stared out of his window, letting his mind wander. Alone with his thoughts.

No one *likes* being lonely, but Ben was at least *used* to being lonely. He spent hours a day running by himself. Although that didn't mean he preferred it. After his sophomore year, Ben's family moved from Downingtown, in the suburbs outside Philadelphia, to Bloomsburg Area, upending the fragile dynamic of his teenage social life. He was naturally shy and often uncomfortable around those he did not know. For that reason, some of his old teammates had nicknamed him Peanut because "you had to crack the shell to discover the nut that lies inside".

However, the nickname probably stuck so well because Ben stood a modest five foot five, had carried little to no muscle and his mounds of long black hair probably accounted for the majority of his body weight. This physique now stood out against the backdrop of strong, rugged Bloomsburg men.

So it was not particularly surprising that, through his first semester of school, Ben struggled to fit in. He had eaten many of his first lunches alone, determinedly looking down at a notebook filled with splits and workout logs, attempting to project that his solidarity was a choice rather than a necessity.

He was also slowly losing touch with his friends from his previous home, the connection between them sustained only by his out of date cell phone's texting capabilities. And, perhaps worst of all, because of its size and budget, Bloomsburg Area High School did not have a cross country or track and field program.

Of course, that did not stop Ben. After meeting with the Athletic Director, he managed to negotiate club status at the school, meaning this "team" would have zero dollars in funding, but could still participate in the Pennsylvania Athletic League events, including the District and State Championships. In the fall of his junior year, Ben competed at one local invitational, funded by the money from his 17th Birthday and then the Small School District Four Championships, where he placed second and qualified for States. His experience at these championships would come to shape the rest of his high school career.

But that wasn't the memory he wanted to clutter his mind. Especially now.

Chapter Five

Ben Havleck, December 2015

It was quiet. It was dark. At first glance, you would think the room was empty, but when your eyes adjusted to the light, you could see the silhouette of a boy. Straining your ears, you'd notice the sound of a drawer sliding open and closed. The gentle pitter-patter of shoelaces piercing the silence. Ben stood from the corner of his bed. His blue ASICS trainers made the floorboards beneath them creak slightly before he ambled down the stairs. From the closet, he pulled a neon orange zip-up jacket, a hat and a pair of gloves before stepping out into the cold.

The weather was manageable beyond the occasional piercing wind. When it picked up, it was like a cold knife, stabbing at any patches of skin that had unwittingly been left unprotected. There were still piles of snow on the ground. Patches of sidewalk were obscured where a neighbor had been apathetic about shoveling duties. The roads were empty and dimly lit by the decorations hanging from the surrounding houses. Only his breathing penetrated the silence. Of course, Ben didn't expect much to be happening. After all, it was 6:30 on Christmas Morning.

Ben Havleck was a runner. For most, this classification simply means that one of your hobbies is running. But for Ben the activity was not merely something he did, but rather something he *was*. So while most ordinary runners were sleeping, cuddled in the warmth of their favorite blanket, Ben was braving the elements and continuing his unyielding training.

This week his goal was 60 miles, an average of close to nine miles each day. Some days were less. But others were more, including today's target of eleven. These longer efforts forced Ben to stretch the limits of his neighborhood, trekking down each cul-de-sac and side trail available. Sometimes he would run until he was lost and then try to find his way home. He found it an entertaining way to let the time pass.

That was the key. Time. Running is repetitive. It is mundane. And, if you are doing it right, it is painful. Couple that with the harsh reality that eleven miles of reasonably paced running will take nearly an hour and a half, and it's obvious why Ben is so unique. And unique may be the kind word for it.

The soft pitter-patter of his stride and a stream of light breathing were the primary disturbances in an otherwise peaceful silence as Ben streaked along the road. He preferred to run without music, citing that it made him stronger and more focused. It also allowed him to better monitor his senses and stay in tune with the rhythms of his body.

He tried as hard as possible to avoid looking down at his wristwatch that displayed the time that had elapsed and, conversely, the time remaining on his journey. It was never satisfying, always less than he suspected it would be.

Ben traversed down Park Ave, then back through a wooded path and down around the perimeter of his new high school. The elements fought him and tried to thwart his quest. He made a few turns into a brick wall of howling wind that slowed him to a crawl. Once he rounded the teacher's parking lot, he narrowly dodged a patch of black ice. With a dry smile, Ben pressed forward.

As he ran along the east side of campus, he gazed longingly at his track, buried under roughly a foot of snow. His mind flooded back to his last race on a track the previous May. He had raced a two mile, running 10:10 at his league championships, and placed fifth. His best time for one mile was just 5:01, but he somehow managed to run an average of 5:05 pace for two.

Ben had very limited foot speed, a fact that frustrated him often in his sport. To date, it had proven his biggest obstacle to success. As much as running was about work ethic and determination, the defining factor was often something given rather than earned: talent.

Frustrated, he attacked the next downhill. As he changed pace, he stepped awkwardly in a stray pile of snow and his right leg tangled with his left, causing him to fall hard onto the sidewalk. His hands stung from the pain of catching himself. He could feel blood trickling from his knee and staining his tights. Begrudgingly, he pushed himself off the ground and back to his feet. He took a quick look around to make sure no one else was reveling in his embarrassment before returning to his mission. His watch only read 58:55.

And he would have to add on extra time to make up for that fall.

Ben Havleck, January 2016

After Winter Break had ended, Ben returned to school for the second semester of his Junior Year. He picked up his updated schedule from the guidance office and set off up the stairs to his first period History Class. As he climbed, his legs ached slightly from his morning run around the campus. Ben was planning to run twice on Mondays and Wednesdays, once in the morning and once in the afternoon. This would allow him to increase his total mileage while maintaining the average length of each individual run.

His hair hung wet after his morning shower, slightly obscuring his face as he slipped into class and took a seat at the back of the room. He preferred to be an afterthought in the classroom. It was not that he was afraid of being called on by the teacher or that he disliked school, but rather he did not want to come across as a know-it-all. Or perhaps worse, a teacher's pet. He was still molding his reputation among his peers and did not want a blemish like that on his record.

The first half of the day was a typical post-break transition. Teachers refreshed the students on what they would be studying during the second half of their courses and returned used textbooks to students who were renting them. Therefore, as Ben walked to lunch, he lugged a backpack about the size of a six year old with an affinity for chocolates. Considering his own height was roughly equivalent to that six year old, he could imagine how silly this looked. Fortunately, his locker was only a minor detour en route to the cafeteria, so he adjusted course accordingly.

As he approached, Ben spotted his locker neighbor, P.J. Danielson, fidgeting with what appeared to be a Chemistry book and a bright blue lunchbox. P.J. and Ben met in last year's fifth period math class and had since got along reasonably well. They were both smart and studious, but that was about where the similarities ended.

"Hey P.J.," Ben said as he approached, giving a small nod of recognition. P.J. looked up surprised and slightly frazzled. His glasses were slightly askew and the collar of his shirt was flipped upwards on the left side.

"Hey Ben," he said exasperated, "Do you think we will need books in both Math and Physics today? Because I'd like to start the Chemistry reading during study hall, but I'm worried the weight of my backpack is going to-"

"I'm not taking Physics this semester actually so I wouldn't be able to tell you," Ben replied as he switched out his first-half-of-the-day books and zipped his now empty pack.

"Oh, ok." P.J. looked slightly crestfallen at the idea the two would no longer be sharing the class: they had the exact same schedule the previous semester before Ben had changed courses. "What are you taking instead?"

"Um … introductory French" He said sheepishly, and added quickly, "Want to go to lunch?" The two turned and headed down the main hallway.

"You know, Ben," P.J. began, Ben's attempts to change the subject thwarted, "Physics is a very useful science and extremely applicable to the world around us. Statistics show that students enrolled in Physics are twice as likely to be accepted into Ivy League institutions … Not that a foreign language doesn't show diversity and worldliness, but as a junior at an introductory level you won't be able to even take an AP test in the subject before you graduate … Unless of course you take some summer courses, but *then* …" Ben let P.J. continue to air his concerns as they walked to the cafeteria, nodding or reaffirming wherever appropriate. Sometimes when P.J. really got on a roll, that was all you could do.

By most definitions, P.J. was the stereotypical television show "nerd". If you didn't know any better, you might think his entire appearance was simply a clever and elaborate joke: the glasses that were often slipping down his nose, the collared shirts, the pencil behind the ear. He regularly misread social cues and had trouble fitting in. Sometimes, Ben got the feeling that, despite their limited contact, he was P.J.'s closest friend.

"I'm just going to stop here for a drink," Ben stooped at the water fountain.

"People often underestimate the importance of hydration during the winter," he replied as Ben straightened up and wiped his face with the back of his hand.

"*People often underestimate the importance of hydration.*" A large senior mimicked P.J.'s voice as he passed, simultaneously miming the act of pushing imaginary glasses up on his face. His friends laughed obnoxiously and pointed, but P.J. was, impressively, unfazed. Together, he and Ben found a table inside the cafeteria and pulled out their lunches.

"Doesn't that stuff bother you? If it was me I'd have been tempted to punch that kid in the jaw." He dumped the contents of a brown paper bag onto the table, catching his apple before it rolled off the table.

"I've learned to ignore it." He responded simply. "It becomes a more amusing hobby if I react poorly." He carefully laid out a napkin on the table and pulled out a perfectly sliced turkey and cheese sandwich. "Besides," he said through his first bite, "The probability of you succeeding in a fight with an offensive lineman on the football team is not statistically different from zero." Slightly stung, Ben fought the urge to mime pushing glasses up his own nose.

The second half of the day began just as uneventfully as the first. In fact, in French class, Mrs. Stillin let the class out a few minutes early because they had finished everything they needed to cover with time to spare. As a result, Ben was the first one to his seventh period Calculus class. Picking his favorite seat in the empty room, he pulled out his notebook and began to sketch the workout he was hoping to do on Tuesday, scribbling down splits and carefully adding up times. He barely even noticed as students started to file in and fill the previously empty room, not diverted from his task until someone sat down in the seat next to him.

He assumed it was P.J., preparing to tell him about whatever riveting physics discussion he had missed an hour earlier. He looked up to check briefly, noticed a girl sitting there unpacking her books and then returned to his work.

Wait, what? He did a double take, checking again to see who was willing to sit next to the new kid. Ben's stomach did a three-sixty flip as he realized it was Nicole Christian: his secret crush since the first day he had arrived at the school. After a moment, Ben realized he was staring unabashed in her direction and frantically turned to start unpacking his own books, stuffing his track notebook out of sight.

The lecture during class was essentially a haze as Ben alternated between sneaking sideways glances at his neighbor and day dreaming about the significance of this monumental event. *But was it monumental? Could it not simply be coincidental? What other seats were left by the time she came in?* He silently cursed his obsession with his track notebook for distracting him.

But the next day, after Ben powerwalked his way out of French to get to his math class first, she sat next to him again, even giving him a small smile before beginning to organize her desk. *She was locked into that spot now*, he thought. *By the end of the second day, the seats you choose essentially become pseudo-assigned seats. It's just basic classroom etiquette.*

With an unprecedented amount of enthusiasm, he listened to the professor's lecture on derivatives.

Chapter Six

Jimmy Springer, October 2013

Jimmy picked nervously at his finger nails. After a brief struggle, he chipped a piece off the end of his left thumb. It flew wildly through the air and hit the man next to him in the side of the head. Matt glanced briefly from the road to look at the boy next to him.

"Geez, Springer, would you quit that?" he said with a slight shake of his head, "Can't you just get your nails manicured like Reggie's?"

Jimmy smiled and pulled his hands apart. "Did he really get a manicure?"

"Nah. Just a pedicure."

They drove down the road slowly, Matt scanning the street signs carefully so that he did not miss his turn. After successfully completing his next right, he played with the radio dashboard, skipping around for a song he liked. Eventually, he settled on a track and adjusted his volume accordingly.

Meet me in outer space ... We could spend the night, watch the earth come up ... I've grown tired of that place, won't you come with me? ... We could start again ...

"Who is this?" Jimmy asked interestedly, his focus momentarily captured. He had been staring out the window as they drove, taking in the unfamiliar landscape.

"It's Incubus," Matt replied. "Probably my favorite band."

"Huh, I guess I'll have to look into them more." He continued to look out absentmindedly from the car, letting his mind wander toward his favorite new daydream.

Meet me in outer space ... I will hold you close, if you're afraid of heights ... I need you to see this place, it might be the only way ...

It was a crisp Saturday morning and the Union Valley Cross Country squad was preparing for the following week's district championships at Lehigh University. This meet would act as a qualifier for the next week's state meet in Hershey with the top five teams advancing. To best prepare, the Vikings were taking a trip to the course itself, located in Bethlehem, to do a final workout. Coach Ames had supposedly been saving a difficult test for his athletes, hoping to put the finishing touches on their fitness before the postseason began.

Jimmy had yet to race across the Lehigh grass, but that had not stopped him from imagining himself breaking the tape as district champion. It was a lofty goal, especially considering his friend, Glenn Fisher, had beaten him in every race so far this year. However, at the team's most recent invitational, the Pioneer Athletic Conference Championships, he had finished second overall and had been gaining quickly on Glenn over the final mile. *If I can make up those three seconds the next time we hit the trails …*

A buzz in his pocket snapped Jimmy out of his revere. He pulled out his phone and swiped onto his home screen. His wallpaper was a picture of himself and Glenn, arms around one another with medals around each of their necks. Tapping a green icon erased the picture and replaced it with a string of text.

"Who's that?" Matt asked, catching Jimmy out of the corner of his eye.

"It's Glenn," he replied, typing out a response message. "Wants to know how far away we are."

"Holy crap, he's there already?!" Matt said in amazement, "Practice isn't for another 20 minutes or so."

"And how far away are we?"

"Like 20 minutes or so, I think." Matt replied slyly causing Springer to sigh in frustration. "What's the matter?"

"I'd rather be early than be late, that's all." Jimmy said sharply.

"But where does 'on time' fall on your spectrum?" Matt asked jokingly. He smiled at Jimmy who apparently was in no mood to return the gesture. "Alright, geez … I'll have to set my watch to match Fish's when I see him at practice…"

"What do you have against him, anyway?" Jimmy responded aggressively. "Why do you feel the need to always disrespect him?"

"You know Jimmy, I think you give Fisher a little *too* much respect. He's not necessarily a great leader just because he's fast-"

"He works harder than anybody else! And he actually *cares* about this sport and this team."

"He's not the super hero you see him as, alright. You could stand to have some better role models."

"What like you?" Jimmy said incredulously. "Messing around during drills? Walking around with your uniform around your neck like a cape because you think it looks cool?"

"You can't take this sport that seriously. It's innately intense. If you aren't having fun, you'll just end up driving yourself crazy."

"Yeah, it was real fun when you guys berated me for the first few weeks of the year. It was like a damn amusement park." Jimmy said coldly. There was a pause as Matt struggled for a response. Eventually he forced out a dry laugh, quite unlike his previous playful ones.

"Had that one in your back pocket, didn't you?" He slowed as the light in front turned yellow and then red. "Look, I'm sorry," he said softly, now looking at Jimmy, "I messed up. I let my ego get to me and slipped into a guy I didn't want to be. And it sucks because I can never undo what I did. I can never undo the pain I caused you. But that doesn't mean I'm not gonna do everything I can to try anyway." The light changed back to green and Matt returned his foot to the gas. "And maybe one day soon, we'll see if Glenn would have handled my situation any better."

They drove the rest of the way in silence before they finally reached the open fields of the Lehigh Cross Country course. The clock read 10:01 when Matt pulled his car into a parking space. One minute after practice was scheduled to begin.

"You're late." Fisher said as they arrived. Matt walked lazily over, trailing Jimmy by a few seconds. The freshman had exited the car as soon as they parked and immediately made his way to the group of boys sitting on the grass ahead. "And what's worse, you are dragging our best young runner down with you."

Matt looked back loathingly. "Shut up, Fish. I'm not really in the mood for your crap right now." He dropped casually to the ground alongside his teammates Dooney and Armstrong.

"It's not 'crap', Matt. We are just weeks away from the state championship and you are being a poor mentor for our impressionable young freshman."

"Don't take yourself so seriously, Glenn," he said with a snarl, his hands now tightly balled into fists. "You might start to think I actually care what you think of me." They glared angrily at one another. The rest of the varsity squad sat in tense silence, unsure of how to proceed. Before either senior could escalate the fight any further, Coach Ames arrived from behind them. He was carrying an orange measuring wheel and a matching orange cone.

The tense air still hung around them, creating an uncomfortable environment. "So what did I miss?" He said with a smile, looking around the circle. "No punches I hope? I'd hate to have missed a good fight."

Jimmy looked across at Matt who realized his fists were still clenched. "We're good, Coach." He said, letting his hands relax. "Fish and I are just a little over excited about this workout." He stared up at Glenn hoping for some support. They locked eyes for a second while Glenn deliberated.

"Coach, Matt was late to practice today." He kept his eyes on Ames and away from the ground where Matt had rolled his eyes and raised his arms in frustration. Coach Ames looked down at his watch to check the time. He seemed fairly unconcerned with this reported indiscretion.

"Well, I guess that means Burke is going to be our guinea pig for today's workout." He said, putting his wheel on the ground and reaching into a black and white drawstring bag for a bottle of water. "15 minutes, boys. I'll meet you at the start line." At his command, the boys on the ground rose to their feet, a few brushing stray grass from their backsides. Then they trudged off into a jog, beginning their warm up routine.

Union Valley circled their route in near silence. Glenn ran haughtily at the front of the pack, controlling the pace, while Matt ran at the very back, looking standoffish. As Jimmy ran, he felt incredibly conscious of his position within the group. If he ran too close to the front or too close to the back, it would appear as if he was choosing a side. The other varsity runners seemed to share his concerns as they dawdled together in the middle.

Over the awkward quarter-hour, they orbited a piece of the course's perimeter and arrived back at the start line. Coach Ames was still holding his final cone, tossing it back and forth between his hands. When his athletes appeared, he looked up for a moment, gestured at the space in front of them, and then went back to his mindless tossing. Jimmy had come to realize that was his coach's cue for the team to begin drills and, as obedient students, the Union Valley boys wordlessly began their walking stretches and plyometrics.

Over the course of the routine, Jimmy was privy to both sides of the Fisher-Burke dispute. "He's just upset because he's racing so poorly," Glenn whispered to Jimmy as they began their high-knees. "Hopefully lighting a little fire under him will get him going in time for districts."

"Maybe he'll also tell Ames how I colored outside the lines in first grade," Matt said shortly after to Reggie Armstrong while Jimmy was doing strides nearby. "Just so we get everything out on the table."

As Coach Ames gathered his troops to explain the assignment, Jimmy could not help but be concerned that this animosity might spill over into the workout. He waited anxiously for his commands directly opposite his teacher. Glenn stood tall to his direct left, Matt to his farthest right.

"Alright gentleman," Ames said, addressing the group with a shrewd smile, "This is going to be a fun one." Jimmy looked around the group. It didn't appear as though anyone was in the mood for fun. "If you take a look behind you, you'll see that I've wheeled off specific intervals and marked them with cones." Springer squinted out from the start line. The sun had risen high above them and shined majestically across the grass. "We will be doing 5 by 1,000 meters along the *exact* district course. And you'll get only a minute rest in between each rep so I suggest you pace accordingly." There was a small stir among the circle.

"I want you to think of this like a race simulation," Ames continued. "I expect each of you to time yourselves. We won't be waiting for anybody else out there. Once you finish your interval, your rest begins. Once your recovery ends, you start your next 1,000. No waiting."

"Coach," Jimmy raised his hand awkwardly. "What if I don't have a watch? How will I know how long to rest?"

"That's up to you, Springer." Ames said simply. It was clear he was not going to elaborate. Jimmy nodded nervously. "Now, as I alluded to before, there will be a little extra bit of madness thrown into the equation." He walked around to a cone on the ground that signified the starting mark. "Burke has volunteered to be our rabbit for the opening 1,000. He's going to help us learn to get out aggressively. And because the state course narrows so quickly," he placed the cone in his hands about an arm's length from the one already on the ground, "we will be starting in between these two cones."

The runners looked around at each other in surprise and concern. *At least it's just at the beginning,* Jimmy thought to himself. *We can spread ourselves out after that.*

"There are a few other tight spots like this," Coach Ames said as if he had read Jimmy's mind. "So make sure you always run through the cones when they appear. Make sense?" His athletes begrudgingly nodded their understanding. "Good. So let's get started. Burke, step on up." He waved Matt forward and placed him in-between the cones. "Scatena and Paulson." Two of the slower runners from the team's varsity stepped into position just behind Matt, standing side by side. The width of their shoulders was wider than the gap between the cones. "Dooney, Armstrong and Wagner," this group was lined three across, "and then Fisher and Springer." Jimmy and Glenn lined up last.

The way they had been organized seemed deliberately inefficient. It would take ages to negotiate the first few steps through the cones. "Everyone set?" Ames said with a small smile. He stepped back to the front of the group and dropped his voice to speak quietly with Matt so that the rest of the runners could not hear.

Glenn shot a contemptuous look at his Coach before turning to Jimmy. "Since I'm faster, I think you should just let me go through first. Rather than waste time fighting over pos-"

"GO!"

Matt took off at his coach's command, but no one else from the team was prepared for the start. Paulson was nearly knocked over as Dooney tried to force his way through him. Glenn hopped impatiently up and down, looking ahead at the ever increasing gap between himself and the tall figure who had broken clear of the madness. Eventually, the next five runners found their way through the cone and broke into their workout pace. Jimmy reacted immediately, sneaking in just after Armstrong and inadvertently elbowing Glenn in the chest, therefore beating him through the opening.

Frustrated, Fisher sprinted madly during the opening stretch, weaving through his slower teammates and making a b-line straight for Matt.

Conversely, Jimmy tried to control himself. He too was aggravated, but this workout sounded incredibly difficult. Wasting his energy now would be costly by reps four and five. Gradually, he passed his teammates, using a well-timed surge to circumvent Reggie Armstrong just before another narrow set of cones.

By the end of the first 1,000 meters, Glenn had somehow caught up to Matt and opened up about a two second advantage. Jimmy finished his interval another four seconds back from the top two finishers. One by one, the Union Valley runners slowed to a stand-still and took their minute's worth of rest. Then, in seemingly the blink of an eye, Glenn was off and running again, beginning his second interval. Matt followed him shortly thereafter. Jimmy looked around as if expecting someone to tell him to begin. Armstrong stepped up beside him and toed the line, still slightly out of breadth.

"What are you waiting for, Springer?" he said annoyed, before he and Dooney took off like their fellow seniors before them. With a pit of dread in his stomach, Jimmy remembered he was supposed to time his own rest. Cursing under his breath, he followed quickly, making up ground in a blur. Realizing how his panic had affected his tempo, he steadied himself with a deep, calming breath. *Don't panic. A lot of workout left.*

He reached the 2k mark about the same distance behind Matt as his previous stop, but Glenn was opening up a fairly significant advantage. In an instant, he was done his recovery period and racing toward the 3k mark. This time, Jimmy didn't wait around for someone to yell at him. As soon as Matt made his move up the starting line, he followed in his wake and copied his stance before they took off together.

"You're … losing some rest … doing that," Matt said as they ran side by side. Jimmy held up his bare wrist in response. The senior nodded his acknowledgement. The duo approached another narrow section of the course and both sprinted hard to try and get there first. But Jimmy was just a step quicker, he slipped through the gap and didn't look back. With another deep breath, he focused his attention ahead. He debated internally whether his tempo was quick enough to begin a comeback against the leader. At the very least, the gap between himself and Glenn was not expanding.

At the 3k, Jimmy estimated he was about ten seconds away from Fisher. However, he had also opened up a nearly equal advantage on Matt who was fading quickly. This left the freshman squarely in the middle. And still without a watch. Glenn stood at the line, watching carefully as the runners started to trickle in behind him. When his minute neared its end, without a word to anyone, he sprang into position to start his fourth interval. Jimmy made to follow him, but Matt grabbed his arm.

"Ten more seconds," he said softly.

"Is that your rest or mine?" Jimmy replied, noticing the relative strength in his own voice.

"Yours ... I timed us both." They waited in silence as the seconds ticked idly by, Springer itching to recommence his chase. "Alright, get ready ... go ..."

Jimmy launched himself into the attack. His legs were beginning to feel heavy and his previously rhythmic breathing was breaking down. He tried to distract himself, keeping his eyes ahead on the tall figure of Glenn Fisher. Despite his struggle, Jimmy could tell that Glenn was hurting worse. Although it wasn't happening as quickly as he wanted it to, he was still chipping away at the ten second advantage his teammate had previously held. He approached a sharp turn into a hill and attacked, taking a quick look back over his shoulder for Matt. A gap had opened between them, enough that Matt wouldn't be able to split his watch and help time Jimmy's rest. *I guess I have to catch Glenn then.*

The fourth rep was by far the hardest, his body weakening with each step. But once he could see the cones that signified the end of his interval, he sprinted as hard as he could to get to the line. He was determined to make up as much ground as possible on this interval. He knew, during the last rep, he would have the extra adrenaline of racing Glenn head to head. This was the stretch that he most had to push himself.

By his estimate, he had closed the gap down to just three seconds by the time he had reached 4,000 meters of hard running. Glenn leaned over, his hands on his knees, his lungs fighting for air. When Jimmy hit the line, the senior looked up startled. It was clear he had not expected anyone to be following him this closely so late in the workout. The two stood beside one another without speaking a word. The only sound to pierce the air was that of labored breathing, which grew in volume as more teammates joined the throng.

This section of the course was relatively secluded, with trees surrounding them on all sides. It made Jimmy feel oddly primal as he watched Glenn, his competitive instincts seeping into his thoughts, contorting his positive opinion of the captain into bitter rivalry. Deleterious thoughts that he had previously shoved aside were willingly brought out of hiding and thrown onto the fires of motivation.

Glenn looked down at his watch and positioned himself in between the next set of cones. Jimmy stepped up just beside him and crouched into a matching starting position. After a few seconds watching his wrist, Glenn took off to begin his final interval. Without hesitation, Jimmy followed, pinning himself to Fisher's shoulder. He felt unexpectedly strong. *You can do this ... You can beat him ...*

After a stretch of patiently waiting, Springer decided to make his bid for the lead. He took a few hard steps and inched himself ahead. Seeing this surge, Glenn put his head down and made a hard sprint of his own, taking back the lead and pushing to try and reopen a gap. Without the energy to respond in earnest, Jimmy clung as best he could to the response, hoping to gather himself for a counterattack at the right moment.

With about 400 meters left, the opportunity presented itself. A final set of tight cones were positioned just ahead of a small, wooded patch of trail. With both runners still stride for stride, the narrow path would slow the momentum of whoever were to hit the gap second. Therefore, Jimmy decided his best chance would be to use everything he had to start his sprint now and get to the cones first. Once through, he would need to hope he had enough in the tank to maintain that pace until the finish.

Gritting his teeth and pumping his arms, he changed gears and began to stride away from Glenn. His opponent fought him for the first few meters, but could not match his top end speed. Gradually, Jimmy began to pull away as they made a slight right and approached the cones. He powered through the cramped space and continued his furious charge for the finish. Completing the turn, he could see the last cones up ahead of him at the end of the straightaway.

Thud. Behind him, he thought he hurt a dull crashing sound, but he was too deliriously tired to process what it could mean. The few particles of energy he could devout to his brain were all focused on getting to the end of the course as fast as possible. And so he sprinted on without so much as a look back.

Chapter Seven

Jimmy Springer, October 2013

After a seemingly endless struggle, he triumphantly crossed the finish line. It was the first time he had ever beaten Glenn in anything. Even on easy days, Glenn had made sure he was the first one to complete the run, sometimes wildly surging over the final few meters. Matt had always found this particularly annoying. *Cross Country is 90% mental,* Glenn would say and Matt would reply, *Yeah ... and the other 90% is physical.*

As Jimmy turned around to look back at the finishing straightaway behind him, he saw the two ideals collide. Glenn was practically crawling toward the finish line. He would run a few steps and then his legs would waiver, causing him to lose his balance and fall to his knees. On all fours, he would continue desperately forward before pushing himself upright and repeating the process. Jimmy gasped and rushed forward to try and help his friend across the line. As he got closer, he could see beads of water dripping down Glenn's face: a mixture of tears and sweat.

"Are you alright?!" He asked anxiously, "Here, let me help you." He stooped toward the ground and extended his arm as support. But Glenn looked at him with disgust.

"Get away from me!" he said with such contempt that Jimmy took a cautious step backwards. Behind him the other runners were beginning to come into view. Matt was first to arrive, pulling up in confusion as he reached the curious scene.

"What the hell's going on?" he asked breathlessly, looking from Glenn, seated angrily on the ground, to Jimmy standing over him in surprise.

"He pushed me down!" Glenn exclaimed furiously.

"No I-" Jimmy tried to interject defiantly, but Fisher cut across him.

"When we went through the last stretch of tight cones, he just knocked me to the ground." He pointed back down the trail. The rest of the runners were now approaching and stopping to see what the commotion was about. Half exhausted from the workout, they trotted slowly forward, creating a circle around the scene. Glenn was still on the ground, wincing and clutching at his leg while Jimmy turned fearfully in all directions.

"I ... I didn't think I did ... I thought I was clear ..." he said, unsure of himself. He looked desperately at Matt for reassurance. "You saw it, right?"

"Well, not exactly. The tree was sort of in my way. Jimmy's heart fell as Matt looked back sadly. However, he quickly turned to the freshman's defense, "But it wouldn't surprise me if Fisher was just making things up because he lost."

"And I'm sure you are completely unbiased." Glenn replied bitterly. He pushed himself to his feet, limping slightly on his right leg.

"Don't be such a baby-"

Glenn ignored Matt's retort and instead looked at Jimmy. "You need to learn to keep your competitive spirits in check," he said condescendingly, "You're not being a very good teammate by playing dirty just to get ahead."

Jimmy looked around at the concerted faces surrounding him. By now the entire varsity had arrived and most, based only on a preliminary scan, seemed to be leaning in favor of the senior over the "hot shot freshman". Lurking a few feet outside the circle, Coach Ames was watching curiously. He seemed content to listen quietly and let his athletes settle this recent row.

After a moment of contemplative silence, Jimmy nodded guiltily. "Sorry, Glenn."

"You got to be kidding me, Fish!" Matt burst out angrily. "Are you really this much of an ass?!"

"Always out to get me, aren't you? Looking for any excuse to gang up on me, even if you are wrong."

"Wrong? You just bullied him into thinking *he's* wrong! All because you can't stand to lose!"

"Really? Who is it that can't stand to lose? Who is it that's a bully? You've been manipulating the kid for as long as he's been on the team! And all the while struggling to even match times from your sophomore season. So I think we know who the bitter loser is." Glenn began to hobble off in the direction of the start line. Matt made a move to lunge forward after him, but Dooney grabbed him around the waist and pulled back. Glenn seemed not to notice.

"Jimmy and I were there-we can settle this without you and your ulterior motives getting in the way. You coming, Jimmy?" He looked back over his shoulder. Matt looked at Jimmy in exasperation. The freshman looked back confused and upset. Then, he turned away from Burke and jogged slowly after Glenn Fisher, extending his arm once again to support his injured captain. The rest of the team followed in his shadow, leaving Matt standing alone in the middle of the field, watching the aftermath of his losing battle begin.

Jimmy Springer, October 2013

After the district championships, Glenn was the most exuberant Jimmy could ever remember seeing him. He was positively bouncing around practice, telling anyone who would listen about the little things they would have to improve upon in order to beat Coatesville at states.

"Dooney and Armstrong, you guys just need a little bit more pop for the sprint at the finish. Really focus on those strides this week." He had said to the team's fourth and fifth finishers. And *"Jimmy, just get out a bit faster and that kick will get you into the state medals."* he added during stretching. Glenn even gave himself a pep talk at the end of yesterday's final strides. *"Just take off up that final hill and break those guys, Glenn. Nobody wants it more than you."*

But he knew better than to try his motivational tactics on Matt Burke. His fellow senior had struggled once again at the district championships and faded hard over the final mile to 31st overall. Reggie Armstrong was closing in on him over the last 400 meters, a fact that had made Matt visibly irate. After seeing the results, he had taken his spikes and thrown them into a creek that bordered the course, leaving them there to soak.

To Jimmy's surprise, Glenn was far from discouraged by his classmate's misery. In fact, he seemed to be slightly smug about Matt's failure. After some thought, it was clear why. Ultimately, Jimmy felt that the disparity between the seniors' performances may have indicated Glenn's approach to the sport was a superior one to Matt's. And he wasn't the only one thinking it. Union Valley was more united than he could have possibly imagined a week previously and Fisher led practice with an air of awed respect from his peers. You could almost feel a big breakthrough was on the horizon for him at states.

The team captain had finished fourth in the district championship, despite an unusually tentative start to the race so there was reason to think he could better his finish at Hershey's championship course. Maybe even win. He seemed particularly sharp in practice early in the week, with no signs of lingering injury from his fall. In fact, Jimmy had begun to wonder how much of the injury was actually physical and how much was simply mental.

Today, the team had scheduled one last workout before the championships. Jimmy's leg felt strong and fresh. His confidence was beginning to regenerate and he was once again setting big goals for himself. As the Vikings jogged around the school's perimeter, he let his mind wander back to his former victorious daydreams.

"Hey Springer," Coach Ames said as the Union Valley boys filed onto the track after their customary 15 minute warm up jog, "Hang back a sec?"

Uncertainly, Jimmy slowed to a stop and dislodged from the back of the pack to walk over to his Coach. Glenn and Matt both watched the pair inquisitively, distracted from their drills until Ames waved them back to work. Only once the team was reabsorbed in their preparations did the coach address his athlete.

"So, as you've probably noticed, I've been extra careful with your training over the past two weeks." He said in a soft voice. Jimmy nodded slightly but otherwise did not respond. "And you also may have noticed … that Glenn seems to have made quite the miraculously recovery. He's certainly back to his old self." Again his reply was merely a nod.

"We have an excellent chance to post a historic finish at states this Thursday. But if we are going to place well, we will need *both* of you to be at your best." The coach spoke very judiciously, taking particular care with each word. "I think we've both seen that Glenn does not, um, *respond very well* when you beat him. And in the interest of keeping him mentally sharp, I think it's best if, at states, you follow in his shadow for the entire race."

"So, let him win?" Jimmy said, trying to wrap his head around the new information.

"Essentially … yes," Coach Ames replied slightly awkwardly before adding, "But stay as close to him as possible. Every point will count."

"But I still don't get it," he said, feeling even more confused than he had previously, "If every point counts so much, why should we not just race all out? So are you just expecting Glenn to-I don't know-*collapse*-as soon as I go by him?"

"You mean like he did in our workout at Lehigh?"

"Well, that was different … I knocked him down-"

"You don't honestly believe that-do you, Jimmy?" And as he said it, the freshman felt his heart drop into his stomach.

"Um … yeah I did, I … well-I …" His lie wasn't at all convincing.

"I watched the whole thing, Jimmy," his coach said softly, "He flopped like an Italian soccer player. You were well past him." He looked sympathetically at his athlete. "I had just assumed you were lying to avoid the impending inner-squad civil war. Our team was coming apart and, whether you knew it or not, you saved it." They stood together quietly, Jimmy staring down at the palms of his hands. The rest of the team was nearing the end of their drills and would soon be undistracted from the increasingly long side conversation between teacher and student.

"Now we just need one more sacrifice. You'll have plenty of chances to do great things when you're older, but for now I need a few more days of acquiescence. For the good of the team. Can you do that for us?"

He looked into his coach's eyes, a whirlwind of emotions swirling through his head. He looked back over his shoulder at the seniors, who were now doing leg swings on the fence bordering the track. Then he looked back at Ames and gave him a small nod of tacit agreement.

***

"You alright?"

"Yeah, I'm good." Jimmy replied bitterly. He and Matt were returning to his car after the day's practice. After his discussion with Coach, Jimmy had tanked the team's workout to try and further Glenn's confidence heading into the race. Ames was doing all he could to fortify the damaged ego of his team captain and number one runner. As a result, his freshman's ego was now the fragile one.

"You got an injury or something?" Matt asked, studying the younger runner.

"Nah, I'm good." This time Jimmy replied with an extra touch of venom. He could feel his temper rising as his frustration continued to mount. *It's not his fault*, he thought, trying to calm himself, *he doesn't know what you're doing. He's just looking out for you.*

As they walked further in silence, Jimmy hoped his teammate would be content to drop his interrogation. He kicked a stray pebble that skipped across the lot and landed beside the wheel of the vehicle they were approaching.

"Look, I can tell something's up." The senior pressed again, unable to contain himself, "I never beat you anymore-"

"Yeah? And who's effing fault is that?!" Any hopes he had of governing his temper were gone in a flash.

"What are you-?"

"You beat me once, remember? And I run every race like you're still chasing me! What the hell happened to that guy from Hershey?" Now that he had begun to yell, all of his suppressed negative opinions came flying to the surface, readily available for an attack.

"You're better than me!" Matt replied with a frustrated laugh, "I'm not an idiot and I'm not afraid to admit it. I'm definitely not gonna let it get in my head like-"

"*Fisher*?!" The name echoed slightly around the open space, "I bet you're secretly thrilled he snapped like he did."

"No I'm not, actually. Because it didn't do any good. You still see him as some *hero*. Not as the lying, fair-weather friend he actually is."

The hidden truth that Matt's suspicions were right ate at Jimmy. A part of him wanted to tell Matt the truth, explain why he was so upset. But another part of him, a more powerful, enticing part, just wanted to be angry. It didn't matter that Matt wasn't the reason he was upset. He was angry and Matt was there to be a target. So he went on the offensive.

"You think you know *sooo* much better than him, don't you? You think he takes this sport too seriously? He's too extreme? Well guess what, you're *just* as extreme. Only the opposite end of the spectrum. It can't be all work, but it can't be all play either. Face it, you're just as bad as he is!"

Both boys looked at each other. Matt was fuming now; any traces of mock laughter had disappeared from his visage.

"Whatever, let's just drop this, alright? C'mon I'll drive us home." He opened the door to the driver's side of the car, but Jimmy remained standing with the passenger's side shut.

"Go ahead just give up again. Same old Matt Burke. Is there *anything* you are going to fight for?"

"Knock it off, Springer," his response was ice cold, but Jimmy's fire burned straight through it.

"When did you quit on yourself, huh? Was it when Glenn started beating you?"

"Just get in the car-"

"He told me, you know. He told me you used to beat him when you guys first started. And then he outworked you."

"Let's go." Matt slammed his door shut.

"Then it was me. And next it'll be Armstrong and Dooney."

"Jimmy-" he was walking around the car now.

"Because deep down you're just some scared, weak little bitch-"

Before he could defend himself, Matt lunged forward and grabbed Jimmy by the shirt up around his neck. He hoisted him off his feet and pinned him against the side door. Matt stared at him angrily while Jimmy returned his gaze defiantly. They were both breathing heavy, as if they had just finished a run.

"Now do you want to apologize to me so we can go home?" Burke said in a soft yet menacing tone.

"Yeah … I'm sorry, Matt," Jimmy replied, "Sorry you're such a little bitch."

It was the last straw. Matt tossed him aside and the freshman staggered to the ground, scraping his hands on the concrete as he extended them to break his fall. He looked up to see his school bag flying through the air toward his face. Holding his arm in front of him, he blocked it down, clearing his line of vision just in time to watch Matt hop in his car and drive away.

Chapter Eight

Ben Havleck, January 2016

After a disappointing race, the worst part is the wait until the next chance at redemption. For Ben, that wait was going to be nearly three months: from November until February. The money he had been saving was enough for only two meet entries during the winter track season. Half the funds were for the PTFCA Indoor State Track and Field Championships on February 28th. But in order to even be eligible for this race, he would first have to eclipse the 9:00.23 standard in the 3000 meter run.

He had targeted the Muhlenberg Track Carnival on February 12th as the meet to chase this mark, feeling that it allowed the best competition relative to his limited resources. Currently, Ben spent a few nights and weekends working at the local *Barnes & Noble* bookstore to pick up extra cash for his racing expenses. His parents would have gladly donated to the cause. Their primary concern had always been the happiness and well-being of their children. But Ben did not want to be a burden. He understood why they had to move in the first place and knew money was tight.

The Havleck family, consisting of Ben, his parents Beth and Paul, and his five year old sister Cayley, had moved out to Bloomsburg in an attempt to cut costs and find work. Paul Havleck's role in the technology and innovation department at Merck Laboratories had been eliminated as the company was making a push to "get younger", improving its technological understanding and embracing the cutting edge, fast moving new generation of workers. As a result, Mr. Havleck had turned to the open market, and graciously accepted a teaching position at Bloomsburg University. With two kids, one of whom burned and refueled calories at an unthinkable rate, and college tuition prices rising, the position was doubly beneficial. As long as he was employed, both children would be able to attend Bloomsburg for free: removing a looming anxiety.

But money was still a concern. Beth had returned to work for the first time since Cayley was born and the family's usual summer beach trip to Sea Isle City, New Jersey was postponed until things were better settled. Ben felt the extra stress of funding a full racing season on top of his sister's gymnastic classes would be an unnecessary strain on the budget. Of course convincing his parents to let him take a job without letting on his reasoning had been a bit tricky.

"Why is it that you want a job Ben?" His father said to him from the head of the dinner table as he spooned a helping of mac and cheese onto his plate. "You made solid money at camp last summer, didn't you?" Ben took a sip of water before responding.

"Yeah it was fine. I'm just looking to have a bit more that I can use when I need it …" he trailed off awkwardly. His mother took the mac and cheese from his sister and passed it along to Ben.

"Honey," she said sympathetically, "this doesn't have to do with college payments does it? I think, with time, your father and I will be able to pay for whichever school you want to-"

"It's not about that," he cut across her more hastily than intended, "I just-well if I go out to eat or need to go to the mall, I'd like to have some extra money to pull from." He was paying particularly close attention to spooning food on his plate, avoiding the gaze of either parent.

"You know you can always come to us if you need something."

"Wait Beth, I think I see what's going on …" Snapping his head up, Ben eyed his father nervously. "You have a girlfriend," There was a bit of an awkward pause. This certainly was not the direction Ben had seen the conversation going. "Well, when you go out on a date, you need to have some money for gas or a nice meal. That's understandable."

"Well … not really, I-there's no girl I just-" He did not know how to finish his sentence. "Um … Not yet, but maybe one day." It was at least partially true and if it got him to where he wanted to go …

He could see his mother eager to ask a multitude of questions, but thankfully, she restrained her impulse and instead chose to smile cheerfully. "Well as long as the job doesn't interfere with your school work … And we still want our family dinners as close to intact as possible."

"Sure, no problem," Ben scarfed down a few more bites of garlic bread. "I have an interview tomorrow afternoon so I figure if you guys can drop me off, I'll bring a change of clothes and then I can just run back."

"Didn't you just run today? And now you're going to run tomorrow?"

"Every day, Mom." He smirked and turned his attention to his salad as the conversation mercifully switched to focus on his sister.

"How was your day at school today, Cayl? Any exciting news like your brother?"

"Well …" Cayley tapped her nose carefully while pondering her response, "Today at recess me and Tommy Finster got married by the swing set," she said matter-of-factly. The family laughed together at the breaking news.

"This is so sudden, Cayley. We didn't even get to meet the guy!"

"That's ok, I saw him picking his nose at lunch time so I divorced him." She nibbled from her meal. "Chuckie Pickering let me share his chocolate pudding so I think I'll prolly marry him tomorrow." As they continued to laugh, Paul glanced sideways at his son.

"We have a few puddings left in the fridge if you want to take them with you on your next date. Sounds like they get results."

"Oh no! My evil step mother stole my car, what will I do now?"

"*MuwHaha you're stuck now! Go back in and clean the house! We are off to the ball!*"

"That's not fair! I'm supposed to meet my Prince Charming!"

"*Have no fear princess! I'm here to save you! Quick, jump on my back I'll run you to the ball*"

"Ben that's not how the story goes. The godmother can't carry Cinderella all the way to the ball!"

"Oh yeah?" And dropping his doll, he scooped up his little sister and hoisted her onto his back. Ben ran around the house as Cayley giggled with glee.

"Ok, now it's time for the ball! I'll go get the dresses!" She exclaimed. When he put her down, she disappeared upstairs. As she left, Ben's mother replaced her daughter in the room.

"Tag in for me, Mom?" He reached into the closet, grabbing a pair of snow boots and his favorite navy blue and gray knit hat. "I have to get to work by 7."

"I'll take over," She replied cheerily, "But only because your evil stepmother voice could give someone nightmares." Noticing the potential tripping hazards, she picked up some of the toys lying on the floor and placed them on the dining room table.

"I think Cinderella is going to wear her *blue* dress because that's the Prince's favorite color!" Cayley called to the two of them from her room.

Ben's mother smiled. "The two of you have always had such powerful imaginations." There was a short reminiscent pause then, "Do you want to pack a snack in case you get hungry later?" She stuck her head into the fridge and searched for something suitable. "Or maybe just a granola bar?" Reaching up she picked a chocolate chip flavored bar from a box above her head and tossed it to Ben.

"Thanks Mom." He walked over and gave her a quick hug, before turning back for the door.

"Bye, Cayley!" he called as he pulled open the front door.

"Bye, fairy godmother!"

Working at *Barnes & Noble* was far from the most glamorous job, but it was neither strenuous nor particularly difficult. This was perfect for Ben, who liked having the down time to let his body recover from the pounding it took during his demanding training. At the bookstore, his tasks oscillated between inventory, cashier work and customer service. On slow nights, Ben had the chance to read from a variety of books including his personal favorite: a training guide written by running legend Matt McWilliams. The book was packed with extensive workout descriptions and other interesting information. For Ben this book was crucial to his future success. He was currently coaching himself, a difficult task for any athlete, let alone a junior in high school.

Unfortunately, tonight he would not have the opportunity to dive deeper into his research. Sundays were typically busy as the store was filled with a mix of students looking to study and adults finishing a weekend of errands. Ben straightened his nametag in the back room mirror and played with his hair until it was to his liking before stepping out onto the floor. Tonight, he would be patrolling the non-fiction sections, an especially popular spot for undergrads looking to finalize last minute history papers.

His shift began when he came across an older lady, looking to buy a book for her grandson. *"He spends too much time playing video games! If I was his mother I would confiscate that z-box and not give it back to him until he ran around outside and ate some carrots."*

Hoping her grandson was an Assassin's Creed fan, Ben opted for a book on the American Revolution. Once he had shuffled her along to the cash register, Ben had just moments to relax before he was quickly engaged by a new customer: an attractive young woman in her early twenties.

"Excuse me-what are your opinions on the power of love?" she asked him, glancing through a row of books.

"Oh-well …um," he was slightly taken aback by this seemingly forward question. For his response, he aimed for something both mysterious and poetic. "Love has lots of powers, some say love at first sight is-"

"No, I mean is it a good book?" she held out a paperback, striped with red and gold that was clearly titled *The Power of Love*. Ben fought the urge to plunge his hand straight into his face. "Valentine's Day is coming up and my boyfriend and I have only been dating a couple months. So I don't want to be too pushy … but I also want him to know I'm cool with things getting more serious-you know?" Ben had a difficult time staring back at her. Clearly, interacting with girls was not among his most marketable skills.

"That's true. Men are beasts that don't like to be tamed." The words left his mouth without him ever meaning to release them. *Seriously?* He thought to himself. *Did you just become possessed by the ghost of Ron Burgundy?*

"Right … maybe just something from the sports section?" And with some direction from Ben on where to go next, she was gone, mercifully saving him from any further embarrassment. With a great sigh, he turned and began re-alphabetizing *The Power of Love* and its companions. Occasionally, he took a covert look at the sports section, watching his co-worker, Neal, function perfectly normally under the same set of circumstances that he had just butchered. After the woman had set off to make her purchase, Neal wandered over to join Ben who was now slumped up against the side of one of his section's bookshelves.

Neal Simons was a few years older than Ben, a sophomore at Bloomsburg University. He commuted from home to school and spent most weekends working at *Barnes & Noble*. This had helped him earn a junior manager position the previous June. Neal was tall and wiry with buzzed black hair. Ben liked Neal. He was charismatic, witty and approachable.

"In the mood for a little romance, Ben?" he said as he approached.

"Look, it was a very confusing book title! Anyone could have made that mistake!" He was in no state to be ridiculed for his previous humiliation.

"Woah there-what are you talking about, man?" Neal looked at him, taken-aback.

"I'm talking about-", his defiance evaporated as he paused in confusion, "Wait … what are *you* talking about?"

"You're leaning up against a stack of romantic novels …" Neal gestured at the shelf Ben was leaning up against.

"Right … Ha … Good one!" Ben produced a half-hearted laugh. *This is the last time I'm working in this section of the store.*

Walking over, Neal joined Ben, leaning up against the shelf next to him.

"What's up, kid," he said, "You seem a little down."

"Well …" Ben subtly checked to see if anyone was nearby before mumbling, "I can't talk to girls." To his frustration, Neal merely chuckled at this heartfelt confession. He returned his manager's grin with a look of exasperation.

"Ben, can you talk to guys?" Neal said seriously.

"Well, of course I can, but I don't see-"

"Then you can talk to girls. It's the same thing. Don't overthink it." He pushed himself upright from his position against the novels. Neal considered his younger coworker briefly. "You play any sports, Ben?"

"Yeah, I run track."

"Close enough," He replied to which Ben shook his head and smiled. "In that 'sport', not every run is a race, right? You have to go out and practice. Well, every night here on the floor? Consider those your practice sessions. There's no pressure. You aren't trying to win. You're just trying to get better."

"Haha, thanks coach," Ben replied sarcastically. Neal extended a hand so that Ben could pull himself to his feet as well.

"Yeah that's a good idea. You can't practice properly without a good coach." Together Neal and Ben began to wander around the store, Neal gesturing dramatically as he spoke. "Plus, since I'm in charge of the floors most nights, I can set you up in the prime locations for maximum female interactions." Ben laughed, amused.

"Are you sure you're qualified to be my coach?"

"I'm not sure anyone is …. I mean, you *are* a beast that doesn't like to be tamed."

Chapter Nine

Jimmy Springer, October 2013

The seventh period bell reverberated through the classroom. It startled the freshman sitting near the back of the class, who had been absentmindedly doodling in his notebook. Getting to his feet, he fumbled with his books and made to stuff them into his bag. Next to him, another freshman with short buzzed hair was also packing his things. The two got to their feet at almost the exact same moment.

"Man, that went slow," Riley Joseph said, hoisting his bag around his shoulders and exiting the classroom beside his slightly taller friend. "I think I looked up at one point and the clocks were literally going backwards."

"They might have been-isn't daylight savings this weekend?" Jimmy replied, leading the way through the crowded hallway.

"I guess so, but today's Wednesday. We still have two days of classes between now and then."

"Oh … right …" he scratched his head absentmindedly, "I can't keep my days straight with all the school I've missed."

The pair cleared most of the traffic as they cut down a side path toward the school's gymnasium. Jimmy shifted his backpack on his shoulder to adjust some of the weight.

"When do you get back from Hershey?" Riley asked as they neared the entrance to the locker room.

"I'll be back Saturday night after the meet. So I'll be around Sunday to hang out."

"Sick, I'll text you." The two extended their hands and half-shook, half-high fived. "Good luck at states, man. You're gonna kill it."

Jimmy smiled. "Thanks, man."

The door fell shut behind him, breaking the silence. The locker room was empty with the exception of the freshman who had just entered it. He sat quietly on a bench and carefully spun the dial in front of him. Once the door was open, he removed a duffle bag and began throwing various objects into it. He added a t-shirt, then socks. Then a pair of pants. A hat and gloves. Finally, he came across his orange and blue cross country singlet. The bib number from the previous meet, the District One Championships, was still pinned to the chest, crumbled and slightly ripped. As he stuffed it into a side compartment of his now crowded bag, Jimmy's mind wandered back to its last race.

The Union Valley team had been aiming for the first district championship in school history. They had dominated the league final, but would have to face other conference winners like Coatesville and Hatboro

Horsham. Despite a tumultuous week, the Vikings were excited to get out and race again.

Not long ago, Jimmy had imagined himself winning this race, but by the time he reached the starting line that dream had been put to sleep. Coach Ames had instructed Jimmy to stay behind his teammate Matt Burke until the two-mile marker, claiming that he didn't want the inexperienced young star to get caught up in the wild opening stretch. Considering Matt's recent struggles, waiting behind him for over half of the race put him way out of position for a run at gold.

From his seat in the room, Jimmy got to his feet and walked across to the far corner. A sheet of paper was taped haphazardly on the leftmost locker. For what felt like the hundredth time, he scanned the results page, soaking in statistics he had already memorized.

2.	**Union Valley 120**
4	*Glenn Fisher, Sr*
9	*Jimmy Springer, Fr*
31	*Matt Burke, Sr*
35	*Reggie Armstrong, Sr*
41	*Thomas Dooney, Sr*
(92)	*Everett Paulson, Jr*
(105)	*Dan Scatena, Sr*

Scrawled across the top of the page, someone had written *37 points*, indicating the deficit Union Valley would need to overcome to win the state title on November 2nd when they raced at the championship course in Hershey. Jimmy liked that course and felt the hills would create a very different race than the flat, speedy surface they had just contested at Districts. That gave him hope for redemption.

He jumped as the door behind him swung open. Matt was walking through, unaware that Jimmy was standing in the corner. Obliviously, he continued forward head down. Then, raising his eyes, he spotted the freshman waiting awkwardly in front of him. Without hesitation, Matt turned around and pulled the door open to exit just as quietly as he had entered, leaving Jimmy alone with his memories once more

Jimmy Springer, November 2nd, 2013
"Did you put in three quarter spikes?"
"Yes, but-"
"I'm assuming you guys have raincoats?"
"Yeah, Coach bought-"
"And extra dry clothes for after the race?"

"Yeah, in the van-"

"And did you-"

"Mom!" Jimmy cut across his mother. She looked angry and her mouth had fallen open, as if she was going to reprimand him. Instead, she thought better of it, closed her lips and smiled at her son.

"Sorry, honey, what was it you wanted to ask me?"

The rain pounded on the windows of the hotel lobby, but otherwise the hallway was quiet. Although Jimmy was now slightly taller than his mother, he couldn't help but feel small looking up into her eyes.

"When you were racing, you said-you said your team's performance was the most important thing right?"

"I always left everything I had on the course for those other girls. It was my biggest motivation."

"But, like, what if you had to choose between yourself and the team. Like, only one of you could do well. Who would you pick?"

Mrs. Springer looked questioningly at her son. "Jimmy, you won't have to pick. The best thing you can do to help your team is run as fast as you can-"

"But what if it wasn't?" Jimmy said exasperated. "What if you *had* to pick?" He looked desperately into her confused face. She paused, studying him.

"Well, if for whatever reason I had to choose, I'd pick my team." She said finally. Her son nodded, slightly solemn. A short ways behind them, the hotel's elevator doors opened up and a pack of boys dressed in blue and orange rain jackets stepped out into the lobby. Catching sight of them, Jimmy crouched to gather up his bags from his feet.

"Well, this is it." He said, nervous energy hitting him like an unexpected punch to his stomach. He looked up into his mother's face again. She gave him another warm beam which he did his best to match. "Love you, Mom."

"Love you too, Jimmy." He began to walk away from her, heading for his teammates who had made their way to the door. Just before he was out of reach, she touched her hand gently to his shoulder, causing him to look back. "I would have picked my team, but I also think my team would have picked me." He grinned and nodded one last time. Then, trailing the rest of his group, he exited from the hotel into the storm awaiting him just outside.

His mother, rooted to her spot on the floor, watched her son go until the van disappeared into the dark and there was nothing left at which to stare.

The rain fell steadily from the sky. Jimmy wouldn't describe it as a storm as there was no thunder or lightening, but it was also far worse than just a modest mist. The course was marred with puddles and the simple act of walking to the team tent splashed mud across his pants. As he approached the shelter, Jimmy lowered his hood and reviewed his surroundings. There were few athletes out in the open. Most were packed together under cover.

One of the few braver, or perhaps more desperate, runners, passed by the opening of the tent so that Jimmy could get a good look at his expression. He looked positively miserable. As he pressed forward, the wind whipped water droplets into the boy's face. He scrunched his nose and lifted his arm in defense. Then, just as the tent began to obscure him from view, the stranger took an awkward step and slipped on a patch of grass. He wobbled for balance and stumbled forward. Fortunately, he was able to keep on his feet. Jimmy could hear the boy swear in frustration as he disappeared out of sight.

The freshman smiled to himself and looked around the tent to see if anyone else had caught this moment of despair. Most of the Union Valley runners looked just as defeated as the sliding passerby, staring blankly at the rainy landscape. But from the opposite side of the tent, he heard a small chuckle. Jimmy locked eyes with Matt Burke and the two smiled at each other for a moment. Then, in a flash, their expressions became stoic and their eyes darted in opposing directions.

Behind Jimmy, Glenn Fisher was huddled in the corner tapping absentmindedly at the screen on his iPod. Springer turned to look back at the senior. He looked slightly panicked, now ripping his headphones from the socket and fidgeting maniacally with the wires.

"Stupid rain," he muttered to himself, "I think my headphones short circuited."

"Here," Jimmy reached into his pocket and tossed his own pair across to Glenn. "Just use these." Relief stretched across Fisher's face.

"Thanks!" He plugged them in hastily and quickly became re-consumed by his music. Watching him, Jimmy's mind flashed back to the bus ride to his first invitational.

Did you say something? Glenn's voiced echoed in his ear. *Sorry, I kinda have a pre-race music routine ...*

Jimmy had been so anxious during that drive. Forced to sit alone with his thoughts, he had worked himself into a fuss. If he had been left in solitude much longer, his first trip to Hershey would have played out quite differently.

You looked pretty bored over here by yourself. Thought you could use a little company. A different voice reverberated inside his head. He glanced vaguely to the opposite side of the tent. But the man he was looking for wasn't there. Instead, Thomas Dooney sat in his spot, plugged into some music of his own. Jimmy looked back out of the tent, checking the immediate perimeter. When his initial search gleamed nothing, he rose to his feet and stepped out into the rain for the first time since their arrival.

Slowly he trudged through the slop. He wasn't exactly sure where he was going. But he liked that. When he ran through his neighborhoods at home, he would wander aimlessly, hoping to get momentarily lost before eventually popping out onto a street he recognized. His feet splashed gently into occasional puddles as he continued on his way. There was something almost peaceful about the scene. The *tip-tap* of the rain on his jacket created a pleasant rhythm. A natural pre-race music routine.

Continuing on his stroll, he spotted a crowd of people gathered near the bottom of a large hill. The sounds of cheering floated to him and, as he squinted for a closer look through the precipitation, he could just make out figures running up the hills. Curious, he walked forward to the site of the commotion. A string fence with flags hanging from it separated the spectators from the athletes. As he got closer, he determined the runners' were girls: their longer hair was a giveaway.

This must be the Large School Girls Championship, Jimmy thought. He positioned himself a few yards above the base of the hill so that he was facing the competitors. He wanted to watch their expressions change as the reality of their painful ascent set in for the first time.

After a couple seconds of watching, he realized there was a puddle in the small valley before the hill. Most of the runners dodged it, running tight around the turn and causing a pile up, but occasionally a particularly plucky girl would run wide, splashing straight through and up into the incline. These same athletes were more likely to attack the hill head on rather than wilt at its feet.

Jimmy fixated on one runner with long, black hair that was tied up with a red hair tie to match her uniform top. She came flying through the valley before the hill, somewhat madly racing through the mud. It splashed off her feet and onto a few other competitors who cringed as the ricocheted dirt flew in their direction. The girl in red tried to sprint aggressively, straight into the hill, but the slick ground caused her to slip and fall.

Around her, the crowd groaned as she lay sprawled on the wet ground, her face catching mud kicking off other's shoes. But surprisingly, as miserable as the fall looked, she smiled. And Jimmy watched in awe as she rose back to her feet and once again began to sprint into the hill with the same reckless abandon. He watched as far up the hill as he could, counting the number of girls she passed as she went. *2 ... 3 ... 4, 5 ...*

"Wow," a voice said quietly from just behind Jimmy. He whipped around, slightly scared and looked up into the hooded face. Its eyes were following the same girl plow through the field. Slowly, she disappeared out of sight. "C'mon," the man said, beckoning for Jimmy to follow. "If we leave now, we can probably catch the finish."

They jogged together side-by-side through the rain. Jimmy paid particular attention to the puddles, taking extra care not to splash the man beside him. The rain and wind made enough noise to drown out the silence between the pair. After a few minutes, they reached the apex of a steep hill lined with spectators. It was the race's final and most grueling challenge, "Cardiac Hill", and Jimmy remembered it well from his first trip to the course. He did not have particularly fond memories of it.

"This hill sucks," Matt said, pushing forward to get a better view, "And it looks like it's extra sloppy today." He touched the ground with his hand and tracked a thick streak of mud.

"Awesome," Jimmy said sarcastically, looking at Matt's dirty hand apprehensively.

"It kinda is though," Matt replied, seriously, a slightly manic grin stretching across his face, "Everybody is going to be so psyched out dealing with these conditions. All those kids with the fancy gear and carefully constructed race plans? They got no chance today. This kinda stuff," he held out his hand, "It's a great equalizer."

As Jimmy considered his words, a string of cheers pierced the air from the bottom of the hill. The first few girls were racing into sight, making their final surge for a state championship. A girl in orange with dark black arm sleeves was leading, followed closely by one in a dark blue singlet. They battled hard with one another through the climb, both gritting their teeth and pumping their arms furiously. Next was a runner in green with short blonde hair, a small gap, a pair in black and then, gradually, more and more girls began flooding the course.

Standing out among the group was a familiar girl in red with a matching hair tie. She was sprinting quickly through the herd, rolling past the other runners. While the others around her were merely specked with small globs of dirt, her jersey and face were caked in it. But she didn't seem to care. As she came up the hill, Jimmy found himself cheering for her, trying to will her forward past even more runners. Once she crested the incline, he turned to follow her sprint down the last straightaway.

"Did you see that?" Jimmy exclaimed, looking around for Matt, who had removed himself from the crowd, "What did she get? Like 15th?" His smile faded as he made eye contact with Matt.

"Don't do it, Jimmy," he said seriously, looking the freshman straight in the face.

"What?" He looked back, startled by the abrupt change of tone.

"Don't go out there and sandbag this race."

"Um … I'm not sure what you're talking about," he lied.

"I know you're pissed at me. You might hate me for a while for going at your boy again-"

"-He's not-"

"-But I'd hate myself even more if I let you throw away a chance to do something great just because you might *think* it's going to help the team. There's no reason to hold anything back. Every point counts, doesn't it?"

"Yeah, but it's different-"

"Why?" he said emphatically, "Screw Glenn. Screw Ames. In this sport, everyone goes out and fights until they can't fight anymore. And at the end of the race, when you shake hands with the guy who finishes next to you, there's a mutual respect between you both. It doesn't matter who finished first. That's not why you respect the other guy. You respect him because you know that he pushed you to the limit. And he respects you because you pushed him right back.

"To give anything less than your best is to sacrifice the gift."

They stood face to face, Jimmy seemingly at a loss for words, Matt clearly finished with his. The cheering of fans thundered around them as runners continued through the concluding straightaway. Then, Jimmy stepped forward and embraced his friend. The rain fell across his face, mixing with a single tear.

"I'm sorry about what I said," he said faintly.

"Are you kidding me?" Matt said as the two broke apart, "I'm not. I've got my swagger back thanks to you." He put his arm around Jimmy and led him back towards the tent. "And you better watch out, 'cause I'm coming for you today."

Jimmy smiled up at the senior, "I don't know man, after that pump up speech, I'm feeling pretty fired up. That was one heck of a line at the end. '*To give anything less than your best is to sacrifice the gift.*' Damn. Did you come up with that on your own?"

"Jimmy, how much do you know about Steve Prefontaine?"

"Steve Charlemagne? Never heard of him."

"Then to answer your question, yes, I came up with that quote all on my own."

The final hour before the race was the slowest of Jimmy's life. They pushed their warm up routine back as far as possible to maximize their stint under cover, but eventually it was time for the ceremonial 15 minute trot. Ames had them jog through the parking lot to try and keep away from the mud and so they traversed the perimeter of the large, concrete space.

While on their jog, they crossed paths with many of the other top programs including the District One Champions, Coatesville. They were the early favorites for the state title and the school Glenn had preached about all week in practice. The Coatesville team, dressed in matching black uniforms with the *Ares* insignia in the top left corner, attempted to look fierce and stoic as they passed the Union Valley boys. Their front runner, Dan Capriotti, looked quite convincing. He was surprisingly bulky and muscular for a distance runner and had a particularly imposing presence in a race. But Jimmy noticed a few other runners near the back of the pack who were unable to hide their discomposure in the storm.

A short while later, they came across the green and white jerseys of the Catholic League Champions, Monseigneur Bonner. Jimmy recognized a couple familiar faces from the Pre-States Invitational he had raced in September. Unlike Coatesville, they waved and smiled at the Union Valley team. Just after they passed, Jimmy heard a *splash* and turned to see that one of the Bonner runners had purposely stepped in a puddle to try and soak his teammate. Naturally, his target mounted a retaliation. He felt the laughter from their team nicely accented the tense, melancholy tone in the black parking lot.

"Such immature idiots. They're going to get themselves soaked," Glenn muttered to himself, "We don't have to worry about them beating us, I'll tell you that." Matt looked as if he had a retort in mind, but he bit it back and replaced it with a smile, continuing the jog in satisfied silence.

Somehow, Matt managed to maintain that smile throughout the Viking's pre-race preparation, despite the disastrous final minutes. The weather continued to be miserable and there was little relief available other than their small tent. Therefore, they had to continue most of their prep within the elements. Reggie Armstrong slipped and face-planted during the team's plyometric drills. Shortly after, while they were changing into spikes, Everett Paulson lost his balance and stepped directly into a mud puddle, soaking his left sock.

Due to the storm, the PAL had suspended the usual restrictions on team clothing. That meant each runner was free to wear mismatching long sleeve shirts, running tights, or pants under their uniform, as long the official race singlet was the top most layer. Jimmy decided to wear a hat and gloves, but would otherwise wear only his customary top and shorts. Most of his teammates added long sleeve undershirts while Dan Scatena donned a pair of dark blue tights. Only Matt opted to sport the official team uniform with no additional clothing. Depending on who you asked, he was either the stupidest (Glenn) or the bravest (Matt) of the bunch. When everyone eventually stripped down just before the starting gun, he had to hop up and down and rub his hands together to keep from shivering.

Jimmy was so distracted by the uncomfortable cold in which he was standing that he had nearly forgotten he was on the verge of the biggest race of his life. Just before the gun, as the starter called them into a crouch and the familiar nervous energy and adrenaline kicked in. He smiled, took a deep, calming breath and then, just like any other race, they sprinted off the line in a wave of bodies.

Despite the depressing conditions, the crowd erupted into massive cheers like Jimmy had never before experienced. He fought the urge to sprint all out for a brief moment of glory at the front of the state championship field and instead followed just behind Glenn, gliding along like his shadow. He could feel his teammates just behind him, all taking an aggressive approach to the start. Union Valley's starting box on the far right meant most of the other competitors would be collapsing down upon them, so Jimmy ran with his elbows out, protecting his position. A pack of runners in red and white jerseys ran beside him, trying to slip into the ever narrowing path. As one of them tried to fight in between Jimmy and Glenn, the freshman stepped hard and stuck his elbow directly in his chest. He felt a hand on his back as others ran up from behind, but there was no pushing and he was able to maintain his balance.

After the opening 800 meters, people seemed more comfortable in their space. Jimmy began to glance around for familiar jerseys, particularly Coatesville. Looking ahead, he saw Dan Capriotti running in second place overall, trailing in the wake of another runner in a red, black and yellow jersey. The pair had already opened up a small gap on the rest of the field and Capriotti looked a little uncomfortable with the aggressive pace the leader was setting. However, he seemed determined to keep him close. Two other Coatesville runners were near Jimmy as well. He monitored them as best he could from the corner of his eye.

They made a slight right turn and runners began to wobble tentatively in the slop. Edging to his left, Jimmy made sure to take the turn wide and avoid the pile up on his inside. As he did so, Glenn caught sight of him running in front. For a nervous second, Jimmy watched Glenn, trying to gauge his reaction. To his relief, Glenn appeared unfazed by his presence. With the tiniest of surges, he dodged the traffic and led a path for Jimmy to follow through a few more runners.

They approached the mile marker that sat at the bottom of the course's first steep hill. Although he had been mentally preparing for it, he also had spent a lot of energy getting into the lead group. He typically didn't start his 5ks anywhere near this quick. As they made the turn into the hill, he scanned the side path for the clock. The rain fell on his face, causing him to squint. A string of beeping filled his ears as the horde of runners cycled across the timing mat that had been positioned at the one mile marker. *Shoot*, he thought as he cleared the mat and charged into the hill, *I missed the split.*

"4:55 ... 4:56 ... 4:57 ... 4:58 ..."

He caught the string of numbers, coming from a coach behind him. *I must be at least three seconds faster than that*, he thought, *So 4:52? Is that right? Can't be.* He took the number with a grain of salt. Even still, he understood he was running very fast through rough conditions. Which made him feel better about how tired his lungs were.

At the top of the hill, they made a quick right. On the turn, he looked back down the hill and watched as a sea of bodies traversed the incline. A few orange jerseys were peppered near the front. Plenty of black. A patch of green. He didn't have time for anything more than that. When he had turned his head, he subconsciously slowed and the runner directly behind him nearly crashed into him. For a second, he wobbled in a slick patch of grass before miraculously staying on his feet.

"Focus, Springer!" A familiar voice shouted from somewhere behind him. Internally, he scolded himself and set his sights ahead, searching in the pack for Glenn. Fisher had run the hill hard, opening up a small gap and pushing into the top ten. The lead two were still clear, but they had not expanded their advantage.

The field rolled into a decline and Jimmy moved to the outside once again, opening up his lengthy stride. He felt slightly out of control, especially when the ground was so slick, but he raced on fearlessly, passing those too afraid to fully utilize the changing elevation's advantage. By the time the course flattened out again, he was back on Glenn's shoulder, riding the chase pack toward the front of the race.

The second mile was grueling and, after their aggressive start, the lead pair was really slowing down. At one point, Capriotti looked back over his shoulder and let himself be swallowed in the pack, seemingly unwilling to lead the pursuit efforts any longer. The other runner in red and yellow, realizing he was now alone, decided he should attack the next ascent and try to put away the field. The chase group held steady.

The wind was hitting them hard in this stretch, whipping rain in their faces and punishing whoever chose to set the pace. Jimmy noticed a few runners rotate to the front and then, realizing the conditions were poor, slow down and essentially beg their competitors to assume the pole position. No one felt comfortable leading the race and as a result, the pack around him was growing in size as more and more runners surged into the mix due to the pedestrian pace.

They went back down the hill and Jimmy again tried to move wide and take advantage. But this time he was boxed in. There were runners on all sides, most of whom were tentatively navigating the decline. With his eyes up, he chopped his stride, waiting for an opening. For a split second, a gap between a runner in yellow and black and another in maroon opened and he seized it. Springer stepped hard and slipped narrowly through their shoulders. As his second foot came down, it skidded slightly, but the runner in maroon reached out a hand and stopped his momentum, helping him stay upright. Jimmy gave the runner a small nod of thanks, but then they raced on as rivals.

That was close, he thought to himself, *if you're not careful, you're going to fall* ... The thought of tumbling combined with his location on the course, jogged his memory. He was coming up on another steep climb, perhaps the toughest of the course. Earlier, he had watched the girls' race from the bottom of this hill. Witnessed a girl fall directly in a massive puddle of mud.

Suddenly, he had an idea. This stretch of the course was on a small section of slanted ground. The lower ground was practically a moat as rain and mud had run down to it the whole day. Therefore, most of the field was pinning themselves to the inside. But at the base of the impending hill, Jimmy swung wide and splashed his way through the bottom section. As the field completed the tight turn, the group who had taken the inside ran straight into a massive puddle of mud. The exact one Jimmy had been waiting for.

He sprinted hard around the bend as the frazzled pack tripped over themselves to navigate the puddle. One of the runners in blue tripped and those closest to him were hampered as well. In an instant, Jimmy had opened a gap on the chase pack and was now all alone in second place. His adrenaline spiked wildly as he looked up the hill at the last man he had to pass.

He poured as much as he could into his ascent, knowing he had a huge mental and physical advantage that he could not afford to waste. He was closing quickly on the leader, who, after his front-running escapades, looked completely spent. It was an incredibly taxing obstacle. Jimmy's legs were screaming in protest, but he pumped his arms and let his emotions carry him.

As they crested the beast, Jimmy drew even with the runner in red and yellow. They looked at each other. He looked as tired as Jimmy felt. They were approaching yet another sharp downhill and Jimmy wanted nothing more than to take it easy through this stretch and catch his breath. But instead, he shot into the descent as fast as he could, flying frenziedly down the sloppy surface. The runner beside him forced himself to follow. His leg turnover was quicker and he was able to match Jimmy's momentum. As they approached the bottom of the decline, he advanced ahead. With the lead once more reopened, he seemed to be gaining steam.

Then, just after the base of the hill, the leader fell. The course took a deceivingly harsh left turn that both runners had completely forgotten. As Jimmy watched the boy careen wildly to the ground, he was able to adjust and slow his momentum just enough to negotiate the swerve cleanly. Upon clearing the bend, for the first time in his life, he was winning a race. And only a half mile stood between him and the state championship.

His bold surges through the mud combined with his opponents' misfortune while battling the elements had created a suddenly large lead for the Union Valley freshman. It was literally a perfect storm of good luck. Most of the top names had been slowed or perhaps even completely fallen in the chaotic conditions. Any step on the messy, wet course could be your undoing. But as Jimmy pressed on through one final downhill, the number of steps he had left to take were dwindling.

He approached the bottom of Cardiac Hill with an unbelievable amount of noise rushing to his ears. The rain was splashing hard against his aching muscles. The crowd was cheering maniacally. He could feel his body beginning to quit as he emptied everything he had left into the final climb. *Once you can see the finish, it will get easier*, he lied to himself. *You'll find another gear. Don't save anything here.*

He topped the incline and made the final turn of the course. The finishing banner stared him directly in the face. There was nothing between them. The cheers seemed to be increasing in volume. Increasing in urgency. He strained through the noise, listening for any hint of challengers around him. But it was nearly impossible to utilize that sense under the circumstances.

His strength and his energy were depleted. And for the first time in his season, there was no runner ahead of him to chase. To inspire that furious kick. So he thought back to his first invitational. He thought back to the final meters where Matt had put in one last ditch surge to nip him at the line. And in that moment, an orange and blue jersey appeared at his right shoulder, ready to strike.

"Aggh!" he screamed, digging deep within himself for one final gear. He elevated his sprint and with the extra acceleration he powered through the finish tape, breaking it clean in half. Three bodies came across the line, just behind him. One dressed in blue and red. One dressed in red and white. And one dressed in black. There was only one orange and blue jersey at the front. And it was his.

LetsRace.com Forums, 2013 PA XC State Live Discussion Thread
CitiusAltiusFortius 11/02/2013 12:15 AM
Any last minute predictions?

SidtheKid 11/02/2013 12:47 AM

Kipruto should take this easily. He looked unbeatable at districts and just walked away from Kensington-who is a 4:15 miler. Capriotti is the only guy I think who could challenge, but he looked pretty average at districts.

GBC95 11/02/2013 7:35 AM
1 Kipruto, 2 Power, 3 Johnston

BoroXC 11/02/2013 7:55 AM
Fitzgerald for the upset. He and Tobin should both be in the medals for North Hills.

SFRunner 11/02/2013 8:16 AM
Power looked really good at districts. Beat most of the top ranked guys in the state including jtrain's boy Capriotti and proved he's healthy after missing conferences

CitiusAltiusFortius 11/02/2013 8:33 AM
What about team title predictions? I think Coatesville is probably the favorite, but anyone else worth watching?

YoungD 11/02/2013 8:41 AM
Coatesville will win, assuming they don't choke. Capriotti might win too. I heard his coaches told him not to sprint down the last straightaway at districts to conserve for states.

jtrain12 11/02/2013 8:50 AM
1 Capriotti, 2 Fitzgerald, 3 Fisher
1 Coatesville, 2 Union Valley, 3 Bonner

CitiusAltiusFortius 11/02/2013 9:08 AM
@jtrain Fisher over Kipruto? Wow, that's bold. Speaking of UV, did anyone else see their freshman got 9th at districts? Could he be a state medalist?

BoroXC 11/02/2013 9:22 AM
@CitiusAltiusFortius No way. Freshmen bomb at Hershey. They can't handle the big stage. You gotta look at juniors and seniors for like 90% of the top spots and then maybe a couple sophomores.

FoxCatcher 11/02/2013 9:24 AM

Is anyone at the meet right now? I heard the weather is absolute crap. Lots of rain and the course is a mess. Will they reschedule? It seems kinda dangerous.

YoungD 11/02/2013 9:36 AM
The PAL doesn't reschedule these sort of things. Too much money and effort for those fat cats to care. As long as there is no lightening, they'll just try and power through all the races.

ilikegrass 11/02/2013 9:39 AM
Yeah, I'm here at the meet. It's as crappy as advertised. Small school race preparing to start soon. I'll try to give live updates on the boys.

CitiusAltiusFortius 11/02/2013 9:42 AM
Speaking of the small schools, does anyone have any predictions on this one?

SidtheKid 11/01/2013 9:46 AM
No one cares about small schools. Large schools has all the best dudes.

ilikegrass 11/02/2013 10:16 AM
Lots of slipping and falling in the early races. It's going to be wild for the large school guys. The course is torn up and super sloppy. Wouldn't be surprised if someone unexpected wins this one just because the weather will take out some favorites and keep it fluky.

Shrimp 11/02/2013 10:19 AM
Kipruto will struggle in the rain. Everyone knows Kenyans don't like rain. The winner will be Peter Bosse of McDowell. Kid's a Bosse!

CitiusAltiusFortius 11/02/2013 10:26 AM
@Shrimp Who is Bosse? I've never heard of him.

SidtheKid 11/02/2013 10:35 AM
Don't feed the troll Citius. He's just a random district 10 kid. Didn't race any of the big names all season. Won't be a factor today.

JimDillner 11/02/2013 10:43 AM
Best of luck to Conestoga Valley out of the Lancaster-Lebanon League. I've been following that league closely for years and this is one of our best teams I've seen. Ken Weaver is their front runner and should be a state medalist.

PatM 11/02/2013 10:59 AM
I don't know why people keep picking non-District One teams. District One always wins at states. They'll have the individual and team champions. Surprised Power isn't anyone's pick to win after his awesome district performance. I also like jtrain's Fisher pick. He was second overall at Pre-States where Union Valley edged out the team win against Bonner. Gives him and his team an extra advantage on this specific course.

RJJL 11/02/2013 11:11 AM
Don't sleep on Bonner in the team title race. They have a really strong pack that could surprise. Individually, I normally would pick Kipruto, but under these conditions, I don't see his front running style being effective. Maybe the Union Valley kid can pull the upset.

ilikegrass 11/02/2013 11:17 AM
Race is off! Kipruto in the lead early and Capriotti following! They've got a pretty decent gap on the field already. Looks like CB West, Pittsburgh something and some other school I don't recognize are leading the chase pack. Coatesville has a lot of guys up front, Cumberland Valley got out pretty well too.

YoungD 11/02/2013 11:22 AM
FWIW looks like twitter has some updated splits through the mile. Coatesville with 90 points is leading, but Union Valley has 101 and is a tight second! Fisher is in 7th and their top 5 are in the top 60.

PatM 11/02/2013 11:23 AM
Coatesville with everyone in the top 100. Looks like Cody Leslie got out hard and is their #3. If he hangs on, they will win big.

SidtheKid 11/02/2013 11:23 AM
Bonner in 7th nice try RJJL

ilikegrass 11/02/2013 11:27 AM
Everyone really packing up near two miles. The wind is making it so no one wants to lead. Kipruto out all by himself now. Could end up pulling away.

ilikegrass 11/02/2013 11:27 AM
Huge move just made by the Union Valley kid! I don't think it was Fisher either, I think it was that freshman. He just went all out up the hill and a

bunch of guys slipped in the mud. Looks like Teague from CB West fell hard. He was in the lead pack. Power with a bit of a stumble as well.

CitiusAltiusFortius 11/02/2013 11:28 AM
@ilikegrass Is he going to catch Kipruto? Seems like a suicidal move this early. No one is going to follow that coming off the back hills.

CitiusAltiusFortius 11/02/2013 11:30 AM
Where is everyone now? Any two mile team standings? I need my updates lol

PatM 11/02/2013 11:32 AM
Springer FTW

YoungD 11/02/2013 11:32 AM
Springer wins 15:52 according to twitter. Looked like top 4 were all really tight.

CitiusAltiusFortius 11/02/2013 11:33 AM
Jimmy Springer WTF??!!

Shrimp 11/02/2013 11:34 AM
I guess not all freshman suck at Hershey, huh BoroXC

ilikegrass 11/02/2013 11:36 AM
Springer came off the final hill with a decent lead, but Fitzgerald, Capriotti and a Conestoga Valley kid were sprinting super hard after him. It looked like they were going to catch up and then all of a sudden Springer just found one more gear and somehow got to the line first.

ilikegrass 11/02/2013 11:36 AM
They are saying he's the first male freshman to win the state championship.

CitiusAltiusFortius 11/02/2013 11:40 AM
What happened to Kipruto?

ilikegrass 11/02/2013 11:40 AM
Looks like Coatesville had three guys in the medals. Probably got the title.

ilikegrass 11/02/2013 11:42 AM
Kipruto apparently fell just before the bridge leaving the back hills.

FoxCatcher 11/02/2013 11:47 AM
Times are super slow. Sounds like lots of falling. A freshman state champ?
Have to wonder if maybe they should have postponed the meet.

SidtheKid 11/02/2013 11:52 AM
That kid can't be a freshman right? There's no way. I want to see his birth
certificate.

ilikegrass 11/02/2013 11:53 AM
Here are the top 25 medalists. Still waiting on team results:

1	Jimmy Springer, Fr Union Valley	15:52
2	Ken Weaver, Sr Conestoga Valley	15:53
3	Josh Fitzgerald, Sr North Hills	15:54
4	Dan Capriotti, Sr Coatesville	15:54
5	Joseph Power, Jr DT East	15:57
6	Peter Bosse, Sr McDowell	15:59
7	Scott Zarniack, Jr Pittsburgh CC	15:59
8	Drew Lassik, So Red Land	16:02
9	Byron Lieberman, Sr Altoona	16:04
10	Lucas Munoz, Jr Nazareth	16:07
11	Elliot Kipruto, Sr Archbishop Wood	16:07
12	Josh Harris, Sr Mount Lebanon	16:09
13	Sean Williams, Jr Coatesville	16:13
14	Teddy Crittenton, So Wissahickon	16:13
15	Tommy Kensington, Sr Father Judge	16:15
16	Josh Hibbert, Sr Hatboro Horsham	16:17
17	Tyler Johnston, Sr Cedar Cliff	16:19
18	Zachary Tobin, Jr North Hills	16:19
19	Brad Hull, Jr Cumberland Valley	16:20
20	Patrick Donaldson, Sr Bonner	16:22
21	Kyle McGowan, Sr Lower Merion	16:24
22	Jeff Goethals, Sr WC North	16:24
23	Owen Ward, Jr Coatesville	16:26
24	Greg Kersh, So Methacton	16:27
25	Matt Burke, Sr Union Valley	16:28

YoungD 11/02/2013 11:57 AM
Bonner upsets Coatesville for the title! 91 to 110!

PatM 11/02/2013 11:58 AM

@YoungD I just saw that too. That's gotta be a type-o or something right? Bonner had one medalist and Coatesville had three. What the hell happened?

SidtheKid 11/02/2013 11:59 AM
Apparently, Leslie lost his shoe during the race. Not sure if that's definitely true, but what I'm hearing.

ilikegrass 11/02/2013 12:01 PM
It's official. Top 10 Teams:

1 Bonner	91
2 Coatesville	110
3 Conestoga Valley	132
4 Cumberland Valley	183
5 Hatboro Horsham	200
6 DT West	216
7 CB West	217
8 Union Valley	222
9 Carlisle	243
10 Mount Lebanon	261

FoxCatcher 11/02/2013 12:03 PM
This is crazy. Full results are now up on RunHigh for those who want to look.

PatM 11/02/2013 12:03 PM
Geez what happened to Union Valley? 8th place? Despite having two medalists, neither of which were Glenn Fisher?

JimDillner 11/02/2013 12:06 PM
Congratulations to Conestoga Valley on their third place team finish and congrats to Ken Weaver on his silver medal. Way to represent the LL league!

ilikegrass 11/02/2013 12:07 PM
Bonner put all five of their guys in the top 50 overall. Leslie finished 137th and Kyle King (freshman) ended up being Coatesville's #5. I'm next to a couple of the team tents now. The Coatesville guys seem shocked.

SidtheKid 11/02/2013 12:10 PM
Glenn Fisher 196th. Ouch what happened to him?

XCmationPoint 11/02/2013 12:14 PM
Not sure how everyone can be so caught up in the bad performances. We just had a freshman win states! How good is this Jimmy Springer kid going to be by the time he's a senior? National champion? Olympian?

Shrimp 11/02/2013 12:17 PM
Calm down. He's probably an age cheat and is already 25.

jtrain12 11/02/2013 12:19 PM
@XCmationPoint Probably the biggest surprise in the history of the state. Can't wait to see what this kid does next. Started a new thread called "Who is Jimmy Springer?" to discuss the meet.

YoungD 11/02/2013 12:21 PM
He probably deserves a "Jimmy MF Springer!!" thread at this point.

CitiusAltiusFortius 11/02/2013 12:22 PM
@YoungD lol so true

ChesmontMiler 11/02/2013 2:11 PM
Coatesville goes home DEVASTATED!

Chapter Ten

Ben Havleck, January 2016

It was a crisp fall day at the beginning of November: stereotypical cross country weather. A long row of boys, jumping up and down to stay warm, was confined on either side by two long seas of fans and parents. A lone man in an orange vest fiddled with his starter's gun about halfway down an empty straightaway of grass. Ben stood alone in a box nearly dead center on the course, wearing a plain, maroon cotton t-shirt, black running shorts and a pair of white gloves. Bloomsburg did not have an official team, which meant they did not have official uniforms. While the other kids wore carefully designed racing singlets, Ben fidgeted in his gym uniform top, trying to adjust the sleeves to his liking. He knew the first straightaway narrowed quickly and was deceivingly short, making the first 200 meters a dogfight for position. He looked at his competition to either side. They seemed much taller than he was. Or at least how tall he felt.

As the gunman raised his arm, a hush fell across the crowd creating an eerie moment of silence. Ben took a deep, calming breath. Then there was a shot. Then an explosion of noise. The crowd erupted into cheers and Ben sprinted as hard as he could, struggling desperately for space. Elbows were flying. Runners were collapsing down on top of him from all sides. Beginning to panic, he stepped wrong and lost his balance. He tried frantically to steady himself. He could feel his position slipping, but he managed to not fall. He was in a decent spot. Probably about 12th. He made to go around the first turn, but as he did so, he took an elbow to the chest and again started to wobble dangerously. Behind him, jockeying had caused another runner to extend his arms out for balance. There was a push in the back and Ben's already fragile balance crumbled away.

From the ground, a stampede of runners were beginning to go by, like a heard of frightened gazelle. He reacted the best he could: dodging and rolling through traffic, shielding his face to avoid being stabbed by shoe spikes. And now there was music playing … loud blaring music … not coming from any source in particular yet sounding vaguely familiar …

… I tried so hard, and got so far … but in the end, it doesn't even matter …

Ben awoke with a start and whirled through his blankets to turn off his alarm, which was loudly trumpeting "In the End" by Linkin Park. Coming to his senses, he checked the clock as it turned from 5:45 to 5:46. He lay flat on his back and stared at the ceiling for a moment, the scenes from his dream still lingering in front of his eyes. Eventually, he reluctantly flicked his blankets away from his body and dressed for his morning run to school.

He pulled out a pair of white gloves and his knit hat from the basket by the door. After a momentary struggle, he was able to corral most of his hair beneath its surface. Ben spared a quick glance at his reflection in the mirror, tied his house key into his shoe and ran off into the darkness. His light breathing and his efficient stride gave a rhythm to his morning, accented by the occasional click-clack of key meeting shoe.

Circling by the school, he checked the status of his track: still covered in snow. He was getting tired of making up workouts revolving around arbitrary distances and longed for a bit more scientific approach to training. His most recent workout had been five repetitions of the school perimeter with 90 seconds of slow jog recovery in between each interval. Before that, he had done an out and back run to Molino Park, running conservatively the way there and as hard as he could for the nearly three miles it took him to return home. He was able to make these tests challenging, but the imprecise nature of their design made it impossible for him to track his progress. He knew he was improving, but he wanted to know how much.

The Muhlenberg Track Carnival was only two weeks away and, although he was confident in his fitness, his goal time was light-years ahead of his personal best from the previous winter. Without any additional data to prove otherwise, he could not fight the notion that he was being naively over confident.

He ran some splits through his head as he circled back through the side neighborhoods of his high school, carefully dodging a student driver absentmindedly rolling straight through a stop sign. *72s per lap outdoors, 36s indoors.* He jogged through the parking lot, imagining himself clicking off the marks one at a time. *36, 72, 1:48, 2:24 …*

With eight miles under his belt, Ben scarfed down a bagel before transitioning to some light core work in the locker room. By the time he had showered and sidled into history class, the second bell that signaled the start of first period was fading into silence. Hastily, he pulled out his notes and flipped to a fresh page. Unlike some other classes, to which he would gladly have been late, Ben immensely enjoyed his history class. It was amazing for him to learn about all the little facts and subtle circumstances that ultimately had a gargantuan effect on the shaping of society.

Currently, they were studying the 1960 presidential election between Richard Nixon and John F. Kennedy. It was an interesting example of the power of public opinion and a good first impression.

"The debates were televised and Nixon seemed nervous and uncomfortable, while Kennedy was just the opposite …" His teacher paced through the rows of still awakening teenagers, "Even if you are a hardworking, dedicated student, sometimes those who are blessed with natural gifts like confidence or charisma will still get ahead … It calls us to question what we *perceive* or perhaps what we *want* to be important and what is *actually* important …"

In gym class, the Bloomsburg students were beginning to prepare for the upcoming Spring Presidential Fitness Testing. At the end of March, each student would be testing their overall ability in a series of exercises: pull-ups, push-ups, sit-and-reach stretching and a one-mile run. As part of the "training routine", each class began with five minutes of jogging. Or as Ben thought: five minutes of unnecessary pounding that he couldn't even justify counting towards mileage. Then, the period would end with some type of fitness contest in the final few minutes. It was designed to incentivize everyone to give their best effort, a difficult thing to salvage from a high school gym class.

Today's lesson was scheduled to end with a pull-up contest which was ideal for someone like Ben. His ratio of strength to body weight was spectacular and this was an area he had been focusing on improving during the winter.

Spreading out to the different pull-up bars in the room, groups of students began to take their turn in the challenge. A few students took their turns ahead of him. A girl from the field hockey team did five. A boy from Ben's French class did two. Once they had cleared, he jumped up to the bar and began to churn out reps.

He wanted to carefully gauge his effort. His competitive fire drove him to make sure he posted a respectable number, but he also did not want to be seen as a try-hard gym class hero. Therefore, he settled on a strong, round number in ten and then dropped to the ground, letting the next person in line step up. The girl originally slated to go after him refused to be the one who followed a performance like that.

Eventually, the class reconvened at center court to discuss the results and end for the day. Ben tried his best to seem passive and disinterested, but was secretly eager to learn the outcome of the challenge. He scanned around the gym, picking out a few athletes from the other clusters who could have potentially topped his mark.

"Alright, how's everyone feeling? Anyone's arms burning?" There was a murmur of unenthusiastic response before Miss Cross, the class's instructor, resolutely pressed on. "Now, I'd like you to raise your hand if you did at least five pulls ups." A little less than half the class raised their hands, including Ben and the girl from the field hockey team who had preceded him. "How about six?" A few hands went down, "Seven?" Quite a bit more fell, "Excellent! Did anyone get to eight?" Now there were only four left, "Nine?" Only Ben and one other boy continued to hold their arms in the air while the other two students dropped their outstretched hands, trying to hide mildly disappointed looks behind apathetic demeanors. "Wow that's really great you two. Excellent work. How many did you do

Tyler?" She spoke to the other boy, Tyler Lloyd, who was the star shooting guard on the Bloomsburg basketball team.

"I did ten, Miss C." he replied with a slight air of cockiness.

"Very good! And Ben?" she turned her attention to him now. He paused, slightly uncomfortable with the gaze of the class focused on him.

"I also did ten." He looked down sheepishly at his feet as he spoke.

"Well how about that, a tie! Marvelous work, gentlemen. Now for next class I'd like-"

"Wait, we aren't going to have a tie-breaker?" It was Tyler who spoke up. Then he added in something of a mock whisper that was loud enough for everyone to hear, "*I think we would all like to know if this kid can repeat his magical feat.*" A couple of his friends snickered at his side.

"Well … I suppose there is no good reason not to …" Miss Cross looked slightly nervous as she spoke. Clearly, she had also been wondering if Ben's result was artificial and did not want to risk embarrassing him in front of the group at large by asking him to try again. But amidst the turmoil, Ben found himself suddenly confident.

"Sure, I'll do it." He stepped forward to the front of the crowd, smiling at Tyler as he spoke. It was as though this slight on his strength had awoken a slumbering beast within him. There was a slight twinge of anger, but the predominant emotion was excitement. At first, Tyler looked somewhat taken aback by the sudden surge of confidence from his opposition, but he swiftly distorted his face into a smug expression of self-assurance.

Walking up to stand beside Ben, he said, "Ladies first" and playfully bowed, extending his arms and gesturing towards the closest pull-up bar. Joking or not, it was a smart decision: going second was a decisive advantage. The first to grip the bar was competing against only himself, but the second was competing against a concrete, objective standard. The same reasoning applied to running. *It's easier to lead then to follow.*

But Ben did not have the natural closing speed to wait around and let others lead. He had to take hold of a race and win by crushing the spirit of his opponent. Shaking out his arms, he walked forward. His strategy was set. Before Tyler could find out the number he had to surpass, he would hopefully have already given up.

Ben hoisted himself onto the bar. The plan was to go quickly, confidently and smoothly. He sped rapidly through the first five, then through five more, all while trying to relax his body. He wanted it to appear as though his pull-ups were as effortless to him as standing there watching was to the crowd of his peers. Whispers of surprised admiration were beginning to grow behind his back, urging him on, fueling his adrenaline. As he approached 20, Ben could feel his muscles starting to fatigue and his body beginning to breakdown. Eventually, he accepted that he was running out of gas. With concerted focus, he clung to proper form just enough so that only he could tell how physically drained he truly was.

He thumped out the 25th rep as aggressively and then dropped as casually as he could manage to the ground. Collecting his thoughts and calming his face, he turned for the first time to see a mixture of shock and awe from his classmates. He smiled and, although it was quite painful, mimicked Tyler's earlier bow while gesturing at the bar. There were a few chuckles from the crowd, but none came from his opposition. Lloyd's previously smug grin had been replaced by an ugly mixture of shock and anger. He took a tentative half step towards the bar, before pausing and then relenting.

Frazzled and desperate, Tyler reached down for some shred of remaining arrogance and retorted weakly, "Yeah well … I could do all those pull ups too if I weighed 60 pounds." And he trudged into the locker room defeated.

"To be fair your mass and height do likely give you a substantial advantage in body weight exercises." P.J. and Ben were at their usual lunchroom table in the cafeteria. He had overheard of Ben's triumph during the prior period's Chemistry class. News was traveling quickly.

"Well maybe if he spent a bit less time doing bicep curls while staring at himself in the mirror …" Ben's arms were aching from his efforts and the lactic acid build-up was making it hard to eat his lunch. Of course, he viewed it as a more than worthwhile sacrifice in exchange for the pride of sticking it to a schoolyard bully. He bit down into his apple, trying to avoid spraying juice all over himself. A group of girls from the basketball team was sitting across the room and he could have sworn he noticed one point at him briefly in the middle of the conversation, causing her friends to turn and stare as well.

Ben focused his attention deliberately on his fruit, attempting to ignore the sensation that he was being watched. He opted for a change in subject. "Did you hear they're making another Transformers movie?"

"I did notice that. They showed a trailer last night on the Discovery channel." The two began to pack up their things as lunchroom dismissal was beginning. "What did you think of the first films?"

"Eh, they were fine. Mostly just … loud. Too intense for me. I tend to leave Michael Bay movies feeling like I just got into a boxing match at a Linkin Park concert. Think I'll withdraw from round two." They funneled themselves into the exodus of bodies from the cafeteria. This particularly narrow stretch of hallway usually caused a post-lunch traffic jam.

"I think writing those scripts has to be difficult. I mean, how are tiny humans supposed to have any sort of realistic impact in a battle between gigantic, super-powered monsters?" Before Ben could respond, three hulking figures forced their way through the crowd, pushing P.J. aside into a group of freshmen as they lumbered forward.

"Talking about us, Havleck? Although 'super-powered' may not be a strong enough verb to describe how we operate." It was Tyler Lloyd, flanked by two of his cronies from the basketball team.

"I think you may mean 'adjective'. 'Super-powered' is a descriptive word which-"

"Oh I'm sorry, nerd," Tyler reached over and plucked the pencil from behind P.J.'s ear. He snapped it cleanly in half and casually tossed it over his shoulder. "How about 'destroyed', want to give me a lecture on what part of speech that is?" His cronies laughed harshly. P.J. muttered something about it all depending on context while staring blankly at the floor, avoiding the groups gaze.

Ben stepped in between them. The hallways were starting to clear as the crowd around them evaporated. "Hey, why don't you guys back off?"

"*Why don't you guys back off,*" the taller of Tyler's two friends mimicked him shrewdly while the other laughed.

"Feeling like quite the tough guy after today, huh?" Tyler smiled maliciously. "Well don't get too comfortable-pull-ups ain't gonna help you win a real fight." The hallway was empty now and the second bell for class was likely to ring at any moment. Tyler started menacingly at Ben, who stared back, unwavering.

"I saw you're true colors today, Ty. You're not so tough yourself-you'll quit as soon as things get a little uncomfortable. Looks like you're more afraid of me than I'll ever be of you."

"Sounds like Mr. Big Shot needs a little reminder of how things work around here." His friends on either side cracked their fingers aggressively and moved to surround Ben and P.J., the latter of which was slowly cowering further and further into the wall behind him.

"Hey!" There was a yell from down the hall and a teacher came running behind the echoing voice. It was Ben's history teacher, Mr. Cook. "What do you think you're doing? Get to class! All of you! Or I'll be writing detentions for next week!" The group scattered to their respective hallways, P.J. positively sprinting away from the showdown. The heavier of Tyler's thugs brought his thumb threateningly across his neck. Ben ignored it and coolly turned the corner for class. *This isn't over, is it?* He thought to himself. And with a groan, he turned the handle and opened the door to fifth period English.

After a fantastically ordinary afternoon, Ben slugged his way into Math class to close out the day. His arms were still bothering him and the weight of carrying an afternoon's set of books was not easing his pain. He dropped into his usual seat and slipped off his bag, halfheartedly preparing for class. As he absentmindedly massaged his left shoulder muscle, a voice next to him snapped him back to reality.

"Still sore?" Nicole said playfully. Ben quickly tried to think up a clever response, but his mind was blank. He settled on a noise that ended up being part-laugh, part-grunt of affirmation. *Very smooth*, he thought to himself. But she seemed unfazed, continuing as if it was normal for a teenage boy to make the same sound as a dying animal. "Tyler has always been a little too cocky for his own good. It's nice to know someone was able to put him in his place." She flashed a beautiful toothy smile. "I'm just upset I wasn't there to see his face when it happened."

Ben laughed. Although it sounded nothing like his normal laugh. "Well-you know-we were just doing some pull-ups ... I'm sure in the grand scheme of things he-" As he gestured with his hands, he knocked his pencil off the table. Frantically, he reached down to get it and, in his haste, nearly slipped out of his chair onto the floor. He emerged back to visibility red in the face. In an attempt to save an ounce of dignity, he responded, "I guess I have a talent for pull-ups."

"Yeah it sounds like it. Did you really do 25?" He felt his face continuing to redden as she looked at him impressed. "What are you some type of gymnast or something?"

"No ... Actually, I'm a distance runner."

Looking puzzled, she opened her mouth to respond but instead was interrupted by the second bell and the arrival of their teacher at the front of the classroom. She gave him another small grin and then returned her focus to the lesson: a lecture on the "chain rule". Ben took careless notes for the rest of the class, the highlight being when he wrote the derivative of sin(2x) was equal to "Nicole".

Well, today could have been much worse, he reflected on the afternoon's events while jogging to work. *I could have been punched in the face by Tyler Lloyd.*

On second thought; I think I might take a shot to the nose if it meant I could sit in a chair without falling ...

Chapter Eleven

Ben Havleck, February 2016

Ben came to a stop outside the tall, locked gate. Face to face with the concealed entryway, he paused to examine his predicament. He checked briefly over both shoulders. No one was within sight. Of course, he didn't expect anyone to be at 5:30 in the morning. He tossed the shovel he held in his hands over the fence and then stretched out his unburdened arms. Climbing quickly, he scaled the obstruction and jumped down to the ground on the other side. Next, he removed the drawstring bag from his back and sat down, unlacing his blue running shoes and switching into a pair of dark brown boots. Then, he finally turned his attention to the track.

As he trudged through the snow toward where he suspected the start line was, a small gust of wind sent a shiver down his spine. Besides the crunching of snow beneath his feet, he walked forward in silence. Eventually, he paused and picked his spot to begin. Pointing the shovel down, he struck into the snow for the first time, scooped up a pile of white and flung it to the side. And then again. The sound of shovel and snow echoed eerily around the empty stadium.

After he had made five or six incisions, Ben paused for a moment and put down his shovel. Reaching into his pocket, he pulled out his phone and flipped it open, shining a dim light through the darkness. He had to bend to his knees to properly examine the surface of the track as he scanned for any recognizable marks or patterns.

Finally, he spotted it: the edge of a black mark bordering on the otherwise red surface. Quickly, he grabbed his shovel and chipped away at the area of snow surrounding his discovery. Now, again lowering his eyes and his makeshift flashlight to the ground, he could make out the features of a large, bold number two.

"Could have been worse" he mumbled into the cold morning air. Turning to his left, he reoriented himself and returned to his tedious task.

***

Ben stepped off the bus into the cool, night air. His legs felt fresh and bouncy, his body relaxed and strong. He removed his headphones from his ears and tucked them away inside his coat pocket as he walked through the front doors of the Muhlenberg College Athletic Center. Immediately, he heard the echoing sounds of cheering he had come to associate with indoor track. Peaking in through the first window, he soaked in the packed facility, filled wall to wall with athletes, coaches and spectators. A smile stretched across Ben's face as he continued to wind his way through the building, walking toward the official meet entrance. A brief look at his watch told him he had made perfect time.

The Muhlenberg Track Invitational was not the most prestigious meet, but it would feature a variety of top small school athletes. Ben had already analyzed the performance list and been happy to recognize a few names that would be shooting to hit the state qualifying mark in the 3,000 meters just as he was. It was a talented group, but, just as importantly, it was an ideal level of competition. No one was so far ahead of Ben that he would be overwhelmed.

As he picked up his hip number at the officials table, he could feel the pre-race jitters crawling around inside his stomach. He couldn't help but be excited about this opportunity: his first race of the indoor season. There was something special about a track or cross country meet. It was an atmosphere in which Ben felt truly at home. Here, he was comfortable in his own skin, not concerned with fitting in or being cool. And certainly not the new kid.

Positioning himself on the track's backstretch, he sat up against the wall and watched as the boys 400 meters took to the track. He stretched out his legs, relaxing his body and trying to fight off the ever increasing nervous energy coursing through his body. He removed his navy blue hat from his head and traded it with his water bottle, tucked within his drawstring bag. Casually, he took a sip, watching a tall, powerful runner in a red and black jersey grind down the backstretch into a commanding five-meter lead.

Time seemed to pass slowly as he sat, eagerly awaiting his chance to race. About an hour before he was scheduled to compete, Ben would leave to begin his warm up routine with a jog around the campus, but he was still 90 minutes from his seven o'clock start time. Already he was growing tired of watching the sprints. As yet another heat of runners positioned themselves on the track, he decided to kill additional time by meandering over to the bathroom. He took another sip from his water bottle and pushed himself to his feet.

Ben wandered back past the registration area into the hallways of the athletic center. He had no idea where the bathroom was, but was in no particular rush to find it. In fact, he kind of liked the idea of exploring. He walked down a long, narrow path, passing a room filled with stationary bikes and followed by a set of coaches' offices. Then he rounded the corner, past some indoor racquet ball courts and up a flight of stairs. This new floor featured a plethora of exercise equipment, including treadmills and ellipticals. Cutting down a vestibule off to the side, he found a few more offices, including the one he had subconsciously been searching for: the head cross country and track and field coach.

"David Ames," he read quietly to himself, before pressing his face up against the glass window to the office. The lights had been turned off, but

Ben thought he could make out a few items in the room. There was a pair of running shoes in the corner, a desktop computer, a clipboard with lap splits and a picture of a tall runner in an orange uniform with a medal next to it. There was also a poster on the wall of a pair of runners he didn't recognize. Both were wearing singlets prominently featuring the signature *Ares* insignia.

Ben imagined the coach as an older man with gray hair and glasses, firing instructions and creating inspiring race plans. He vaguely remembered his previous high school coaches from his old school, but they were in the picture before he became truly passionate about running. Before he had been able to appreciate just how important a coach could be.

"Looking for the coach?"

Ben nearly jumped out of his skin as the voice struck him out of his revere. Walking towards him from the opposite end of the hallway was a taller girl dressed in white and blue sweats. "Um, not exactly-I was just … well …," he trailed off looking for the right explanation. He didn't think, 'I was looking for a bathroom' would be suave enough. Or particularly plausible.

"Are you a recruit?" She looked to be about the same age as Ben, perhaps a year or two older. She stared at him with piercing blue eyes that closely matched her clothes.

"I-well, are you a recruit?" he tried to sound curious and interested rather than accusatory, but all the same the girl looked slightly taken aback.

"Um-yeah, I am actually. Well, sort of," she paused awkwardly, searching for the right words. "I wasn't technically *recruited*, but I-I really wanted to compete collegiately. So I just emailed the coach to ask what it took to be on the team. And-well-it turns out I was a pretty good recruit for them." She finished sounding self-conscious. "So, are *you* a recruit?" She grinned, "Or are you going to keep dodging my questions?"

Ben laughed. "No … and no," he replied. They both laughed again and Ben began to feel a bit more relaxed. "I just was doing a bit of exploring and thought this might be a cool place to visit." He nodded his head in the direction of the window.

"I've never seen his office actually, is it cool?" And she walked up next to him to press her own face up against the glass. Ben could smell some type of perfume on her clothes. "I kinda wonder what he's like, you know?" She turned to face him and Ben's stomach did a somersault that had nothing to do with his upcoming race.

"Dunno. Shame he wasn't here, I would have liked to ask him a couple questions."

"Yeah … oh well, maybe next time. You headed back downstairs?" She asked over her shoulder as she turned to go.

"Yeah, actually I've got a race soon," he remembered with a jolt. He checked his watch, but, gratefully, still had time to spare.

"Ooo, what are you running?"

"The 3k." Together they walked back down the stairs to the first floor.

She smiled. "Had you pegged for a distance runner from the start. Well good luck …" she trailed off indicating he should insert his name.

"Ben," he said stretching out his hand.

"Katie," she replied taking it. "Nice meeting you, Ben."

***

Even during his most painful and exhausting races, Ben did not truly appreciate how incredibly long 400 meters was. After almost an hour of work, he had barely cleared 150. His back ached from stopping and his hands were throbbing and cracked from gripping tightly to the shovel. But he continued to press on. Every time he wanted to quit, he thought of his 3,000 at Muhlenberg. He thought of the nine minute state qualifying barrier. It bounced around his brain, motivating him to clear each layer and carve out a bit more of his path. He drove his shovel back into the snow, creating a weak crunch, pulled back the pile and tossed it to his inside, producing another dull thud. It became almost rhythmic and with each chunk he moved, he seemed to hear his goal time. *Nine … Minutes. Nine … Minutes.*

The sun began to rise as he closed in on 200 meters, shining light along his path. He stopped for a moment to look around at his work. *Sometimes,* he thought, *you need to take a moment and appreciate how far you've come. Rather than worry about how far you still have left to go.* He chuckled to himself about his philosophical subconscious. "I'm going crazy out here by myself," he muttered. Ben tossed his shovel off to the side and let himself fall back into a pile of snow on the inside of the track. The cold felt good on his aching limbs.

"Comfortable there, Havleck?"

Ben sat up in a panic and lunged for his shovel when he heard the voice. His manager from *Barnes & Noble*, Neal Simons, was standing in the middle of the turn, leaning on a different, larger shovel that he had rammed into the snow.

"Neal?" Realizing he wasn't in any danger, Ben's fear turned to curiosity. "What are you doing here?"

"The school is on my way to the gym. Saw you when I drove by. Looked like you needed some help." He shrugged. "Nothing to write a novel about." Neal scanned the track as Ben continued to look at him in surprise. "This isn't really a one person job, you know."

With more of an effort than he would have liked, Ben lifted himself out of the snow and got to his feet. "But … it's like 6 o'clock in the morning, aren't you supposed to be sleeping in or having fun or …" He looked around bewildered. "Doing literally anything else?" But Neal didn't respond. Instead, he took up Ben's former position at the 200 meter mark. "And where did you get a shovel?"

"Remember, I commute to school every day. Gotta be prepared to battle the elements." He plowed his tool into the snow and cleared his first patch. Then, Neal paused dramatically. "Satisfying … but not sure it's the most efficient workout."

"I'm not doing it as a workout I'm-"

"Shoveling out the track so you *can* do a workout. Yeah, I know. Again, seems a bit inefficient, no?" Neal smiled and took a few steps forward in the snow to clear a spot for Ben to join him.

"And yet you're still helping me?"

"And yet I'm still helping you." Neal made another dent in the ice before Ben filed in behind him to get to work on his section. "I guess we're both idiots."

With a bit of a renewed spirit thanks to Neal's arrival, Ben found shoveling much more enjoyable.

"So how's that girlfriend of yours doing? Megan … or Courtney … what's her name?" Ben asked as he removed a particularly heavy patch of snow.

"Yes," Neal replied simply, "But I wouldn't really call them girlfriends, I'd say they are just girl friends. Right now I have a bunch of girl friends, but nobody is a girlfriend."

"Wait-what's the difference?"

"I'll tell you when you're older." Neal took a few steps forward to make sure he and Ben were still adequately spread out. "Anything happen with you and that Nicole girl from Math class?"

"No … there hasn't really been an opportunity yet." He tightened his grip on the shovel as he prepared to remove another large pile of white, "I'm not really sure how I feel about her anyway. She's-ouch!" Ben took a snowball to the chest. Looking back, he saw Neal was now preparing a second attack.

"C'mon Ben! With that attitude there's never going to be an 'opportunity'. Sometimes you have to make your own luck!" He fired another snowball, which Ben was able to swat away with his shovel. "Do you remember the stuff I said?"

"Um … there was something about questions right?"

"If you're uncomfortable, start by asking some questions. Keep it off you and on her for a bit. Plus it's nice for you to be interested in *her* rather than be all about yourself. That's just basic Hitch 101 stuff." Neal paused to hoist another, more significant stack of snow from his path.

"Compliments are always good- but appropriate compliments there, Denmark, no more complimenting old ladies on their youthful figure."

"OK, that was one time!" Ben threw his pile of shoveled snow in Neal's direction. "And why exactly did you just call me Denmark?"

"You know, your name is Ben. Like 'Big Ben', the big clock?"

"Yeah …"

"Isn't that in Denmark?"

"You're kidding right?"

"Denmark-England, it's all Asia you know?" Ben merely stared at him half smiling, half angry. "Sorry, I know you are super into that social studies stuff." Ben launched another pile of snow at Neal which he deflected easily with his shovel. "Hey, speaking of clocks! Remind me again about this race you're planning to do?"

***

Ben jogged along the sidewalk surrounding Muhlenberg College, careful to avoid any stray patches of ice. This was perhaps the most nervous he could ever remember being for a race. He had psyched himself up for weeks. Every decision he made always centered on the question "How will this affect my 3k?" His stride was crisp and smooth, his workouts had been very strong and his confidence was high. This was his moment.

After his jog, exactly 15 minutes, he went into the gym to begin his stretching and drills. A few other, long, thin runners were populating the gym with their own version of plyometrics. He recognized a few from cross country, including Wyomissing's Terrence Griffin, who had finished fourth at the small school state championships. Griffin was the top seed on this meet's performance list at 8 minutes and 55 seconds. Also in the gym was Colin Brett from Notre Dame in Easton. Brett had finished one spot ahead of Ben at states this past fall.

When his drills were completed, he cruised one up-tempo stride along the sideline before transitioning into the field house. Once inside, he laced up his spikes and knocked out two more strides, accelerating gradually through the turn while traversing the outside lane. He felt strong and powerful. As he walked back toward the starting line, he noticed Terrence Griffin striding gracefully in the opposite direction. His speed was impressive, but Ben was not concerned. His focus was only on himself and hitting his splits. *36s. 72s.*

The officials lined up the athletes on the starting line. It was a twelve-athlete race. By this time in the night, many teams had chosen to leave the meet early and begin their weekend rather than stay until the invite's longest distance event was completed. Yet there was still a healthy buzz in the fieldhouse. Considering essentially everyone who wasn't racing the 3k was finished competing, they were enthusiastic and willing to cheer on the athletes with unabashed enthusiasm. As he walked into position, tucking in his maroon t-shirt, he noticed Katie out of the corner of his eye, standing on the first curve with a few other girls.

"Good luck," a runner with an orange and black jersey remarked, extending a hand from Ben's right.

"Gah la," he replied with a small shake and a nod. It was all he could muster through his nerves. Ben tried in vain to steady himself, breathing deeply and slowly. After what seemed like an eternity of waiting, the starter took his position.

"Runners set …."

Bang!

Off the runners went, jockeying for position around the first turn. Ben charged forward, but was knocked out of position by a bigger runner to his inside. Keeping his balance, he navigated smoothly into a mid-pack position just off the rail. He had a comfortable pocket, able to run freely without chopping strides. *Heck of a lot better start than the last time I raced.*

At the front of the pack, he recognized Griffin in white and blue controlling a quick pace. He was flanked by a pair of runners on either side with a small gap already beginning to open up behind them. Patiently, Ben waited until they rounded the track's second turn and then calmly inched himself forward so that he would not lose contact. A quick look at the clock as he passed by told him his feel for the pace was almost perfect. 35 ticked to 36.

Returning to the first bend, a wave of noise filled Ben's ears, overflowing into his thoughts. He tried to keep his head clear and focused, to hold diligently to his pace. Although the top pack was increasing their lead, Ben was content to let them escape. The 3,000 meters was a long enough race that, if he held form, he would have time to reel them back in. *36s. 72s.*

As he pressed on, keeping a consistent clip, he gradually began to pull away from his pack. But, the trio of leaders was still far enough from his grasp that Ben could not draft off them or gain any substantive advantage from chasing. Determinedly, he pressed on, running solo. He glanced again at the clock as he went through lap five, hitting his split in roughly three minutes. It was exactly the pace he needed for a state qualifying mark. But he still had not made up ground on the leaders.

Terrence Griffin continued to hammer from the front, looking relaxed and smooth. His tall and powerful figure glided along, showing little sign of weakness or fatigue. His two closest pursuers, however, looked neither as graceful nor as comfortable, each fighting desperately to keep contact near the leader's shoulder. It was these runners that Ben focused his intensity on as he approached the 1600 meter mark. His mouth was beginning to dry and he could feel sweat dripping from his long hair, but he had yet to budge from his consistent pace. *36s. 72s.*

With over a mile gone by, the race was now adequately spread out and the cheering became more defined. It was now becoming difficult for Ben to hold form and his most recent lap had slipped a second off his target pace. Ahead, Griffin's furious early pace had allowed him to pull free with a five meter lead. His two closest opponents had slipped dramatically out of contention, but Ben could not find the extra gear he needed to get after them. The monotony of running nearly nine laps by himself was beginning to take its toll on his mind.

"Go Ben! You can do it!"

Rounding through yet another lap, Ben could have sworn he heard someone urging him on by name. A small extra fire ignited in his stomach, and he forced his legs to turnover a bit faster. His head wobbled slightly from side to side as he pressed forward. A stream of spit had worked its way outside of his mouth along the side of his face. His shoulders were tightening and his form had lost much of its fluidity. But despite it all, he had worked himself back within pace through ten laps. And better yet, he had made his first pass since the early stages of the race, moving into third place overall.

It was an exhilarating feeling to pass another runner, to feel the thrill of competition once again. It was such a rush, such a high, that he had to experience it again. Holding his head high and keeping his eyes forward, Ben continued to grind around the oval. His mind was spinning and his breathing was heavy. The back of his throat burned from the indoor air. Forcing himself into a steadying breath, he focused on making another pass. As he hit the eleventh lap, he found himself in second place.

Many in the crowd had begun to take notice of Ben's furious charge in the second half of the race. Having finally usurped both stragglers, he was free to focus everything he had left on Griffin. Although Ben's charge from the middle of the pack had been arduous, Terrence Griffin's journey through 2400 meters had perhaps been more challenging. Since the race's start, he had led the entire way, establishing a blistering pace with no help and no one to chase. Subconsciously, he had become complacent in the middle stages of the race, feeling victory was nearly assured. This small moment of mental weakness had provided Ben an opportunity to surprise.

As the duo approached the finish line for the 13th time, Ben had made his way within a few short strides of Griffin's hip. *I have to make a pass now and pass hard. Otherwise, I won't be able to kick with him on the last lap.* His eyes wandered once again to the clock, which read 7 minutes and

47 seconds. If he kept up the pace he had held over the most recent mile, he would punch his ticket to the state championships. *But I'm on pace, I don't need to do anything crazy.* The searing pain in his throat whispered to him, hoping he would relax rather than press on. *36s. 72s.*

He sat just behind Terrence, both runners pressing around the track, the noise increasing around the fieldhouse as the battle neared its climax.

"Go Terrence! Come on, Ben!"

For the first time, Terrence checked over his shoulder, finally realizing there was danger present behind him. He and Ben locked eyes for a brief moment, the latter noticing a combination of surprise and panic in the eyes of the former. In an instant, Terrence was off and sprinting and Ben, who lacked the gift of speed, felt suddenly powerless. *I can't stay with him,* he thought, *but it's OK. I just need to hold pace, anyway. Winning doesn't matter.* However, his body was becoming increasingly tired with every step. The energy and spark he had been utilizing laps earlier had faded into complete flatness.

He heard the last-lap-signaling bell ring ahead of him as Terrence powered through the line, exploding with one final surge. The gap had swelled once again to an insurmountable margin. Ben, his head now flailing wildly, had eyes only for the clock as he checked one final split. *I just need a 36! That's it! You can do this!* He screamed inside his head, chanting positive thoughts, doing everything he could to will himself to a state qualifying time.

The final lap seemed to stretch on endlessly, with Ben pumping furiously to get to the finish. He was lapping slower runners now, moving slightly to the outside of lane one, trying to use every remaining pass as extra motivation. When he finally turned onto the last straightaway, his eyes went instantly to the clock. Griffin had already crossed the line, but the electronic timer continued to tick. *8:56 ... 8:57 ...* Ben prayed for it to stop moving so fast ... *8:58 ... 8:59 ...* he tried to throw himself forward, watching in agony as his last seconds ticked away ... *9:00 ... 9:01 ...*

***

"My official time was 9:01.50. So I missed the state championship qualifying time by a little over a second." Ben spoke the last words with a mixture of venom and disappointment, accenting the conclusion to his story with a particularly angry bit of shoveling. "I only had enough money saved up for one qualifying race and then the state championship. Which would have been today up at Penn State."

"So you used the rest of the money on this next race you're doing? Take another shot at the states time?" Neal asked. He was sitting in a pile of snow, his shovel laying to his right, as he listened intently to Ben's story.

"No, I decided to save it. Wait for something important. If I wasn't going to be able to run states, I didn't want to waste money trying to get a qualifying time." Ben chipped away at another patch of white snow, grimacing slightly. His hands were sore and callused, but it was an invisible wound that stung him most.

"So I'm confused ... what's this next race you said you were planning?"

"It's here." He cleared another block of ice. "Tonight." With one final strike, Ben removed the last bit of white that had concealed lane one of Bloomsburg track. "I'm time trailing another 3k here on this track."

"Tonight? Are you crazy? After all of this shoveling?" Neal touched his own pulsing arms gingerly. "Why not just wait?"

"It has to be tonight. Same day as the state meet. I'll see exactly where I stack up against everybody else." He threw his shovel down and briefly admired his accomplishment. "Besides, what if it snows tomorrow? And all this hard work is wasted?" Ben plopped down in the snow next to his friend. "No, it has to be tonight."

Together the pair laid in the powder in silence. The sun was now shining brightly upon their work, adding an extra layer of warmth and melting pieces of white that may have escaped their plow.

"I feel like I just need a few extra-long intervals. That should make my finish better." Ben blurted out, half to Neal, half to himself. "Also, I'll need to maybe get out a couple seconds faster ... Or maybe just throw in a surge in the middle laps ..." He couldn't stop himself from reanalyzing his race. Trying to figure out what he had done wrong.

Neal sat up from his position in the snow. He stared down at Ben who seemed lost in his own world, staring at the sky. He opened his mouth, as if he wanted to say something, but then paused. Instead, he pushed himself up to his feet and extended his hand.

"Come on Havleck, let's get you some breakfast."

Ben took it and pulled himself to his feet. Together, the duo gathered up their shovels and set course back towards the fence they had climbed over upon arrival.

***

In a fog of exhaustion and fatigue, Ben stumbled off the track. He wiped the spot of drool from the corner of his mouth with the back of his hand as he hobbled over to the nearest trash can. He coughed violently, leaning over its edge, but nothing came forth. Finally, he lifted his head, looking around for a place he could sit and regroup.

"Great race, Ben!" The compliment came from a high pitched voice to Ben's left. Katie was standing a few feet away and beaming at him.

"Thanks," he said weakly, forcing himself into a small smile. He pushed his arms off the trash can and shuffled slightly so that he was turned towards her. "I heard you cheering. It-um-it helped." He was becoming increasingly aware of how sweaty he was.

"Yeah, you ran great! We were both really impressed!" She turned over her shoulder looking for someone. "Hey Terrence!" Ben watched in confusion as Terrence Griffin turned from a group of well-wishers and wandered over to join them.

"Hey, nice race man," he said, extending a hand to Ben, who took it and shook it half-heartedly. As the pair stood face to face, it struck Ben how much taller Griffin was than him.

"Ben, this is my boyfriend Terrence," she said putting her arm around Terrence's waist. "We run together at Wyomissing." The pair turned and smiled at each other. Despite himself, Ben found it cute. "I saw you were way in the back and then all of a sudden you made up all that ground! You gave me a little scare!"

"Ha, yeah I guess so," Ben tried to force himself into another false grin after his lackluster response. He was having a hard time keeping his frustration out of his voice. The wounds from his defeat were too fresh for anyone to be spilling salt in them, whether intentional or not.

"Yeah, it was kinda a good wake up call for me," Griffin piled on with what he mistakenly saw as a compliment. "Where exactly do you run for?" He added, examining Ben's tattered gym uniform.

"I run for Bloomsburg High … we're a small school in district four." Ben looked at the ground as he spoke, growing increasingly embarrassed by his circumstance.

"Huh, never heard of it. Well, tell your coach, he can get cheap running singlets online. No reason you should have to race in *that*." He gestured at Ben's shirt.

"Yeah, I'll let him know," Ben lied. Flashing one last fake smile, he gathered himself to leave. "I gotta cool down, but maybe I'll see you guys at another meet some time?"

"Yeah, maybe!"

"Sounds good, man. How far are you thinking of going? Maybe I'll jump in with you if you don't mind?"

Of course I mind, Ben thought to himself. "Sure, always nice to have company. I've got another six left to do tonight," he replied.

"Six?!" Terrence looked at him appalled. "Geez, you are on your own with that one man …"

"Haha, fair enough," This time Ben smiled in earnest.

Seven miles later, his cool down was complete and he was forcing himself to think about other things. Like where he might be able to buy a shovel.

PTFCA Indoor State Championship Results, February 28th 2016

4x800m
1. North Penn 7:50.02 (Justin Franks, Brian Davies, Ryan Trimble, Bernard Mirun)
2. Coatesville 7:52.35 (Kyle King, Chris Wolff, Jason Dawson, Sean Dawson)
3. Abington 7:54.16 (Charles Mitchell, Eleazar Cesar, Thomas Moran, Kyle Murphy)
4. State College 7:57.96 (Jordan Douglas, Will Barton, Adam Cather, Peter Wellington)
5. West Chester North 7:59.85 (Will Aldrich, Austin Lynch, Jack Lowry, Andrew Eggleston)
6. Cedar Crest 8:01.53 (Alex Ditzler, Jon Steinbock, Aaron Ditzler, Adam Ditzler)
7. Cumberland Valley 8:01.60 (Chris Fuller, Michael Marquez, Scott Schiller, Caleb Hartzel)
8. Baldwin 8:03.44 (Angelo Jamison, Logan Dennis, James Christopher, JT Wolfe)

Mile
1. Tom Scarsdale, Sr Germantown Friends 4:12.98
2. Drew Magness, Sr Upper Merion 4:13.11
3. Greg McKenzie, Sr Quaker Valley 4:13.25
4. Liam Conley, So Methacton 4:16.43
5. Dathan Kaulbach, Jr Germantown Academy 4:17.18
6. JT Wolfe, Jr Baldwin 4:19.62
7. Teddy Crittenton, Sr Wissahickon 4:20.00
8. Billy Wilson, So Garnet Valley 4:22.36

800m
1. Andrew Mallon, Jr CB East 1:51.87
2. Joseph Rotz, Sr Lower Dauphin 1:52.05
3. Anthony Moore, So Penncrest 1:54.74
4. Peter Wellington, Sr State College 1:54.99
5. Justin Franks, Jr North Penn 1:55.18
6. Bernard Mirun, Jr North Penn 1:55.92
7. Alex Murphy, So Carlisle 1:56.35

8. *Brad Francis, Sr Bensalem 1:56.72*

3,000m
1. *Jayson Miller, Jr Manheim Township 8:35.16*
2. *Andrew Rosato, Sr Coatesville 8:37.82*
3. *Daniel McGee, Sr Bonner 8:38.90*
4. *Tom Seeley, Sr Bonner 8:42.44*
5. *Henry Gonzalez, Jr JP McCaskey 8:48.66*
6. *Noah West, So Mount Lebanon 8:50.11*
7. *Chase Morgan, Sr North Allegheny 8:52.67*
8. *Terrence Griffin, Sr Wyomissing 8:56.79*

Ben Havleck R2W Log, February 28th 2016

Not a bad run. Weather was a bit cold and body was aching a bit from shoveling. Lucky enough to have Neal there to time and give splits. Ran pretty even, just trying to focus on holding form and running strong. Splits of about 3:00/2:58/2:56 for 8:54.8h. Two mile warm up, six plus mile cool down. Plus two this morning for 12 on the day. Good start for 70 next week.

Ready for outdoors.

Chapter Twelve

I always found road trips rather enjoyable. Being trapped in a car isn't ideal, but it does force you into conversation. Sometimes it's nice to just talk to people. Plus, after a while, you have to get creative with your discussion topics and that's when you can really make a special connection.

Zat and I have had our fair share of road trips. Some of my fondest memories of our friendship feature the two of us sitting in a car and talking. Honestly, I don't even remember where we were driving to half the time. I guess it's nice to avoid distractions and actually have a worthwhile-wait a second are those runners?

"Pull over," I said, twisting in my seat to try and get a better look at the gaggle of harriers now in our rearview mirror.

"What-why?" Gary asked, slightly perturbed. "Elizabeth is gonna kill us if we are late for graduation."

"Actually, she's gonna kill *you*. I doubt she's too invested in whether or not I make an appearance. Sucks to be you."

"Touching."

The runners were getting further and further away from our car. "Just pull in up here," I said hastily, "We can park in the lot." On command, he drove past the exit I had pointed out. "Dude, what the hell?"

"Can you at least explain to me what you are doing?" He asked. Admittedly, it was a reasonable request.

"I'm looking for someone."

"Who?"

"Ben Havleck."

"Still? I thought you found him months ago?"

"No, just another false alarm," I replied disappointedly, "I've got a couple more leads, but I'm not sure how promising they are." We pulled to a stop in front of a red light. I watched the runners increase in size as they continued forward.

"Well, I hate to burst your bubble," Zat said, his eyes on the mirror above his head, "But those look like high school kids."

"High school?" I remarked confoundedly, "But I thought Bloomsburg High didn't have a team?"

"Maybe they added one," He shrugged, unconcerned. "Regardless, none of those are Havleck." Flicking his gaze back to the road, he prepared for the light change. I probably only had a moment to react. Even if none of those kids were the guy I needed, maybe they had some information I could use to help me find him. Unclicking my seat belt, I made to open the door and escape. As the light turned green, I threw my weight into the side of the car as I pulled on the handle. My shoulder collided hard with the door as it stayed firmly in place.

Smirking, Gary put his foot on the gas and drove away. "You good, Train?"

"Forgot to check the stupid lock," I mumbled in aggravation. "Can we just pretend I did something awesome instead?"

"Sure, buddy," He replied sympathetically. "Maybe you should just relax a bit until we get there."

"They make it look so easy in *The Fast and the Furious* movies …" I re-buckled my seatbelt and leaned back lamely in my chair. "So what time does graduation start again?"

"Ten o'clock," Zat replied, checking the clock on his dashboard, "So I think we will make it assuming we find parking reasonably quickly."

"Did you build in time to buy flowers?"

"Flowers?" He replied, sounding slightly concerned, "Should I have brought flowers?"

"I mean, it's your girlfriend's graduation. I feel like you should be bringing flowers."

"Crap, you're right." He slowed down the car, scanning the sides of the road. "If you see a grocery store or something, let me know."

"Will do," I took up duties as watchdog. There wasn't too much that looked promising. We passed a liquor store and a pizza shop before turning into a residential neighborhood. No sign of stores back here, although there were some cool houses sitting in large yards with well-kept gardens. Hey, well-kept gardens!

"Pull over."

"You're kidding, right? What is it now? Please tell me this isn't about runners."

"The only person that's going to be running around here is me," I replied, unclamping myself from my seat once more. "I'm getting you your flowers."

Gary cautiously wheeled toward the side of the road. "How exactly are you going to do that?"

I hopped out of the car. "Just be prepared to drive the getaway car."

Shutting the door on his confused face, I turned toward the nearest yard. A colorful set of daisies was positioned not too far away. It would just take a short sprint, a small tug and then another sprint. I checked to both the left and right. The block appeared empty. Mentally, I prepared myself, just as I might before a race. Then, I took off.

Just as I reached the "small tug" phase of the plan, I heard the front door of my target house creak open. Standing in the entranceway was an elderly woman, looking down horrified at the stranger robbing her carefully constructed garden. She let out a single scream of terror as I turned and sprinted back to the car.

"Go, go, go!" I hopped inside and slid onto the seat, slapping repeatedly on the dashboard. Gary didn't need the hint as he put his foot to the gas, pulling away from the disheveled shrubbery and its perhaps equally disheveled owner.

"Well, that could have gone better," I said once I had caught my breath. Leaning down, I examined my shoes and the dirt tracked into my friend's car. Then, I looked back at the fistful of flowers I had retrieved. "But hey, mission accomplished."

"You're a crazy person," Zat replied, shaking his head. "But you're a good friend."

"It's the least I could do considering I'm the reason you're stuck with this girl in the first place," I joked.

Gary and Elizabeth had first started dating almost a year ago after a chance encounter at a bar nearby campus. After a little prodding, I successfully convinced Gary to ask her out … so that I could try and make contact with Jimmy Springer. Little did I know, there was an authentic connection between these two lurking beneath the surface. With a successful school year's worth of a long distance relationship, we ended up here, at Elizabeth's graduation from Bloomsburg.

All I can say is if they end up married, I think I've earned the title of best man.

"How are things going with Springer anyway?" Zat asked as we neared our destination.

"We still chat from time to time," I replied, "He's a pretty cool dude." Up ahead, we could see lines of cars already parked along the street. Thus, Zat took the next spot available.

"Plus, he's crazy fast." I continued as we prepared to exit the car, "I was looking at some of his workout logs from sophomore year of high school-they're absurd!" I grabbed the handle and prepared to push, "Honestly, it's some of the most impressive-agh!" As I tried to open the door, I jammed my already sore shoulder into the still locked exit.

"Did you just-"

"I don't want to talk about it."

"But you literally *just* did the same-"

"I don't want to talk about it." Now properly unlocking the door, I slumped out onto the sidewalk. As we started our trek to the stadium, I rubbed my shoulder gingerly. "Anyway," I persisted, trying to distract myself from the pain, "After his freshman year, most of the team graduated. And the guys who were left weren't particularly impressive runners. So at that point there wasn't much reason to hold back."

A light buzz of noise drifted to our ears as we neared the stadium. Checking down at my wrist, I saw that it was five minutes to ten.

"So how'd he end up doing?" Zat asked as we handed our tickets to the attendant at the gate. "Was he happy with his sophomore year?"

"Well … that's kind of two different questions …"

Jimmy Springer, December 2016

"Would you rather never be able to bend your elbows or never be able to eat cheese again?" Riley Joseph kicked the black and white soccer ball diagonally the turf. It rolled swiftly across to his friend who stood waiting for it.

"That's easy, I'm giving up the cheese." Jimmy controlled the ball, kicked it twice back and forth, and then sent it to his partner.

"No cheese? That means no nachos. No pizza. No milk-"

"Wait a second, no milk? You never said anything about milk."

"Oh, milk is definitely part of the equation," Riley dribbled the ball in a small circle before firing it in the air to his friend. "Milk is cheese, isn't it?"

Springer expertly controlled the ball with his chest and let it drop down toward the artificial grass. "I'm pretty sure that cheese is milk, but milk isn't cheese. It's like a rectangle-square thing." He juggled the ball on his cleats for a few touches. "Regardless, I'll just switch to soy or something. I *need* to be able to bend my elbows."

"Do you, though?" Riley replied seriously. "Here, send it to me." He focused all his energy on keeping his arms straight as the soccer ball came flying in his direction. With his right arm, he smacked the ball down and corralled it with his legs. Then, he dribbled forward, his arms swinging ridiculously at his sides as he ran. Jimmy laughed hysterically at the absurdity of his friend's display.

"Hard to believe you just turned 16. You're old enough to drive now!" Jimmy shook his head in disbelief. "For the record, there's no way I'm getting in a car with you."

"I've seen you play Mario Kart: you're better off riding with me than driving yourself," Riley said, kicking the ball over, this time utilizing fully functioning appendages. "Speaking of which, I think a couple of the guys are coming over tonight to hang out and play video games. You should come by-assuming you don't have any races or anything."

"Nah, I'm free for the next couple months, actually. I'm not racing again until the spring. Focusing strictly on training." Jimmy dribbled ahead toward the nearest soccer goal. "Got some big goals for next season." He took a hard jab against an imaginary defender, then stepped into a shot.

With a powerful swing of his right foot, he launched the sphere into the top corner of the net.

"Big goals?" Riley said, walking forward to retrieve the ball from the net. "How do you top a state championship? What are you going to do-win the race twice?" He rolled the orb back to Springer, who was waiting for it at the edge of the penalty box.

"Something like that," He replied coyly. "You finally gonna come watch me race this year?"

"Hmmm," His friend paused, stroking his chin as though he was deep in thought, "No, I don't think so. I'm not really interested in competitive exercising."

"Oh, I'll show you competitive exercising," Jimmy grinned. "Come guard me." He waved his arm, encouraging his comrade to step forward. With a smile, Riley shook his head. But he couldn't resist a challenge.

Casually Springer dribbled the ball back and forth, then when Riley stepped close enough, he launched onto the offensive. With a big kick, he shot the ball ahead of his opponent, who was caught with his momentum in the wrong direction. Seizing on this advantage, Jimmy set course straight ahead for a shot. However, as he lined up his foot, Joseph came sliding into his path, blocking the attempt just after it left his friend's cleat. Both chased after the deflected ball, but Riley reacted a fraction quicker and, therefore, corralled it first.

"You've lost a step, Jim," He teased, now gathering himself for a counterattack. He didn't have the same speed with his first step as Jimmy did, but he had great control over the soccer ball. Moving to his left, he stuck the ball out in the open before slinging it back underneath his body to the right. Springer quickly responded to the move and realigned himself defensively.

"Don't speak so soon-" But at the moment when Jimmy retorted, Riley struck. He popped the ball up in the air over his opposition's head and darted after it. Caught completely off guard, the cross country runner did not have time to get back in front. Before the ball even landed on the turf, Riley had kicked it straight into the back of the net.

"What was that you were saying?" he mocked, standing triumphantly in front of the goal. "Something about not speaking too soon?"

"Well played," Jimmy smiled. He followed the path of the shot and scooped up the ball. "You're going to get our soccer coach fired."

"What do you mean?"

"Well, clearly he doesn't know anything about the sport," He said, straightening up and walking back toward his friend. "How did he think it was a good idea to cut you from the team?"

"He didn't cut me," Riley replied awkwardly, "I didn't try out this year."

"Oh, right," Springer fidgeted uncomfortably. He found it odd that his friend would quit his favorite sport, but he didn't think it was necessary to press the issue right now. "Anyway," he continued, changing the subject, "Who all is coming tonight?"

"A couple of the other sophomores from my biology lab group: Corey Smith, Jeremy Seidel, and Grant Rosen."

"Ah, gotcha," He tried to keep some mock enthusiasm in his voice, but his tone still seemed lackluster.

"I know you think these guys are trouble, but, trust me-they've just been getting a bad rep. They're actually really cool and super friendly. We've got a decent amount in common." At this, Jimmy gave a small dismissive snort which his friend picked up on immediately.

"See this what I was worried about. I knew you wouldn't get it. Looking down on the rest of us from your golden throne." Riley continued defiantly, "Not everybody lives a perfect little life like you. Sometimes you need something to take the edge off."

"Give me a break, my life's not perfect!" Jimmy replied tossing the soccer ball aside angrily.

"Oh please, there's people lining up to fill your shoes! What's so crappy about being a state champion? Living in a big house, with nice cars and fancy toys?"

"I've got my stuff like anybody else! I just handle it differently. I think there are better ways-"

"Better? Better for who?"

"Well, I just mean-like," Springer sputtered, "It's the right thing to do, I guess."

"You act like we exist in this just place where good things happen to good people. Well, I've got news for you: that's a fantasy world. Every day, there's 'bad' guys getting ahead and you can be damn sure there's good people suffering. So you can keep living your life trying to live up to some standard that somebody told you was 'right' when you were a little kid, but me? I'm gonna go ahead do what's best for me.

"Because at the end of the day, that's all anybody really cares about."

"I guess I just have a little more faith in people than you do," Jimmy remarked proudly.

Riley considered him with a long meaningful look. When he finally spoke, his tone was no longer angry, but more sympathetic, almost pitying. "Yeah, that's how I used to be too. I just hope they don't let you down."

Chapter Thirteen

Jimmy Springer, May 2015

He sat on the edge of the bed. Outside he could hear the laughter and joy of the other athletes on the lawn. *It must be nice*, he thought to himself. His face became warm once again. If the tears came with another surge, he may not be able to fight them off. Blinking furiously, a few drops slipped through his defenses and splattered the sheets beneath him. It wasn't fair. This was supposed to be the moment that would make everything right. When everyone would be happy again.

A knock came at the door and startled the boy on the bed. The palm of his hand wiped his face before turning its attention to twist the knob. Standing in the entranceway was a shorter man with glasses and wild, messy brown hair. He smiled, holding up a stack of papers. "I thought we should discuss some strategy for tomorrow."

Jimmy Springer and Coach David Ames entered the stadium at Shippensburg early the next morning. It was already packed with reporters, fans and parents, but Jimmy wasn't too concerned about the pressure or the "bright lights". He had already succeeded on the big stage.

He watched the other runners as they walked in. Some looked nervous, others overwhelmed by the mass of spectators, the stadium, or the atmosphere. Springer had long passed that stage of inexperience. He had even passed the sadness he felt the previous night. Now he was simply angry. If no one cared about him anymore, he would make them care. He would make history.

Together he and Coach Ames sat quietly, almost awkwardly, as time slowly ticked down. Eventually, Springer rose to his feet, throwing his jersey around his neck like a cape and grabbing his spikes. Coach Ames rose as well.

"Remember Jimmy-ten minutes is full recovery."

The 3200 was first on today's agenda. An eight lap race covering about two miles of running. He jogged carefully onto the infield, stone-faced, trying to project an air of invincibility to those around him. Stretching. Drills. Strides. All in silence and seriousness. As they lined up the competitors for the event, someone stuck out his hand.

"Good luck James." It struck him the wrong way. *James*. Something burned slightly within him, his eyes briefly stinging.

"My name is Jimmy." And he ignored the outstretched arm of the blonde haired boy so that he could turn his face from him. They took seeds one through six and walked them up to the top of the waterfall, pulling Jimmy and a few other athletes away from the majority of the field. He took a deep breath to calm himself, wiping a trail of sweat from underneath his eye. Or at least he pretended it was sweat.

"Runners to your marks …" He took a long step forward to the line. "Get set …" A slight look to his right revealed five nervous faces. A quiet confidence emerged inside of him. *BANG!* The crowd erupted and Jimmy sprinted coolly through traffic to take up a spot at the front. Around him, the field fought for position, but subconsciously everyone was defaulting to the defending champion.

There was no doubt the first 200 meters was fast. Maybe a 29 second bend. *They are scared now*, he thought to himself. Casually and easily, he took his foot off the gas.

Coach Ames was waiting for him near the 300 meter mark as planned. He didn't open his mouth, instead giving a simple nod. Springer glided along at the front. The first 400 would still appear quick, but really they had gone down from four minute pace to five. He knew it. *If the others do, they sure aren't acting like it.*

No one so much as challenged him down around the back stretch. Or by Coach Ames. Or again into the straightaway. This time, when they passed the start the clock read 2:23 and the reality of the situation was etched clearly for all to see. It spelled out the dramatic change the pack had underwent from meet record pace to above state qualifying pace over the course of the first two laps and it kick-started the field.

Panic was setting in from all sides. Coaches were screaming for athletes to quicken the tempo once more. Frantic jostling and positioning recommenced within the pack. Yet Springer was clear of it all at the front, just as planned. He had wasted no energy and stayed out of traffic. As they made their way into the backstretch for a third time, a few runners came swinging wide. Scott Zarniack, the Western Pennsylvania champion in this event, surged wildly to the front, dragging Owen Ward of Coatesville with him.

The blistering early pace had resumed. Runner after runner seemed to be flying by on Jimmy's outside. He was in fifth. Then eighth. But every time he passed the 300 mark, his coach spoke the same barely audible word: "Wait".

Jimmy was keeping an eye on his 400 splits as he came through. He had dipped his pace evenly down over the next three laps, while the runners at the front had burned themselves out going from 76 down to 66. As a result, most were already slowing back down. Just as easily as he had been passed, Springer floated back towards the front. Every runner he overtook sent a new burst of energy through his body. The adrenaline of his race was empowering, wiping clean the pain of his daily life and replacing it with the ecstasy of competition and the thrill of impending victory.

He was right on the shoulder of the leaders again, closing in on the race's final two laps.

"GO NOW JIMMY! IT'S TIME TO GO! PUSH!" For the first time, Coach Ames was positively shouting, a far cry from his silent, stoic demeanor he had maintained in the race's early stages. Springer responded, pressing for a brief moment and breaking loose of the field with an impressive surge. A pair of Coatesville runners, Sean Williams and Owen Ward, were his only real competitors now. He could hear their strained breathing as they doggedly followed him. A slight wheezing was coming from Williams. Ward's arms were beginning to flail. But their spirit was more broken than their actual bodies.

Jimmy held the lead around the turn of the penultimate lap. *I can't believe it*, he thought to himself. *They bought it*. He smiled to himself as he effortlessly loped down the back straightaway, Williams and Ward running steadfastly in his wake. However, the lead group of three was increasing in size. The chasers were making a surprise bid to join them. Williams looked wildly over his shoulder, confused by the turn of events.

Springer's initial burst. Ames's wild cheering. It was all a ruse. Jimmy hadn't gone to the front to start his kick: he'd gone there to delay it. Faking a surge then slowing the pace back down fit perfectly with his plan to save as much energy as possible. It simultaneously guaranteed a true kicker's finish, the type of race he was confident he would win.

Stunned by the turn of events, Sean Williams desperately rushed to the front, going back ahead of Springer so that he held the lead into the bell. The sophomore from Union Valley held his ground, stepping slightly sideways to avoid becoming boxed in on the inside rail. They were sprinting in earnest along the far straightaway, but Jimmy knew he still had gears left in reserve.

The roar of the crowd grew in intensity as the runners rounded their final turn. Jimmy tried to remain patient, but he could feel opposing sprinters closing in on both his inside and outside. Plus, Williams was noticeably slowing. His push from home had come too furiously and too soon.

"GO JIMMY, YOU GOTTA GO NOW!" This time Ames's screams were authentic. Seizing the moment, Jimmy flipped on his switch. Slingshotting himself off the bend, Springer came flying into the straightaway, a slight breeze brushing across his face, wind whipping gently through his hair. He tried to remain smooth, to keep his face calm. 75 meters. 50 meters. 25 meters. He chanced a look to his outside. There was no one. He chanced another to his inside. All clear. The emotion of the moment hit.

With a dramatic fist pump and a scream of triumph, Jimmy Springer won the state championship at 3200 meters.

There was nothing like the feeling after a good race. The young sophomore from Union Valley had a certain swagger about him as he walked the perimeter of the track at Shippensburg. Jimmy was wearing a gray, long sleeve t-shirt with his navy blue racing shorts and carrying a lemon flavored Gatorade in his right hand. His 3200 gold medal was tucked away inside his backpack. *One down, two to go.*

As he continued to make his way back towards the tent, he noticed a few heads turn in his direction. A few whispers of his name. It was difficult not to let the attention flood to his head. Of course, as any 16 year old would do, he thoroughly enjoyed his newfound fame. It fit nicely into the place in his heart that had once been filled by the comfort of his family.

Coach Ames was waiting for him at the team's tent, a shaded space already carved out for Jimmy to stretch. "C'mon Springer, let's get you off your feet." He hastened his athlete under cover, removing the backpack from Jimmy's shoulders. "How are you feeling?"

"Not bad ... Definitely better than districts," He sat down gingerly and began to stretch his hamstrings. "It didn't hurt that the two mile was like ten seconds slower this time around."

"Yes, I'd like to think we learned a lot from last week." Coach Ames flipped through the meet program. "By the looks of it, you've got a little less than an hour before the mile. In a bit, we'll have you go for a brief jog. You're already warmed up at this point." He watched as Jimmy switched legs. "Think of this as a workout where I felt extra generous on the rest."

His athlete rolled over onto his stomach and pressed his upper body up to stretch his back. He could feel a slight tug and let out a barely audible groan. As he relaxed back to the ground, he noticed a few runners from yesterday's trials of the mile jogging outside the stadium.

"What's the plan, Coach?" He took a sip of his Gatorade before he rotated his body so he was sitting up again, facing his teacher. For comfort, he folded his shins beneath his hands.

"Well, we have a couple of guys to worry about. There's this kid from Cumberland Valley, Hull, who is pretty quick ..."

Before long, Jimmy was re-lacing his spikes on the infield. His mind wandered to and from his race plan. To his right, Brad Hull was striding powerfully towards the 50 yard mark. Last week, he had won his district championship on this very track in 4:10.57. Hull eyed Jimmy as he made a return stride.

Behind his stare seemed a forced attempt at intimidation, causing Jimmy to smirk as he finished tying his left spike. *Why do distance runners think that's a good idea? I'm not going to be scared of some scrawny kid. A shot putter maybe, but not a distance runner ...*

He popped to his feet and took his first stride with about 75 percent effort. As he finished, he noticed a runner behind him sprinting quickly to his left shoulder. "Good luck out there Jim-bo." The athlete gave Jimmy a small pat on the back, before turning to walk in another direction.

This was Upper Merion's Drew Magness, the only runner to beat Jimmy over 1600 meters at the District One Championships last week. Magness had impressed with a blistering finishing kick to beat the other competitors to the line, winning with a 59-second final lap. As Jimmy watched, Drew violently shook out his arms and legs, mixing in a few light slaps to his face. Springer shook his head. *Distance runners ...*

The wait to start his second race was agonizing, time passing impossibly slow. But eventually, it was time to line up. Springer and a group of eleven other runners made their way down the front straightaway. Some mixed in an extra, light stride; others were doing plyometric drills like high knees or butt-kicks. Jimmy was rather calm. His nervous energy had evaporated with his first race. His orange top clung to his chest, wet from a combination of sweat and water that he had doused himself with to keep cool.

A gentle hum was projecting from the stands, now packed to the brim with spectators. Jimmy briefly admired the mass of fans before turning his attention to the official at the starting stripe. When they lined up, he saw that Scott Zarniack, who also raced the 3200 meters, was positioned directly on his inside.

"Ready to do this again?" he asked with a grin, sticking out his hand. Jimmy took it and shook.

"No," he replied, returning the smile, "Think they would consider pushing the start back for us?"

As if in reply to his joke, the starter had taken his position on the first curve. "Runners set!" In the instants before the gun, there was complete silence. Jimmy enjoyed the momentary calm before the storm.

The shot was followed promptly by an eruption of noise. The calm was gone and in its place was a frenzied jockeying of sprinting athletes. Jimmy carefully avoided the horde, moving himself to the back of the field. He, Magness and Zarniack were situated in the last three spots while Hull had assertively taken up second position, just behind a runner Jimmy did not recognize.

Hull took a brief glance over his shoulder, curious about his competition's whereabouts. He looked uncomfortable, uncertain whether he should press the pace and take on the lead this early. The pace was moderate, but nothing herculean as Jimmy ambled through 300 meters. Despite the fact that he was trailing at a pedestrian pace, his body still didn't feel particularly comfortable. His legs seemed reluctant to turn over quickly.

Things were still bunched together after the first lap, but now Brad Hull was beginning to get anxious near the front. Every second the pace slowed would give the kickers an advantage against him on the final lap. After another 200 yards at a manageable pace, he finally succumbed to impulse and charged to the lead. The injection of speed transformed the field from a clustered pack to a straight line and, sensing that he was losing touch, Drew Magness stepped outside to move his way through the crowd. Without hesitation, Springer mirrored his tactic.

The field seemed to be wilting under the strain of the new pace: Zarniack was off the back in last place, clearly tired from his efforts an hour earlier. A few others were beginning to falter as well, yet Magness still looked incredibly smooth. Much smoother than Jimmy felt. Although his legs were loosening, the increase in pace was taxing to his fatigued body. He tried to forget about those reservations and focus instead on the small "UM" insignia stitched into the back of Drew Magness's jersey.

At the 800 mark, Hull surged once again, cementing a gap between him and the field. Running along the far straightaway, it seemed like he might simply ease away from his competitors and seal the victory. For whatever reason, Magness was still content to wait in fourth and Jimmy, bound by his pre-race strategy, was locked on his shoulder. His mind was telling him to go, although his body was perfectly happy to sit back. *I can't just settle here, Hull's getting away.*

On the bend, Springer looked for his coach and spotted Ames leaning along the fence. *What do I do Coach?!* He tried to scream it with his eyes. But his concern was not matched on his coach's face. Ames remained completely silent. He simply held up a hand, indicating the sophomore should stay put. Frustrated, Jimmy rounded the turn. Surprisingly, Coach Ames had said nothing to him the entire race. *Is this some type of test? Because this feels like the wrong time ...*

With one lap to go, the official rang his bell and once again, Hull snuck a look over his shoulder. He had run the entire lap completely unchallenged. The surprise at his dominance was unmistakable. Magness cheated up a bit and made one more pass just before the turn, taking over third place, but he still was not making an honest attempt at the front. *What the heck is he waiting for?!*

Meanwhile, Hull's gap was widening. His stride, formerly crippled by hesitation was now emboldened with confidence. One final surge along the far straightaway would surely clinch the championship. Jimmy's body ached, but it had at least adjusted to the pace. The gradual build-up to speed had not been a significant shock to his system and, as a result, he was ready to turn things up a notch for the finish.

Screw this, I can't just wait here. I have to go. Although it was specifically against his coach's pre-race orders, he stepped to the outside, ready to go by Magness and unleash whatever speed reserves he had left to go after Hull.

Then, it happened. Jimmy had been told just how absurd Drew Magness's finishing burst had been at Districts, but watching his ability unfold right in front of his eyes was almost indescribable. In an instant, Magness had completely changed gears, dropping into a sprint and powering his way through the remaining straightaway into the curve with half a lap to go. Jimmy reacted as best he could, trying furiously to latch onto the move. Now they were running in second and third, Hull still holding a lead, but his advantage was beginning to shrink.

As they approached the final 100 meter straightaway, the crowd had taken notice of the two oncoming kickers and the cheering was intensifying. Magness, arms pumping, powered his way off the turn while Jimmy tried desperately to hang on. Drew embraced the roar from the stands, feeding off the sound and moving onto Hull's shoulder with just 50 meters to go. Both men were dead even, Hull calling on his final ounces of fight, determine not to let his once insurmountable lead be completely diminished. Each runner was completely absorbed by the finishing close of the other, unaware that a third athlete was split out to their left.

Jimmy grit his teeth, digging in, demanding his body to turn over just a bit faster. He watched as Magness broke the draw that was just ahead of him. Watched as Drew's final push broke Hull's spirit. And Drew seemed to know it. *He thinks he has it won.*

For a split second, Magness lifted his foot off the gas, easing away from his former intensity, preparing for a victory celebration. And in that brief lapse of concentration, Jimmy made one ultimate drive to the line. Throwing his body forward into a concluding lean, his legs gave out beneath him and he tumbled forward across the finish line, falling hard to the track.

"How long?" Jimmy stepped down from the podium to meet Coach Ames who had been snapping pictures of the awards ceremony.

"About 45 minutes I'd guess. Maybe less." He replied casually, fixing the lens of his camera.

"You're kidding, right?" Jimmy walked with a slight limp, his calf wrapped in a bandage. A painful abrasion stung his right hip. As he continued back towards the tent, he removed his gold medal from around his neck and passed it to his Coach. "I still don't get why you made me go to that awards ceremony. I would have rather been off my feet."

Ames smiled. "You'll thank me one day. Winning a gold medal is a fantastic achievement. You have to enjoy it while you can. Who knows when you could win another one?"

"I was thinking about 45 minutes from now. Maybe less." He flopped down on his back and stretched out his aching limbs. Now that the adrenaline of his victory in the 1600 meters had evaporated, he could feel all the places his body had been ripped open by his fall. The most painful was his calf, which he had clipped with his right spike as he spiraled out of control. "So what's the plan for this one?"

"Give whatever you have left and see what happens," Ames shrugged.

"Ah, so this is why they pay you the big bucks."

"Haha how about, don't be an idiot and chase Hadrick again?"

Now it was Jimmy's turn to laugh. He had attempted this same triple last week at districts as well, taking first and second before crumbling to seventh in his final event, the 800 meters. Lewis Hadrick of Springfield had taken the pace out in a blistering 52 seconds and, as a result, Jimmy's legs had been blasted to pieces. After a painfully slow last 200 meters, he made it to the line less than a second ahead of ninth place and barely secured his spot at states. Considering the effort he had put forth obtaining his gold medals thus far, he would need to go out much slower than 52 if he were to have any hopes of even finishing the race. Let alone winning it.

"At this point, the only thing you can do is relax and have fun." Coach Ames took a seat so that he was facing his athlete. "Go out at the back, get your legs underneath you and then use whatever you have left at 300 meters to go." He gave Jimmy a long searching look before adding softly, "Live in the moment. This is your escape."

He barely even jogged before entering the check-in zone. Aerobically, he felt strong and recovered, but physically, his body refused to cooperate. After a lackluster set of drills, he threw on his spikes and laid face down on the ground, waiting for the officials to call them together for the start. Occasionally, he picked his head up to look around. Lewis Hadrick was powerfully going through drills on the far corner of the infield. A few other runners he recognized from his preliminary runs were also dancing about, looking incredibly springy and fresh. Jimmy was unsure he would ever feel like that again in his life.

"LARGE SCHOOL BOYS 800 METERS!" An official in a bright orange shirt was waving a white flag near the 100 meter mark, calling the competitors to assemble. Reluctantly, Springer lifted himself from the ground and slowly made his way to the gesturing man. He tucked his singlet carefully into his shorts as he walked. Most of the runners were already gathered together, eager to begin the race they had waited all day to start. A few others came flying by Jimmy as he walked, either completing a final stride or recycling a pre-race drill.

His seed for this race placed him all the way on the outside curve, meaning he would have a long, crowded way to run if he wanted to grab a spot on the rail for the first bend. *Great. Because I was worried this race might be* too *easy*, he thought to himself as he settled in next to a short, muscular runner with a black and red striped jersey. The raising of the starting pistol drew little reaction from Jimmy, who took a nearly imperceptible step forward, gingerly balancing on his left calf.

Bang!

In an instant, the field had shot out five meters ahead of him. Getting to the inside quickly became the least of Jimmy's problems. He ran through the turn in dead last, no hope of keeping pace with the effort Hadrick was throwing down out front. *I've got nothing,* he thought hopelessly, *I can't even dream of matching this right now*. He eyed the turf just to his left. It would be easy enough to drop out. He would barely have to change course. One step off the track and his suffering would be ended in an instant.

As he began to relax, he could hear 200 meter splits for the leaders ahead of him. "23 … 24 … 25 …"

"27 Jimmy!" Coach Ames was sprinting clockwise around the outer fence to get within earshot. "They won't hold this! Stay focused!"

Hadrick had set out at a suicide pace and the field had been unafraid to follow. At least a second behind the next to last athlete, Jimmy willed himself to press on, his mind pleading with his body to cooperate. *They're gonna come back. I promise they're gonna come back. Just keep fighting.*

A wall of wind was waiting for them as the runners made their way onto the home stretch. Jimmy put his head down and charged ahead, trying desperately to make contact with the next athlete in front of him so that he could draft his way through to the bell. He caught sight of the clock up ahead as he finally made his first pass, quickly followed by a second. As he moved wide to go by a pair of competitors, he glimpsed the leader cross the start line for the pen-ultimate time. *Holy shit....*

"49 SECONDS AT THE BELL FOR LEWIS HADRICK!" The announcement reverberated around the stadium as Jimmy pressed on, struggling through the line at maybe 56. Those seven seconds seemed like an eternity, yet he couldn't dwell on Hadrick. He still had to pass six more runners just to get into second place. Fortunately, the excitement of the chase was propelling him forward, distracting him from the screaming pain in his lower body.

Rounding the bend into 300 to go, he felt a surge of energy pulse through his body. With the wind now at his back, he let himself drift wide to open up his stride and pass a trio of struggling runners. Then, just before the 200 meter mark, he picked off one more, navigating his way back to the inside as he prepared to run his final turn. There were still three runners left to catch if he was going to earn his coveted third gold.

His legs were beginning to rig, but he knew his anguish would be nothing compared to the runners who had pressed so vigorously early on. Despite this advantage, he could not close down the gap more than a few inches. The others were simply too quick.

Hadrick was flanked on either side by his two main pursuers, one of which was the short runner that Jimmy had started next to, dressed in red and black. This boy was pinned to the inside with no room to maneuver to his right. The third member of the group, sporting a yellow jersey, was positioned perfectly on the outside, ready to strike with his finishing kick.

With 100 meters to go, it became clear that Hadrick was now spent. His courageous start had been too ambitious and his pace was rapidly slowing towards a crawl.

From his position, Jimmy watched it all unfold. As Hadrick wearily drifted into the outside of his lane, the runner in red and black stepped hard to his inside in an attempt to split Lewis and the rail. However, in his fatigued state, he stepped awkwardly on the track's metal barrier, rolling his ankle violently. He crumbled towards the ground and, as he leaned forward, made contact with the already wobbly frame of Lewis Hadrick. Together the two collapsed to the track. The runner in yellow countered instinctively, hurdling the fallen duo, but his balance and momentum were thrown out of rhythm. Springer, on the other hand, had time to react, smoothly transitioning to the outside.

The fall had been enough to bring him within striking distance of the new leader. Enough to shift the momentum in his direction. The taste of victory was on the tip of his tongue again. He grit his teeth for one final, unthinkable push and powered through the straightaway, pumping his arms dramatically, hoping their momentum would transfer to his leg turnover. In the final meters of the race, he surged triumphantly from the wreckage behind him and tore through the line first.

I did it! He screamed inwardly as he fell to his knees, desperate for breath. *I did it!* He looked up at the stands, scanning the faces for two people he hoped might somehow be there. His victory solving their issues, reminding them of what once was. But they were not there.

Like an ocean wave, the realization that his family was split in pieces rushed over his body. With his face in his hands, he celebrated his last gold medal with tears.

Jimmy Springer, August 2015
   ... Pardon me while I burst, into flames ... I've had enough of the world and its people's mindless games ... So pardon me while I burn and rise above the flame .... Pardon me, pardon me, I'll never be the same ...
   "Who sings this?"
   "It's Incubus, man. You don't remember them from back when we used to drive everywhere together?"
   "Nah, not really …"
   "Times aren't like they used to be, huh?" Matt glanced sideways at the boy seated next to him. As they drove further, the street was flanked by the high school on their right side and a construction site to their left. "Wait, they closed the old library, too?"
   "Yeah, they knocked it down a couple months ago. Probably right after your spring break ended." Jimmy scratched his arm absentmindedly. "Remember when you locked me in the car before our first cross meet?"
   "Oh yeah," Matt laughed, "You were such a little baby back then." He glanced quickly to his left before returning his gaze to the road. "Heck, I almost beat you in a race."
   "You *did* beat me," Jimmy said, smiling back. "And I never forgot it." Flashing across his memory was their epic finish in Springer's first invitational. After a wild sprint, they had crossed the line at essentially the exact same time. Each was convinced the other had beaten him, but to this day, neither had confirmed it in the official results.
   Foolishly, Jimmy had let up a few steps before the finish line, allowing Matt to catch back up in the final meters. Now, whenever he struggled to find the drive to push himself in practice or a race, he remembered the anguish he had experienced following that performance and it motivated him. Looking back, the race felt like it happened a lifetime ago.
   "You know I used that same move on Magness in the 16. Same thing you did to me at Hershey that race. Waited until he eased up-then nipped him at the line." He mimicked a dramatic lean from the passenger seat to accent his statement.
   "That must have been sick," Matt wheeled his car carefully into the school parking lot. A few other runners were already stationed there. "Wish I could have been there to see that." He removed his keys from the ignition and opened his door. Simultaneously, both men exited the car.
   "Can you pop the back?" Jimmy called.
   "Why?"

"My shoes are back there." Matt looked down to see a pair of flip-flops on his friend's feet. With a small sigh, he clicked his keys so that Jimmy could open the trunk.

"Why didn't you just wear your shoes to practice?"

"I don't like the way running shoes feel. Too constricting. I want my feet to breathe a little bit. Makes me feel more comfortable and free."

Matt rolled his eyes. "Somebody around here needs to bring you down a peg," he said as Springer slipped on his socks. "You've kind of become a tool since I graduated." They laughed as Jimmy finished pulling on his shoes. He laced them up before rising back to his feet.

A few more runners had joined the cluster in the lot since Matt had first parked. With the pair's addition, the group totaled about 12 runners. Jimmy glanced around the assembly, looking for someone.

"Hey, what time is it?"

"How do you *still* not have a watch? Aren't you supposed to be like, a runner or something?"

"Adam, what time is it?" Jimmy said, ignoring Matt and instead directing his attention towards one of the runners in the circle.

"It's 6:05," the boy responded, looking down at his wrist. Jimmy frowned slightly. Again he scanned the parking lot. "Did Ames tell you if he was coming today?"

"No," Jimmy responded, giving up his search. "Well, it wouldn't be the first time he was late … I'm sure he'd want us to get started." His voice became more assertive sounding as he pressed on.

"Younger guys, you guys can do four. Spencer, you can lead them down toward the River Trail. And then the rest of you get in five or six. No heroes out there, alright? It's a recovery day." At his command, the groups assembled and prepared to begin their assignments. Many of the younger athletes looked at Jimmy with awed respect. He wondered just how blindly they would be willing to follow him. Just because he had run a couple fast times.

Together, he and Matt set the tempo for the longer group, who had subliminally defaulted to Jimmy's leadership. Everyone was running about the same pace, but there was a small, three second space between the front pair and the next five. Matt looked over his shoulder in confusion before pressing on at Jimmy's side.

"What's up with the gap?" he asked, "Do you not shower anymore?"

Jimmy half smiled, "They're all scared of me or something. They just assume because, you know, I'm so much faster than them, they should never be running with me. Like, they don't even want to try." He couldn't hide the disappointment in his voice. "Times aren't like they used to be, huh?"

They ran on in silence, the distance between the leaders and the followers now slowly beginning to expand. Jimmy kept absentmindedly drifting a couple steps ahead of Matt before catching himself and slowing back down to stay even.

"So which loop are we doing?" Matt said as Jimmy led him into a right turn. They were exiting the neighborhood closest to the school.

"I was thinking we'd do the Blue Jay Park Six Miler," he looked back over his shoulder to check for cars before crossing the street. "Haven't done it in a while. You cool with that?"

"Sure. I'll probably have to add on afterward though. I'm supposed to be getting up to like 70 miles this week."

"70?!" Jimmy looked stunned. "That's like ten *per day*."

Matt laughed. "Yeah, well that isn't even that much honestly. Relative to a lot of schools. Like when *you* get to college-at Stanford or Oregon or wherever-you'll probably peak at like 90 or 100."

"How could you even run 100 miles in a week? I don't think that's physically possible."

"Glenn Fisher always used to say he was going to run 100 in a week during the summer. But to be fair, he was a crazy person."

"What's he up to these days?"

"Heck if I know." Matt shrugged his shoulders, "Haven't talked to him since we graduated."

Jimmy clicked down the pace another notch as the duo entered into a wooded trail. The soft surface crunched gently beneath their feet. The two remained quiet as they ran single file through a narrow stretch before emerging in a short, grass field. Matt's breathing had grown more strained as the pair reverted to running side by side.

"So ..." he said, "Tell me ... more about states ... You never gave me the ... full breakdown."

"Well I was exhausted after districts, not gonna lie. I didn't even really want to try the triple." They turned into a sharp downhill and Jimmy unfurled his long powerful stride, forcing Matt to press a bit more. "Ames told me he wanted me to promise to at least start each race, but after that I could drop out if I wanted to-"

"-But he knew you'd never drop out."

"Exactly. I think he always believed I could pull it off. He just didn't want any extra pressure on me." Jimmy paused as they approached the base of a hill. Shortening his steps, he charged strongly forward. Matt did his best to keep up, head down, breathing unsteady. Once they had crested the hill, Jimmy resumed his story.

"The 32 was pretty different than last year. Last year, they all just let me run away with it. They just kinda assumed I'd come back. Since I'm established now, we knew that would never happened this year so we had to switch it up." Jimmy glanced sideways at his former teammate. It was past the point in the run where he would be able to contribute to the conversation. By now Jimmy estimated, they were over five miles into the loop.

"The other races, I just got lucky, honestly. Magness messed up in that 16. That was the hardest race for sure." They crossed back over the street, the outline of the school now coming into focus. "And the 800, if Hadrick doesn't take out half the field with his fall …" He shrugged rather than finish his sentence.

They ran the final stretch without speaking. Jimmy strode along comfortably as Matt struggled to hang on beside him. When they reached the parking lot, the four-mile group was stretching on the ground. The sound of the quick turnover of feet on concrete quickly captured the attention of the young runners who watched in amazement as Jimmy cruised to a stop a few feet in front of them. Meanwhile, Matt crumbled over, putting his hands on his knees and gasping for breath.

"You still adding on?" Jimmy said, fully appreciating his friend's suffering for the first time. Matt weakly dropped himself to the ground and laid down on his back.

"Yeah …. I just …. I'm just … Just give me a second here …" He rolled onto his side and curled slightly into a ball. Smiling, Jimmy dropped into a squat at Matt's side and patted him on his shoulder reassuringly.

He pulled back his hand just after touching him. "You sweat a lot. You might want to see a doctor about that." Jimmy smirked as his old teammate raised a single finger to express his dismay. Springer checked the watch on Matt's wrist and read a final time of 35:48 for the six mile distance, was under six minutes per mile.

Extending himself back to his full height, Jimmy checked around the parking lot. "Do you see Coach Ames anywhere?" He asked, a small note of concern in his voice.

"Little busy down here," Matt replied with a slight moan of discomfort.

Jimmy ignored him and began to wander around the lot. "I know he's usually late, but kinda feels like this would be pushing it …" He approached the pack of four milers, looking for an older face among the youth. But he found nothing besides high schoolers. "Have any of you guys seen-"

"Springer!" A strong, deep voice echoed across the parking lot as a man approached. He wore a dark blue sweat suit with an orange U and V stitched upon the right corner. His hair was dark brown and he sported a thick mustache on his upper lip. Jimmy recognized him as a teacher from the Union Valley history department. "Where have you been?!"

"Uh, I've been running." He responded flatly "Who are-"

"I don't appreciate your behavior, Springer. I'm sure you had free reign back in the day, but I can assure that I will be holding a much tighter leash-"

"Back in the-wait, what's-" Jimmy could feel blood rushing to his face, a combination of confusion, nervous energy and anger. In the commotion, Matt had sat up from his position of misery to follow along. His mouth was hanging slightly agape, a mixture of shock and fatigue.

"Please don't interrupt me, Springer. Just because you're some hot shot state champion doesn't mean you can order around my athletes and skip out on our team's practices-"

"*Your* athletes?"

"Yes, Springer, *my* athletes! I'm sure you don't like the idea of having a new coach that isn't going to be your best buddy, but that's no reason to stage a coup and have everyone meet at the tree instead of the track where I was wait-"

"Why would we meet at the track? This isn't track practice-"

"DON'T INTERRUPT ME, SPRINGER!" He pressed his face close to Jimmy's as the latter stood his ground. Matt had jumped to his feet now and was moving quickly to his friend's side. "*I'm* the coach of the cross country team now and you will play by *my* rules!"

Jimmy felt his heart catapult straight into his throat. "What happened to Coach Ames?" He asked quietly, his face feeling warm and clammy. He took a step back and turned to look at Matt who stared back, mirroring his look of confusion. The man opposite him was briefly bewildered as well, but then his expression turned to a broad, mischievous grin.

"He didn't tell you?" He asked sinisterly. His voice had lost its booming sense of power and transformed into a quiet, evil whisper. It was somehow more frightening this way. "Your precious coach quit, Springer. Probably didn't want to have to put up with some show off, hot shot-"

But Jimmy was done listening. He had turned and began walking purposefully toward his friend's car. "Matt, take me to Ames's house." He said sternly as they walked side by side.

"Jimmy … I know you're upset but-" He was practically jogging just to keep pace with Springer's brisk stride.

"Matt, take me to Ames's house." A few other runners were just finishing their five-mile loop, but Jimmy ignored them, pressing forward.

"Jimmy, wait," Matt sprinted ahead to block his friend's path. "Just listen to me-" They could hear the mustached man laughing crudely behind them.

"I said, take me-"

"This isn't about you alright! It's not your fault!"

At those words, Jimmy's eyes flashed dangerously. He picked up Matt by the shirt and slammed him up against the car door.

"If you aren't going to help me," he whispered menacingly, "Then you better get the hell out of my way." And he turned and sprinted off, spinning just before the first tears left his eyes.

He was just a few minutes away now. He certainly could have gotten there faster, but he had decided to cut through woods and backyards to ensure that Matt could not cut him off half way. It was better that he was going alone. Better to push away his best friend. At least for once he could be the one leaving instead of the other way around.

As he continued through creeks and shrubs, his mind cycled through a variety of memories

It was the summer after his freshman season. He set out running into the hot afternoon air. He had needed to get out of the house. Each piece of bickering was like a small prick to his skin. The feeling of euphoria he experienced while training was his escape. He lost himself in its tranquility. Without this sport, he knew he would crumble away, ripped to pieces by his own doubts and insecurities.

After a long stretch of peace, he soaked in his surroundings for the first time. Nothing looked familiar. The calm was replaced suddenly by fear. Scrambling, he ran down the next street, searching for a main road. He could feel his stomach grumbling, hunger beginning to set in. Then, by some miracle, he came across a familiar face biking through the neighborhood. Before long, he was eating a home cooked meal with the man and his wife. Smiling. Feeling like a part of a family again ...

... He was on the track. It was empty with the exception of athlete and coach. The shouting of splits echoed eerily around the stadium. Darkness was creeping in as the sun began to set, but Jimmy continued the workout. His coach split his watch as he crossed the starting line and drooped to his knees.

"That one was 69.2. Close. But I'm gonna need another repetition."

"Coach," *Jimmy said his outrage evident even through his shortness of breath,* "We've done 20 of these-"

"But not 16 reps at 68 seconds. Now get ready, your rest is ticking down."

"C'mon the last two have been 69, isn't that good enough?"

His coach smiled. "Of course, it's good enough."

"Well then-"

"Jimmy, you've always been 'good enough'. You could have stopped ten laps ago and you would have been good enough. But I don't coach my athletes to just be good enough. And more importantly, you don't run to just be good enough. There may not be somebody in this district as good as you or in this state as good as you, but there will *always* be someone better. Short of a world record and an Olympic gold, you can always be better. Like Viren in the Olympics.

"And heck, even Viren ran the 5,000 a few days later." *He looked down at his watch.* "Now get up to the line. You're getting an extra five seconds of rest, so this has to be at least a 65."

His next rep was his last. 59 seconds …

The familiar house was now just ahead of him towards the end of the block. As he approached, he could see a man standing outside, waiting for him. Jimmy slowed to a stop at the edge of the lawn. Coach Ames stood just before his front steps. The door was open behind him and Jimmy could make out the outline of Mrs. Ames washing a dish in the kitchen. Her round belly protruded noticeably as she turned to place the plate in the drying rack.

Now that he was stopped, he realized how ragged his breathing was. He panted heavily as he stood across from his former advisor, who watched him silently from his position. Neither of them spoke; they simply stared across the grass at one another. Jimmy waited in frustration for some type of response to his arrival. An apology, an excuse, anything that he could attack. That would give him the justification to shout and scream. But he received nothing. Nothing beyond a soft, searching gaze. The gaze that had followed him in every practice, every workout, and every race for over two years.

Finally, he could no longer contain his emotions and they spilled over. "You're not even gonna say anything?! You're just going to stand there like-like … without the decency to even apologize! " They remained ten feet from one another, an awkward distance for a normal conversation. But neither took a step forward.

"Of course I'm sorry," he replied gently, "But I don't think you ran all this way for an apology. You came here to yell at me. To be angry with me. " He smiled sadly. "And I'm going to let you." Then, he paused, deferring to Jimmy who was at a loss for words. He was taken-aback by Ames's passive demeanor. He was expecting an argument. His blood was boiling and he wanted a fight, not a tacit surrender.

"Why did you do this?! Why are you abandoning us?! Just leaving?! Without even having the guts to come tell us to our faces-"

"Certainly you don't think that was my choice?" Ames asked simply.

"Well I-I …" Jimmy was caught off guard again, struck dumbfounded by the smooth counter. "I wouldn't have let it be somebody else's choice!" He recovered weakly.

"Unfortunately, you've always had more heart than me, Jimmy." He flashed another sad smile, but he left his lamentation vague. Again, the conversation lapsed into uncomfortable silence. Jimmy's mind continued to race, his anger continuing to hover near its boiling point. "Do you want to borrow my phone?" the Coach asked, "I'm sure your parents are worried sick-"

"Ha!" Jimmy exclaimed dramatically, "My parents?! You think my parents give a *damn* about where I am?!" His head was pounding as his voice continued to elevate. For the first time, Ames's calm demeanor began to deteriorate into confusion. It incited him further, his rage continuing to overflow. "They could care less about what I'm doing, where I'm going-whether I'm happy!" He blinked furiously. "They're getting a divorce-Did you know that? My Dad moved out last week." He paused to catch his breath. His shouting was stealing the wind from his already depleted lungs.

"I'm sorry, Jimmy," Coach Ames said comfortingly. His wife had made her way to the window, checking on the noise. "But this doesn't mean they love you any less. This is not your f-"

"Fault?" He laughed coldly. "I thought you might say that. Everyone *loves* to say that. Like it wasn't *my* fault with Fisher, it wasn't *my* fault with them and it wasn't *my* fault with you." He threw his hands forward before letting them fall hopelessly back to his sides. He could feel the tears charging again, but he fought fiercely to hold them back.

Coach Ames approached cautiously. "It's going to be OK. Let me drive you back home." But Jimmy took a big step back, away from his Coach and into the middle of the road. A car was maybe 40 seconds away, making a left turn onto their street. He considered the oncoming vehicle for a second, before turning and dashing off to the opposite sidewalk.

"You remember how you told me running could be an escape?" He called, looking back over his shoulder as he prepped to sprint again, "Well I've escaped. This is my home now." He opened the door and threw himself back into his safe space, taking off at a sprint back the way he came.

Chapter Fourteen

John Trainor, March 2021

"So you're a runner, huh? How fast can you run a mile?"

I rolled my eyes. This was probably the least enjoyable question I ever had to answer. Should I get into the details of specializing in an event? Should I explain the relationship between 1500, 1600 and the mile?

Should I stop overthinking this? Let's be honest, we all know she's going to say "Wow, that's fast" and then probably move on immediately to something she *actually* finds interesting.

"My best time is four minutes and 30 seconds," I said nonchalantly. That was probably the only fun part of this question. Saying it nonchalantly.

"Wow, that's fast!" She replied, looking impressed. "In high school gym, I knew this guy who did like a 5:40, I think? So that's pretty much the same thing, right? Only a minute's difference?"

There were so many things that upset me about this statement. First, and most obviously, it's not a minute. It's a minute and ten seconds. There's a difference. Of course, ten seconds wouldn't seem like a lot to someone who doesn't think a minute matters much. How long has this conversation been? Probably only a minute, but it still feels incredibly long and painful. Just like an extra minute of running the mile ironically. I could keep going, but I'm assuming that if you have made it this far into the story, you're likely sympathetic to my aggravation. Besides, it's not like I actually said any of this out loud.

"Yeah," I smiled wryly, "Pretty much the same." Thankfully, this was the end of our chat. As I finished my sentence, I noticed a tall, wiry boy walk into the bar. That was my cue. "I'm sorry, but I've got to run." I said getting to my feet.

"Haha, nice one," The girl at the bar laughed. It took me a second to catch on.

"Oh, yeah," I fake laughed. Not particularly convincingly either. "Anyway …" I didn't have time to stumble into any more puns. I chased off after the boy, trying to make sure I caught him before he disappeared. I weaved through bodies, covertly following him up toward a separate counter.

"Pick up for Mark, please." I could barely hear his voice carry within the crowded room. He waited there, tapping his fingers patiently on the table in front of him as the man behind the counter walked away to retrieve whatever his order was. I had him alone. Time to pounce.

"Excuse me, can I-um-can I buy you a drink?" Not the brightest choice of question.

"Uh, sorry man, I'm … well, I've got a girlfriend so …"

"No, no, not like that," I said, my face growing red as I fumbled flustered. "I just need to talk to you. I've been searching for you all day." At this point, he looked absolutely terrified. I don't really blame him, I was doing an incredibly creepy job trying to get my point across.

"One large pie for Mark?" The man remerged from the back carry a rectangular pizza box.

"Yeah, that's me," Mark said, taking his food. He looked grateful to be one step closer to escaping this awkward situation. He pulled out a 20 dollar bill and threw it down on the counter. "Keep the change."

"Wait," I called as he made his way back to the exit, "Maybe we could just exchange phone numbers?" Well, that was the icing on the stalker cake. Mark sped up his walk, taking one last look over his shoulder before disappearing through the door with his pizza.

I debated chasing after him. Honestly. It didn't occur to me that it would be a terrible idea. Thankfully, I resisted. At this point, I couldn't afford another restraining order against me.

Mark Miller, November 5th 2016

"Did they taste any better the second time around?" Mark asked as Ian lifted his head, looking up at him with a mixture of disgust and discomfort. "Wait, you got a little something on your face." He reached out and wiped something from the corner of his friend's mouth.

"It's disturbing how comfortable you are with all this." Ian's face was pale and he still looked slightly sick, but he had managed to put on a smile. "How are you not nervous?"

Mark shrugged. "I am," he said simply, "I just prefer to save my puking for *after* the race." Slowly, the duo resumed their trek along the lower level of the course. They were the only members of the varsity squad who had not run here a year ago and Coach Vanderweigh had wanted them to preview things briefly upon arrival.

"Are your parents coming down to watch?" Mark said, dodging a small mud patch. Ian simply walked straight through it.

"Are you kidding? My parents, my grandparents, maybe a few cousins I've never met. I haven't done a lot of impressive things in my life." They smiled. Mark was worried if he had laughed, butterflies would fly forth from his stomach. "How about you?" Ian gave his teammate a covert sideways glance, before refocusing his gaze on the path ahead.

"Yeah, my parents are coming with Jayson …" His voice was slightly shaky as he finished. Together, they crossed a bridge and walked up yet another hill in momentary silence. As they continued to ascend, their collective breathing became louder and more strained.

"We have to be the stupidest people on the planet ..." Mark was panting in between sentences, catching his breath, "This hill is torture ... I'm literally ... voluntarily ... torturing myself." They finally crested the hill, adjusting course back to the team tent.

"And to think, racing is supposed to be the fun part."

Chapter Fifteen

Mark Miller, April 2016

"Three … Two … One … STOP!" The voice echoed around the fields to a circle of runners who, on command, stopped running. A few were forcing themselves into a slow jog; others had their hands on their knees, leaned over, desperate for breath. Eventually, each forced himself to amble back in the direction of the man who just called them to a halt and his makeshift start line of water bottles and discarded warm-up pants.

A blonde haired boy, tall and long-limbed, had positioned himself at the front of the joggers. He took a quick glance at his watch before slowing to a walk. He took up slow pacing around the start line, relaxing his breathing as he went. Compared to many of the others in the pack, he seemed fresh, motivated and eager.

"Ten seconds," The man spoke softly this time. The blonde haired boy responded by taking up a ready position, one foot in front of the other, just behind an empty Gatorade bottle. Reluctantly, the other boys filed in behind him, many holding their fingers over wrist watches as they stood perched. Waiting.

"Three … Two … One … Go!" And they streaked from the line, up a short, quick hill and towards the first goal post.

Although the weather didn't always suggest it, the Manheim Township boys were entrenched in the Spring Track season. Commanding the troops, Coach Vanderweigh stood, twirling a stopwatch around his finger, carefully monitoring the packs emerging in front of him. The task he had assigned to his warriors today was an interval workout. Five repetitions, three minutes each, of hard running. They encircled the high school's sports facilities, a soccer field and a pair of baseball fields, running loops just under 800 meters in length.

Everyone started at the same time, finished at the same time and had the same amount of rest in between-regardless of their pace. The point of the workout was not to finish a distance in a certain amount of time, but rather to finish a time with a certain amount of distance. In theory, Coach Vanderweigh wanted his runners to get a little farther each interval, with the last rep being the furthest. However, in practice, trying to get a pack of competitive teenagers to control their efforts was sometimes a lost cause.

"Come on now, don't settle here. This is the hard one!" The blonde haired boy was powering along at the front, towing a pack of three gasping for air behind him. He rolled through the short hill once again and willed himself past a small orange cone. "Three … Two … One … STOP!" Another interval had ended. The lead runner turned, picked up the cone and moved it a few paces forward to where he had just finished. Coach Vanderweigh smiled to himself. There were, of course, exceptions.

Mark Miller jogged back towards the start line, joining a growing mass of bodies who were heading back for the start line. Only one rep remained and, although his legs were heavy and his thoughts were cloudy, there was a ray of confidence piercing the fog. As the seconds of rest continued to tick, his breathing inched closer and closer to normalcy. *One more ... Just one more ...*

"Three ... Two ... One ... GO!" And again, the runners were in stride, stampeding up the hill and around the first turn. Mark guided his body into a rhythm, moving slightly to the outside of his teammates to ensure he had room for his legs to stretch. His body hurt, but it was a good kind of pain. It was merely a reminder of his perseverance, rather than a crippling burden.

He let his momentum carry him on the downhill and then forced himself to hold that pace as he approached the baseball field. There was still a little bit more in his tank, enough to unleash a finishing kick once he hit the lap marker. Mark pushed past his coach, now gritting his teeth, sprinting towards the hill once more. Smooth and controlled was gone: his arms losing form, his legs losing lift. But he focused on the target. There likely wasn't much time left.

"Three ..." He was steps from his previous mark, "... Two ..." Digging desperately for one more gear, "... One ..." Nearly throwing his body forward now, "STOP!"

Letting his upper half wilt, he placed his hands on his knees, wavering slightly as he stood. He glanced sideways, looking behind him at a brown leaf that signified his furthest previous interval. A small flux of elation had arrived, helping to fight the post-workout pain. Up ahead, he noticed the blonde haired boy trotting back past his orange cone. Slowly, the team's fastest runner corralled his teammates, gradually prodding everyone into a cool-down jog. As they approached, Mark wiped a strand of dark hair from his eyes and tucked inside the growing pack with a few of his friends from the Junior Varsity team.

His blonde brother Jayson took-up his usual position at the front.

John Trainor, June 2021

"I feel like we may have gotten off on the wrong foot," I said in perhaps the biggest understatement of young life. I sat across the table from Mark Miller, a man who I had seriously frightened in our first encounter some three months earlier. "Assuming you can even call it a foot."

"It's alright, man," Miller replied, chuckling at my joke. "First impressions can be misleading sometimes." Ironically, as he said this I was forming my own first impressions of him. From the preliminary data I gathered, Mark seemed like a fairly likable guy. He laughed at my joke so right away we were on good terms. It seemed like he was easy to talk to, probably a great running partner. Miller's presence in the room was not overly commanding, I'd guess he had a knack for fitting easily into any situation. But this was mostly conjecture at this point. I reached into my pocket and pulled out my tape recorder.

"So, you ready to do this?" I asked, placing the device in front of me on the table.

"Hit me with your best stuff," He responded simply, making himself comfortable in the chair. Like I said, easy to talk to.

"OK, this is kind of a classic," I clicked down the "on" switch, "In your early running career, what do you think is your most defining moment?"

"Like early career as in high school or-"

"Before that even. Like tell me about your first big race."

"Ah," He pondered for a second before an idea seemed to click inside his mind. "I wouldn't necessarily call this 'defining' per se, but it's a good one." He straightened up a bit in his chair, apparently a little more invested in the interview. He must have been excited about the story.

"So in middle school, we had this race every Thanksgiving called the 'Turkey Trot'. It was this loop around the campus, probably like a mile long, and all the kids would compete right we before went on break. The winner got a free turkey, but I didn't really care about that. What I really wanted was a t-shirt. The top five in each grade got one and they put your place on the back. It was just, like, a simple cotton shirt, but for whatever reason, I really wanted one.

"I was 12th the year before for sixth graders so I figured if I trained hard as a seventh grader I could move up the standings enough to get that shirt. So I did some runs-it was just middle school so I wasn't doing anything crazy-and I showed up at the end of the month ready to crush it." He paused, smiling as he was transported back to this memory.

"It's about an hour until I'm supposed to race and the eighth graders have just finished competing. While me and my fellow seventh graders are all sitting in history class, waiting for class to start, my teacher Mrs. Klotz walks in with this big smile on her face. She looks straight at me and says 'Mark, I have great news! Your brother just won the Turkey Trot!'. Unabashedly, in front of the whole class. No pressure, right?

"Well, after that I think my swagger or whatever it is that makes you run fast drained out of me. I raced like crap and I never got that t-shirt."

He paused. I wanted to ask him more about the story. Why it jumped so readily to his mind. But I waited. Unlike the first time I met Mark Miller, I played it cool. Eventually, he spoke up again.

"Looking back, it's so obvious now why I ran poorly, but at the time I probably had no idea. What I sometimes wish I could go back and tell young me is that running isn't about what you've got here," he pointed down at his legs, "it's about what you've got up here." He tapped twice on his head. "The sooner you figure that out, the better."

Chapter Sixteen

Ben Havleck, May 2016

Ever since I could remember ... Everything inside of me ... Just wanted to fit in (oh, oh, oh, oh) ... I was never one for pretenders ... Everything I tried to be ... Just wouldn't settle in (oh, oh, oh, oh) ...

Ben turned down the volume slightly on the radio. Cautiously, he turned into the driveway, put the car in park and then felt around in his pockets for his phone. Finding it on his left side, he reached down into his pants and pulled it out. He stared down at its screen, focused on the contact list, flipping through names. The door opposite him opened and a man entered, but Ben didn't seem to notice. Instead, he pressed the green call button, having finally happened across the name he had been seeking. He put the device to his ear and looked up for the first time since his arrival.

"Hello," Neal said, purposefully answering the phone. Ben shuttered violently in fearful surprise and dropped his phone beneath the driver's seat.

"Geez, you scared the crap out of me ..." he replied, fumbling under the chair. "How did you get in here without me noticing?"

"Because you text like my grandma," Neal returned humorously. "It takes all of her focus just to press the buttons, too." He pulled out his own cell, as Ben emerged victoriously holding his.

"It's harder than you think," he said with a slightly embarrassed smile. "It's not one of those new iPhones with the 'touch screens' and 'automatic correct'."

Neal snatched the phone from Ben's hand. He typed quickly with his left hand on the stolen device while holding his own in his right and scrolling through the screen. Without glancing at it once, he passed the older flip phone back to Ben. "How'd I do?"

Ben looked down at the screen and read aloud, *"I'm going to ignore the fact that you just said 'automatic correct', because I don't want it to spoil the kick abs night I've planned."*

"So close."

***

Ben walked over to his backpack and sat on the ground beside it. He carefully unlaced his blue training shoes and slipped them off his feet. Then, he let out a deep breath and took a swig from his water bottle, which was nearly empty. He tossed the depleted container aside gently, letting it fall on the turf with a dull thud. Carefully, he removed his spikes from their bag and gently slipped them onto his bare feet. Pulling each section of laces in order, he tightened the racing shoes until they fit snugly. A rush of adrenaline hit him and he let out another steadying breath. Standing up, he bounced twice on the balls of his feet before launching himself into the air and raising his knees as close as he could to his face. He felt springy and confident.

"Gooo Ben!" A small girl cried out from the stands. Her two parents laughed and smiled down on the infield as their son beamed back. He spared them a brief wave before turning toward one of the field goal posts a few feet away. Here, he held onto the base of the post for balance and swung his left leg back and forth.

Another boy wandered over to join him, sporting a pair of black tights and a dark blue t-shirt. He seemed quiet and nervous, similar to Ben. The stranger mimicked his swinging on the post. The two athletes exchanged a curt nod before each alternated legs.

Wait a minute, Ben thought. He looked back up and saw his own thoughts mirrored in the face of the boy across from him.

"Peanut?" the boy said, smiling broadly. He removed his hand from the post and extended it.

"What's up, Sean," Ben responded, returning the grin. He took his friend's hand as they pulled each other together for a brief embrace. "You running this two mile?"

"Yeah man, are you?" the boy named Sean responded, now stretching his left arm across his chest.

Ben nodded. "Yeah, I'm in heat two, how 'bout you?"

A moment of shock flicked across Sean's face, but he recovered quickly. "Me too man. I guess we get to race again!" He said still grinning and now switching arms. They stood briefly facing each other, each somewhat surprised to run into an old friend at this unlikely moment. "You know a bunch of the other Downingtown guys are here too, I'm sure they'd be psyched to see you." He nodded back over his left shoulder at a patch of grass just outside the fence. "We post up out there. You should come by after the race and stuff."

"Yeah definitely, man." They each started to walk in opposite directions, preparing to finish up the last details of their warm up routine. "Good luck!"

"You too, Peanut."

***

"Pull in here. There's a back lot that nobody uses," Neal directed Ben from the passenger seat. He flipped on his turn signal and set course down a side street in between a pair of apartment buildings. "Yeah, just go right in there." Neal pointed at a small lot with a few older-looking cars parked close to the left edge.

"How far is the field from here?" Ben asked as he navigated into central spot. He put the car into park and raised the windows, using a small manual crank on his door.

"It's not super close-maybe a couple minutes," Neal responded, opening his door and stepping out of the car. "I assume you of all people don't mind walking a little bit?" He smiled at Ben who had also emerged from the car. They shut their doors almost in unison and turned north, Neal leading the way. The sun shined brightly on their path. Neal pulled a pair of sunglasses from his pocket and placed them over his eyes.

"Here, cut up through this," Neal turned right and began to climb a hill towards a small stretch of trees. Behind the leaves, Ben could hear a small chorus of cheering, but its source was obscured from view. "Now I hate myself for doing this," Neal continued, brushing aside a particularly large branch as they began to crest the hill. "But I figured you might want to check this out before we head to the game."

As the pair moved through the last stretch of trees, Ben saw a dark red oval, surrounded by a short gray chain-linked fence. A pack of men were traversing the perimeter of the field as a tiny group of supportive fans urged them on. With a surprised smile, Ben looked at Neal who shrugged. "I saw they had a home meet on the schedule," he said as they made their way to the fence's edge. "This is supposed to be the '10,000 meters'."

"They race *10ks* in college?" Ben said excitedly. He looked out at the runners grinding around the track. He followed them as they passed by the finish line and watched the lap counter tick from 12 to 11.

"I figured, 25 laps around the track? Sounds like Ben's kinda Friday night."

The lead pack was made up of about seven at this point with a few others fading from the back. Pain was etched across some faces as they looked up at the runners ahead longingly. Ben split his watch carefully as the first runner crossed the finish line. The stop watch feature sprang to life and the seconds began to flash across the screen. He wanted to estimate the pace at which the competitors were running, trying to compare it to his own racing effort.

75-76, that's-what-5 minute pace? ... So maybe 15:40s for 5k, he calculated quickly in his head. As they approached his section of fence, he carefully examined the expression on each runner's face. A few that had looked promising earlier were now fading hard, while other former stragglers were making encouraging surges back through the ranks.

Ben looked intently at his watch for each lap, even tracking the 1,000 meter splits produced every two and half times around. Neal seemed more amused watching Ben than the race. As one runner with a thick dark brown beard surged to the front, Ben gave a barely audible cheer of excitement, causing Neal to break his silence and laugh.

"I'm not sure I'll ever understand your fascination with running in circles …" Neal said smiling at Ben, who was blushing slightly, but still diligently calculating each runner's pace.

"To be fair, you're taking me to a baseball game," he said, still not breaking eye contact with the track. "It's pretty much the same thing. Except they only *sometimes* run in circles."

Neal smiled and turned his attention away from Ben and toward the race. "Give me some insight here," he said watching as one of the trailing runners passed at a painfully slow crawl, looking incredibly fatigued and strained. "Where's the strategy? What's the nuance?"

"Well," Ben began matter-of-factly, "See this guy?" He pointed at the bearded man controlling the pace, "He's putting down a surge- that's, like, speeding up the pace-to try and tire out the rest of the field for the sprint to the finish."

"So he's running as fast as he can? Seems like the optimal strategy …"

"It's mainly about timing." Ben pressed on unperturbed, "If he puts too much energy into the surge, he'll have nothing left for the end. But if he waits, then somebody who has better sprinting speed will go by him on the last straightaway." There were now two runners who had separated themselves from the field as the clear leaders. The bearded runner and another, slightly taller and lankier fellow. The trailing runner looked comfortable and at ease, despite the surge. The bearded runner's face was determined and stoic, but there was also a layer of strain poking through to the surface when the harrier's concentration lapsed.

"This guy in second here," Ben pointed as the runners came by for the penultimate time, "looks like he's sitting on the dude in first."

"If that's sitting than what were just doing in the car?"

"No, not that kind of sitting. He's kind of … drafting off him. Letting him do all the work because it takes more energy to lead than to follow. Then at the end," the officials rang the bell to signal the final lap of the race as the boy in second charged past into first, "He'll sprint away." Ben finished frustrated.

"Why do you sound so upset?" Neal remarked as the lanky runner began gliding away from the former leader on the back straightaway, "Seems like he's going pretty fast!" He clapped and cheered as the runner came sprinting around the turn.

"Because it's lame. He didn't even try and help the other guy make it fast. He just rested until the end."

"But he's gonna win isn't he? I thought the goal was to win …"

"There's more than one way to win," Ben said sourly, watching the bearded man cross the line in second and crumble into a heap on the ground. "C'mon," he said now turning and walking away from the track, "We're gonna be late for the baseball game."

"We're gonna be *really* late if we walk that way." Ben turned around, half frustrated and half amused. Neal returned a broad toothy grin. "Cheer up, kid. I promised you a kick abs time, and you're gonna get it."

***

Ben fidgeted with his new dark maroon singlet, tucking it carefully into a pair of short black shorts. He taped a white and black sticker of the number 11 onto his left leg and placed an identical one on his chest. Then he jogged slowly over to the starting line, joining the string of runners preparing to start the race. He was greeted with a polite nod from the athlete to his left. None of the faces looked very familiar to him, but he hadn't been expecting them to: it had been over a year since he last raced at Coatesville High School.

Scanning the upper stagger, a line of the top four seeds, Ben found Sean, sporting a dark blue and white jersey and a number three sticker. Two spots to Sean's left was a tall, imposing figure with a navy and orange jersey. Ben thought he had recognized him from pictures of the indoor state meet that had been posted online at VaniaRunning.com.

The back row of runners all had their unique, individual pre-race ticks. Some would slap their legs, others would jump up and down. One boy was even hitting himself in the face and muttering profanities under his breath. For whatever reason, Ben felt calm and self-assured. He could feel his family's positive energy from just a few feet away and it gave him an extra spark.

The sun had set now, leaving the air cool and comfortable. A pair of towering stadium lights illuminated the surface below. About half way down the bend, an official hoisted a starter's pistol into the air, paused and then fired one sharp blast into the night. The crowd erupted, matching the intensity of the previous shot, as the runners sprinted into the first turn.

Ben calmly drifted to the back of the pack. In a field of this size, he was not interested in fighting for position due to his limited foot speed and slight frame. There were still eight laps available for him to move through the 18-man field. As he jogged comfortably down the back stretch, he was greeted by a wave of cheers from the inside of the track. Runners who had raced earlier in the meet had come out in droves to support the last competitors of the night, urging their peers on wildly from just inches away. Specific sounds were essentially imperceptible to Ben at this stage; it was simply a wave of noise that washed over him, sending energy pulsing through his body.

Patience, Ben. He thought to himself, continuing to hold position at the back of the pack. He didn't want to let himself get caught up in the aggressive early pace that had been driven on by both the legion of screaming fans and the hype surrounding the meet's signature event. As he hit the line, finishing lap one, he caught a quick glimpse of the clock. His first split was about 71 seconds. The lead pack was nearly ten seconds ahead, controlled by the runner in blue and orange who was sporting the number one stickers. Sean was near the front as well, in around fourth or fifth, looking smooth and graceful, even at this fast tempo.

Ben ran the second lap in a similar pace, finding a consistent rhythm to his stride. While he could feel the gap between himself and the leaders continuing to expand, his confidence in his strategy did not waver. His parents, however, weren't quite as at ease. When he finished the second lap, he could hear both of them urging him to move up, a small note of panic in their voice. He resisted the impulse to give them a wink or a thumbs up, something to calm them down. *They'll have to just be surprised.*

As the race continued, Ben cut his pace down ever so slightly. One by one, he picked off the runners in the field. His curls bounced wildly around his head as he picked up steam, gaining momentum from each pass. A few other students in the crowd had seemed to notice his surge as well. He caught a glimpse of some hands pointed in his direction and random cheers of support for "maroon kid" were peppering the air.

By the time he hit three laps to go, he had moved from his humble beginnings at 18th place up to fifth and he was still feeling strong. He had run nearly perfectly even splits and, although he was beginning to feel his form break and his breathing weaken, Ben was confident that he was in better shape than the ragged looking runners trying to keep pace with him.

The man in blue and orange was well clear of the field now, running alone and running very quickly. He seemed like an unattainable goal. But second was definitely possible. And second was Downingtown West's Sean O'Neill. Ben grit his teeth and let his head droop for a second, before charging on, moving up another spot as he approached the final kilometer of racing. Fans were now jumping up and down cheering for him when he passed, the first wave of observers recruiting their friends to join in on the fun. People love to root for the underdog.

As he concluded his sixth lap, he could feel his head starting to roll. The spit was flying from his mouth and the familiar burning in his legs was back. But Sean O'Neill was less than a yard away. The crowd was on its feet screaming its approval, but his family's cries were no longer distinguishable in his fatigued state. Ben clenched his teeth fiercely again as he tried to bite through the pain.

600 meters left to go. It was time to make another surge, but his body was fighting him. He had to break down the mental walls in addition to the

physical ones. Ben fixated on the blue jersey in front of him and tried to embrace the frantic screaming to his left. The students were practically on the track now, waving their arms in wide circles and shouting unintelligible words of encouragement. His head drooped forward and then whipped back as he forced himself into a hard surge around the bend, moving directly onto the shoulder of second place.

Together, the former teammates came off the turn for the penultimate time. Ben swung wide to make his bid for second. The bell was already ringing to indicate the leader was beginning his final lap, but he was in a different race. As he advanced in front, Sean looked to his right. He recognized Ben immediately and put his head down to try and keep his pursuer at bay, but he didn't have enough momentum to hold his advantage.

Ben couldn't register anything going on around him beyond Sean's position. With 400 to go, thanks to his struggle, he held about a one second lead. His body screaming and his head on fire, Ben threw himself as best he could down the back stretch, but he could still feel his opposition closing back in, mounting a counterattack.

At 200 meters to go, it was Sean's turn to try for the pass, moving to the outside and getting the slight edge over his opposition. Ben parried as best he could, trying to force Sean to stay wide on the curve and run extra distance. He could feel his head swingy wildly now, but he was long past the point where he could control his body efficiently. They turned into the straightaway, side-by-side, sprinting as fast as they possibly could.

Ben couldn't remember wanting anything more than he wanted to beat Sean. He was sprinting quicker than ever before, gritting his teeth and forcing his feet forward into the track. Despite his best efforts, he could feel O'Neill inching ahead. But Ben fought feverishly to keep pace, pumping furiously. His mind was a blur, his thoughts barely decipherable in his own head. The only thing he understood was that he was going to pass out if he kept this up. This seemed like a worthwhile reason to take the risk.

Driving with one last ditch effort, Ben powered through the last 20 meters and found a previously undiscovered gear. It was a gear that his Downingtown counterpart could not match and, in a fit of agony and pleasure, he crossed the line and crumbled in a heap onto his back.

***

"See now that's called a strike out."

"I know what a strike out is ..." Ben smiled, eyebrows raised. He and the crowd clapped in support of their pitcher as he prepared for the next batter in the order.

"You can ignore him, Ben. Neal's the king of striking out anyway."

"I learned everything I know from you, Bryn."

The man called Bryn put his arm around the woman to his right. "You must have skipped a class or two."

It was warm, but not oppressive. The air was still without any recognizable wind. As each pitch hit the catcher's mitt, it echoed beautifully through the anticipatory silence. The stadium was about half filled with fans, mainly students, sporting dark maroon t-shirts.

Neal lounged comfortably in the stands, stretching his legs onto the empty bench below him. His left sandal was dangling precariously from his foot. His elbows supported him as he leaned backward, resting on the open seats behind him.

To his right sat Bryn, discussing one of the players on the field with the woman who sat next to him. He pointed in the direction of the left fielder, holding a water bottle in the same hand, and mentioned something about an economics class. The woman nodded with interest, looking in the direction he point her. She had introduced herself as Colleen and was later identified by Neal as Bryn's new girlfriend. She was friendly, but quiet, willingly defaulting to the excitable personalities of the boys around her.

Sitting a row below his friends, a man the others had called Jared was focused intently on the pitcher. He followed the ball as it soared from arm to plate, breaking low into the dirt. The batter, wearing yellow and black, swung and missed, prompting Jared to clap politely. He turned to Neal, asking something about the pitcher's number of strike outs. Neal replied simply, letting his gaze drift momentarily from the game before flicking back toward the pitcher.

Ben sat to Neal's left, quietly observing this group of new acquaintances. His eyes were hidden behind a pair of sunglasses which Neal had recently given to him after noticing his strained expression. To then compensate for the absence of his own shades, Neal had stolen the hat from Jared's head a half inning later.

This was Ben's first encounter with Neal's friends from college. He hadn't had many chances to be social since his move to the area. His only friend from high school was P.J. Danielson who was typically very focused on academics and independent research projects on the weekend. Neal was practically a different species in comparison.

Having grown friendly with Ben at the Barnes and Noble's bookstore where they each worked, Neal had invited Ben out to Bloomsburg's home baseball game against Millersville. An invitation which Ben tentatively accepted. It wasn't that he didn't like Neal. Quite the contrary: he found him funny and easy to talk to. At work, when it was essentially just the two of them, they had shared their fair share of laughs. The problem was, he felt that he was closer to the P.J. species than the Neal species. He wasn't sure he was cool enough to fit in with his older friend and his lack of confidence had manifested itself in shy silence through the first five and a half innings of the game.

"What's that seven now?!" Jared asked as the Bloomsburg players trotted off the field following yet another strike out. The crowd had risen to their feet in approval.

"Yeah, I'm pretty sure," Bryn said, sounding impressed. "Three in a row that inning."

After a moment, they returned to their seats and Bryn turned his attention to Ben. "So, Ben what do you think of Bloomsburg baseball?" He opened his arms widely as if he was presenting the stadium as the climax of a magic trick. Colleen smiled and rolled her eyes.

"It's … um … pretty cool-your pitcher's pretty good."

"Yeah, he was first team all PSAC last year." Jared replied enthusiastically.

"In case you're wondering why he's wetting his pants with excitement," Neal whispered quietly, leaning towards Ben, "it's because the pitcher's his roommate." Ben flashed him a covert grin.

"In the game last week …"

Jared continued on devotedly, apparently unaware of Neal's commentary. He outlined the previous victory for the pitcher whose name, Ben was informed, was Charles Woods. The story dragged through the first batter of the inning, who walked on five pitches. He then dropped his bat and trotted easily down the first base line.

"And I'd just like to reiterate the guy's name is 'Chuck Woods'. I feel like there has to be a joke there somewhere." Neal said as Jared concluded his story. Bryn and Ben laughed while Jared's expression sat halfway between a smile and a scowl.

"So what do you think here, J, would you try and pull a hit and run here?" Bryn asked as the next batter stepped up to the plate. Ben recognized him as the shorter, speedy Bloomsburg shortstop.

"With nobody out? No, why risk the double play?"

"I just feel like we need to get something going. The line-up looks a little flat tonight and we gotta find something to spark us." Bryn leaned backwards to speak to Ben, "What do you think short-stop?"

"Well, I'd bunt it down the third base line," Ben said confidently. "The third baseman doesn't have much of an arm and Garcia is quick enough to put pressure on him and speed up his mechanics. At the very least, you've got a good chance of advancing the runner, but I'd bet you could squeeze out an infield hit or a draw throwing error."

There was a general murmur of surprised agreement followed by an awkward silence. No one was quite prepared for such a thorough response.

And no one had a sophisticated enough reply to confidently offer a follow up point. Ben squirmed slightly, uncomfortable with the hush.

Meanwhile, Neal giggled to himself. "Short-stop" He muttered under his breath, breaking the quiet for the first time "Why didn't I think of that?"

The group laughed as they turned their attention back to the game. After taking the first two pitches, which were high and outside, he had taken a big swing and miss on the third toss. That brought the count to two balls and one strike.

"Runner going!" Jared shouted as the pitcher began his wind up for the fourth time. The runner on first base was taking off toward second at full speed. Meanwhile the shortstop had lowered his bat parallel to the plate below, dropping a carefully placed bunt down the third base line and taking off toward first. It was a slow grounder and, thanks to the runner's head start, the third baseman had no play at second. So, sprinting in to grab the rolling baseball, he turned his attention to first base.

It was going to be a tough throw, especially with the bunter, Garcia, moving so swiftly down the line. The opposing defender forced the throw, moving awkwardly to his right and not stepping into his motion. The toss lacked momentum and skipped violently towards the first baseman. He tried to scoop the ball into his glove with a backhanded maneuver, but his heroics were too ambitious. Instead the ball scooted past his outstretched arm and rolled up against the stands. The runners advanced to second and third on the error, giving Bloomsburg two runners in scoring position.

The fans in the crowd rose to their feet cheering ecstatically. Bryn turned quickly to Ben and gave him a hard high five that made his hand burn slightly. But in a good way. Meanwhile Jared grabbed Ben by the back of his shoulders, nearly hopping with excitement.

"That was sick, Ben! Nice call!"

"Yeah, how did you do that?"

"Uh-I don't know. I used to watch a lot of baseball with my Dad. So I guess I picked up a thing or two."

"Hell ya, you did!" Bryn said, getting to his feet, "Neal, switch places with me for a bit. I want to talk more to the baseball savant you brought with you."

Neal rose as well, maneuvering around his friend, "That's cool, Colleen and I could use some time to catch up."

"Save the gossiping for your slumber party, screw-ball," Colleen said jokingly, getting to her feet as well and climb back a row. She walked to her left and sat behind Bryn. "I'm trying to talk baseball."

"She's a keeper, Bryn." Neal said, now standing alone and smiling on the outside of the circle. "Her nicknames need some work though."

"Heyyy, there he is!"

"Go Ben!"

He sheepishly walked over to his family, giving a small wave of recognition and a matching smile. He had just finished a short, post-race cool down run and was back in warm, dry clothes. "Thanks for coming guys! And thanks for cheering so loudly for me Cayley." He said sweetly, stooping down to give his baby sister a hug and a kiss.

"It's three hours past my bed time and I'm not even tired!" She replied excitedly. Ben rose to his full height and gave his parents a slightly guilty look. But his mother only beamed.

"Oh, she'll sleep the whole ride home," she said swatting the air with her hand. "What did you think of the race? Did you hear us? We're so proud of you!" She pulled him into an excited hug, skewing his blue and gray knit hit from its position on his head.

"Yeah, I heard you guys for sure." He said happily. "I had my best race of my life thanks to you." A broad grin had found its way onto his face. His time, 9 minutes and 24 seconds, was a massive personal record. Previously, he had never covered this distance under ten minutes.

"That was some race, son," Ben's father said as he took his turn in the congratulations. He pulled his oldest in close to his chest. "We were worried about you in the beginning. You were waaay in the back."

"And then you just starting passing all those people and we were going *crazy*!" Mrs. Havleck chimed in. "You've always been such a smart boy."

"Just a gutsy run. You've got twice the heart of all these kids."

Ben blushed, but continued to smile. It had been almost a year since his parents last had the chance to watch him race. It hit him just how much he had missed having them there for support. And it looked as if they had missed watching him just as much.

"Ben, was that kid Sean O-"

"Mom," Ben said in a frustrated whisper, scanning his perimeter. "Voice down, please."

"Oh, sorry honey … *Was that kid you were racing Sean O'Neill? You know from Downingtown*?"

"Yeah that was him, I talked to him a little before the race."

"He's gotten so much older since you boys went to school together. Does he have a little facial hair on his chin now?"

"I don't know, I didn't inspect him," he replied, with just a twinge of annoyance. "Why wouldn't he? I've got some chin hair too."

"Sure you do, honey."

Although he rolled his eyes, Ben couldn't help but maintain his smile. It seemed to be plastered onto his face.

"He used to beat you pretty consistently, right?" Mr. Havleck said, picking up on the discretionary tone more quickly than his wife.

"Yeah, he did. Every race." Ben paused, his grin nearly splitting his face in pieces now. "So I was kinda out there gunning for him."

His father shared in his enthusiasm. "You should have seen his face when you went past him the first time, it was great-"

"We all know Ben's really fast, so can we just go home now, please?" Cayley cut in. She had sat back down on the closest bleacher and was rubbing her eyes.

"We'll talk more on the drive," Paul Havleck replied, turning to his youngest. "C'mon sweetie, I'll take you up to the car." Mr. Havleck scooped up his daughter and began to walk away from the track. "You know she's starting to get kinda heavy." He muttered to his family as they departed.

"I heard that!" Cayley exclaimed from over his shoulder. Ben and his mother laughed for a moment, before the latter turned to leave as well. Ben checked over his shoulder in the direction of the Downingtown West camp Sean had pointed out earlier, noticing the final few members of the team were packing up the tent.

"I'll catch up, Mom? I just want to say bye to the guys," he pointed back over his shoulder.

His mother murmured her approval but otherwise did not break stride. "Just don't take too long. Or you'll have two sleeping girls to carry into the house."

"Thanks ma,"

He jogged around the fence, trying to catch his old teammates before they left. "Yo Sean!" He called as the last runner turned to walk out to the parking lot. The boy turned around at the sound of his name.

"Yo, Peanut!" He paused in his tracks to wait for Ben. "Awesome race, man."

"Thanks dude, you too," Havleck replied. He tried to extend his hand, but Sean's were full. The two awkwardly tried to maneuver for the shake but struggled to create the space.

"You know what, screw this," O'Neill threw his bags on the ground and pulled Ben into yet another hug. "That was one heck of a race. I tried everything, but I couldn't get away. You're in sick shape dude."

"Thanks, you guys are too. That was a PR for you, right?"

"Yeah, by like ten seconds haha. You too?"

"Yeah ... by like 50 or so ..."

Sean staggered backward, mouth agape in over-exaggerated surprise. "Are you serious right now? How is that even possible?"

Ben shrugged, "I haven't really run it all out in a while, I guess."

BEEP! BEEP!

The horn of a van parked on the edge of the lot blared loudly causing both boys to jump.

"That's my ride," Sean said, scrambling to gather up his belongings. "They're probably pissed I held them up so long."

"Who all is in there?" Ben asked curiously, looking carefully across at the tinted windows.

"Oh it's uh Jake, Josh, Quinn … You know what-come with me for a sec." And he nodded his head toward the van, breaking into a jog. Ben followed along eagerly in his wake. As they got closer, he could hear screaming and banging on the windows. Finally, someone pulled open the door and a trio of runners stormed out to greet them. All three wrapped him up into a fierce bear hug that nearly knocked him off his feet.

When he recovered from the impact, Ben got a chance to take his first good look at each of them. It had been almost a year since he moved from Downingtown to Bloomsburg and each friend had changed slightly from their days as teammates, yet they were each easily recognizable. It was surreal. These people had essentially become ghosts to him. Nothing more than memories. But now he was staring them in the face and they were staring back.

"Sick race, man!"

"Yeah, that was great!"

"What are you doing back in the area?"

"My sister had a little, like, gymnastics competition and when I saw it was the same weekend as this meet, I knew I had to try and hop in." Ben said excitedly. "How did you all do?"

"Pretty solid," the boy in the middle said as the others defaulted to him. "Josh qualified for districts in the 1600," he said gesturing to his right, "And then Quinn and I each set PRs in the 32," gesturing back to his left.

"I thought for a second she was gonna beat you, not gonna lie," Sean joked.

"Yeah, I think I helped inspire him." Quinn replied, gently punching Jake's arm. They laughed for a moment, letting it slowly fade into silence.

"So your sister is old enough to do gymnastics now?" Quinn asked, turning her attention back to Ben. "Gosh, I can still remember when she was born …" They locked eyes for the first time and Ben's stomach back flipped just like it used to.

"Yeah it's crazy, I slept over at Jake's house that night I'm pretty sure," Ben said pointing across in his friend's direction.

"Oooh yeah wasn't that the first time-"

"-I ever did a 5k, yeah." Ben replied, remembering instantly. "Your mom signed me up last minute to run it with you guys. I had no idea what I was doing." They laughed again. Ben kept that race bib in an album underneath his bed. On the back he had written his time of 24 minutes and 45 seconds. "Who knows, if that never happened, I might never have started running. My whole life would be different …"

"It's kinda freaky how each little decision has a butterfly effect like that." Josh replied, staring blankly off somewhere behind Ben. "Just imagine how different our lives could have been if even one small event was flipped."

"For sure," Ben said, glancing subconsciously to his right. He scanned the faces of his teammates once more, dwelling for an extra second on Quinn. *But maybe that's all the more reason to think everything happens for a reason,* he thought to himself.

***

After a consistent string of runs in the game's final innings, Bloomsburg baseball clinched a decisive victory over their counterparts from Millersville. As students and fans prepared to leave the stadium, spirits were high among the hometown crowd. Ben thoroughly enjoyed himself the second half of the game, pushing himself out of his comfort zone a bit as he talked and joked with Neal's friends.

"You guys coming back to our place?" Jared asked as they walked single file down the aluminum bleachers.

"Yeah, we're definitely down." Bryn said looking back to check with Colleen who nodded in confirmation.

"Do you mind if I invite my roommates to come?" she asked, pulling her phone from her pocket.

"No not at all. The more the merrier. Although if they're guys, that's gonna really push down our ratio."

"If her roommates were guys, our ratio would be the least of my concerns." Bryn joked as Colleen rolled her eyes again.

"Don't worry. They're girls. They're pretty cool actually." She looked up from her phone to make sure she correctly navigated the final steps. "I think Neal would get along well with one of them-what do you think of that match, Bryn?"

"Tiffany or Stephanie?"

"Stephanie."

"Yeah, I was about to say …"

"Sorry to spoil this episode of the Bachelor ladies," Neal said as the group packed up at the bottom of the stairs. "But I won't be able to make it tonight."

Jared's face fell. "Why not?"

"My mom needs me to take care of a few things back at my place." They cleared the perimeter of the ballpark and things began to open up as the crowd spread in separate directions. A yellow and black butterfly flew down and rested on Ben's shoulder for a moment. "And he's my ride," Neal continued, nodding at Ben, "so I'm afraid I'll be stealing him too." Ben stirred slightly when acknowledged, motivating the butterfly to float gently away.

"I honestly don't think I could hate you more than I do right now," Bryn said somewhere between serious and joking. Neal smiled and shrugged his shoulders. "Well, Ben, you should at least come back for the Shippensburg game next week."

"Yeah, that would be awesome," Ben replied as the two parties prepared to walk off in opposite directions. "I'll see you guys later!"

Cutting across the path, Neal and Ben wandered back in the direction from which they had originally came, doubling back toward the first base line. A group of dawdling girls was standing about 50 yards away, having just descended the stadium steps. From afar, Ben thought he recognized one of the shorter girls in the pack. *No ... why would she be here?*

Like Ben and Neal before, two of the girls split from the group to travel in another direction. His direction. Deciding he had imagined things, he shook his head slightly and turned his attention to Neal.

"So what do you need to do for your mom?" he asked curiously.

"Nothing," Neal replied simply. "Just didn't feel like going out." Confused, Ben opened his mouth to respond, but was quickly distracted. The pair of girls was fast approaching, almost close enough for him to clearly make out their faces. As they passed one another, the one Ben had recognized gave him a surprised smile and small wave, which he returned sheepishly. Other than this greeting, the couples passed one another in silence. It was a small gesture, but not so small that it was overlooked by Ben's older friend.

"What just happened ..." Neal said, snapping his head back and forth, "Do you know that girl?"

"It's just someone I know from my math class," Ben said quietly, continuing to walk forward. He was hoping to drop it and move on, but Neal was slowing to a stop.

"Interesting," he said sneakily, "And what's she doing *here*?"

"I don't know-why would I know th-?"

"So let's find out!" And Neal turned around and sped back after the duo that had just passed them.

"Neal ..." Ben said, cautiously following. "This isn't a funny joke ..." But his friend showed no signs of slowing. *"Neal!"* He tried to quietly scream, but it was, unsurprisingly, ineffective. Begrudgingly, he jogged after his friend who was now within earshot of the women ahead.

"Excuse me for a second," he heard Neal say as he approached, "but my friend here recognized you from school-" he nodded at the now slightly out of breath boy beside him, "-and wanted to come over and say hello." Ben gave a slight wave of acknowledgement, feeling his face burn red.

"You know this guy, Nicole?" the taller of the two asked, brow raised, eyeing Neal suspiciously.

"Well um," she replied, "I know *him*, yeah," she pointed at Ben, "but not um-what did you say your name was?"

Neal gave a meaningful look to Ben who, after a brief moment of confusion, realized that was his cue to speak up. "Oh-um-this is my friend Neal," He said awkwardly displaying the collegiate, who smiled at Ben encouragingly. "We were just at the baseball game. Were-uh-was that why you're here?"

"Yeah, the girls thought it would be fun for me to see some Bloomsburg athletics while I'm visiting. I'm here on a recruiting trip with the soccer team." She gestured at the older woman beside her.

"Funny you should mention that," Neal said, jumping in enthusiastically, "Ben is here doing a recruiting trip as well!" Ben looked incredulously to his right, but thankfully Nicole seemed to have missed it.

"Oh, really? For … what was it you said you did-distance running?"

"Er-yeah, Neal's hosting me for the-" he glanced quickly at Neal before forcing himself to continue with the lie. "-the Cross Country team."

"Oh, Cross Country?" the taller soccer player spoke up again, "I had a couple friends who ran in high school. How fast can you guys run for a mile?"

"Well, my best is 4:49-" Ben began.

"Wow, that's really fast!"

"-but I just ran a 9:24 in the 3200 so realistically-agh!" Neal stepped hard onto his right foot: a signal to get him to stop talking.

"Sorry man, I lost my balance for a second there." Neal lied, straightening up. "I got one of those runner's cramps. You know how it is." Ben fought the overwhelming urge to laugh. "I'm more of a six minute guy myself," Neal continued. "Not quite as fast as my friend Ben here, but he's top notch. State caliber kind of runner." He patted Ben on the back affectionately.

Six minutes?, Ben thought to himself. *For a college guy? You're killing us here, Neal.*

But apparently the older soccer player was not as skeptical. "That's still a good time," she said reassuringly, giving Neal a consoling smile. "You're still *way* faster than I am."

"Well that's awfully nice of you to say-" He paused to let her insert her name.

"Kim."

"Well, it's nice to meet a fan, Kim." He said, shaking her hand. "After struggling through a 10,000k race, it's just nice to feel appreciated." Ben somehow managed to keep his palm away from his face. "Anyway, are you guys headed back up toward campus?" Neal asked, sensing the skepticism from his partner.

Nicole looked to her hostess for guidance. "Yeah, we are heading up to Kehr actually." Kim replied, her previously hostile tone seeming to soften. "Are you guys going this way?" She pointed in the opposite direction of Ben's car.

"As a matter of fact we are," Neal said springing up past Ben to walk alongside the soccer player. "I pretty much live at the snack bar. They're considering naming a sandwich after me …" He walked at a quick pace, but kept his classmate engaged in conversation. Slowly, a gap emerged back to Ben and Nicole.

"So," she asked smiling, "Why are you *actually* here? Because I don't think it's for cross country."

"What gave it away?" Ben asked in a mixture of amusement and surprise. "Was it the runner's cramps thing? Because that's real. Don't get too close to me in the hallway."

She laughed, flashing that toothy smile of straight white teeth. "Not sure I can sit next to you anymore in math class." They walked in the shadow of their two older comrades toward a building lined with large glass windows. "Speaking of which, I'm definitely not ready for that Math final. How complicated do you think he's going to make the derivatives section?"

"Probably nothing crazy. Hopefully it's something comparable to the last couple homeworks which weren't too bad." Ben pushed open the door for Nicole who followed him through.

"You didn't think those were that bad?" She asked, sounding impressed.

"Oh-well … I mean relatively to, like, fighting a shark or … something." He laughed uncomfortably. Glancing quickly around, he realized they had completely separated from Neal and Kim. Then he looked back at Nicole who was scanning around the unfamiliar room as well, likely sharing his concern. "You know maybe we should meet up some time," Ben blurted out before he could stop himself, "To, like, study for the final and stuff." Once again, he felt himself blush uncontrollably.

"Yeah, that would be cool," she said and Ben noticed that her face also had traces of red. "Do you have my number or-?"

"Um, I don't think so …" Ben fumbled nervously with his pocket. Finally, he removed his phone and clicked onto his contacts section. "You want to read it off?"

"Sure, it's 642-6532. Usual area-code." Ben carefully typed the numbers into his phone.

"Alright awesome, I'll-" But before Ben could finish his train of thought, Neal came flying back into view from around the corner. His hair was slightly disheveled and his shirt had a small rip in it.

"We gotta go," he said, stopping for a moment beside Ben. "Don't have time to explain." He looked back over his shoulder and then dove across the room and under a couch. Emerging from the hallway that Neal had just exited were two, large collegiates, each nearly double Ben's size in both height and weight. They scanned the room quickly before trudging off down a side hallway. Once they were out of sight, Neal carefully crawled out from his hiding spot and sprinted for the door.

"I guess that's my cue," Ben said as he stood dumbfounded a few feet from the doorway Neal had just escaped through.

"Make sure you tell your friend to hydrate. Wouldn't want any more runner's cramps."

Chapter Seventeen

John Trainor, April 2022

"Can I get you anything? Like water or coffee or anything?"

"Nah, I'm good. Thank you, though."

"Alright, just let me know if you change your mind." He sat down across from me, his long legs folding underneath him. "So where would you like to begin?"

"Well, I'm trying to piece together some things-" I stopped as the baby in his arms stirred slightly. "Oh, sorry, should I speak more softly?"

"It's OK, I think he's just having a dream. He's usually a pretty good sleeper."

"Alright cool." It was odd. I was interviewing this person who I considered a peer, yet there he was sitting with a newborn boy. I felt so unprepared to be a parent-I was still a kid myself-how could someone my age be going through this? Of course, from everything I had heard about Matt Burke, he was a natural father.

"So like I was saying, I'm trying to piece together some more information about what things were like for Jimmy after you graduated. Kind of in that sophomore-junior window."

"Well, I'm sure you've heard about his sophomore year at states?"

"Oh yeah. But I was thinking more his progression *away* from the track."

"Ah, alright I see what you're saying." He paused, inspecting me with a long searching gaze. Eventually, he made up his mind about how well-intentioned I was and spoke again. "Now, as you know I wasn't around much, so a lot of our communication came through phone calls ...

Jimmy Springer, November 1ˢᵗ, 2014

"Hello?"

"*Hey, what's up, superstar?*"

"Haha, I assume that means you saw the results?"

"*I've been sitting here refreshing the page all day. I know being a state champ is probably getting old to you by now, but I wanted to call and congratulate you anyway ... And, of course, I wanted the details.*"

"Well, thank you! Give me one sec-I just want to get in a comfortable story telling position," Jimmy lounged on the couch, letting his sore feet hang off the edge. He repositioned the phone carefully by his ear. "Alright, you ready?"

"*Hit me,*" Matt's voice replied.

"So, for starters the weather was *way* better than last year. That got me pretty excited. Besides that, I was just zoned in on my race plan. Ames and I figured Zarniack would probably take it out since he likes to go out fast."

"Yeah, didn't he take it out in like 4:41?"

"Yep. Crazy fast. So I just sat back by Power 'cause he typically runs a pretty reasonable pace. Then we went into the back hills and I could feel things slowing up a bit-just like last year. I was itching to go earlier but Ames really wanted me to wait until like 800 to go before I made my move."

"I'm guessing you didn't make it all the way to 800?"

"Well, I would have but this random dude from, like, Crestwood or something started to try and surge for the lead. And I was just like, 'no way is this kid running a single step ahead of me'. So that's when I dropped the hammer. A few guys tried to come with, but they paid the price at the end."

"Did you realize how fast you were running?"

"I had no idea until I saw the clock honestly and then I lost it. I was amped, man. Running 15:11 on that course blows my mind."

"That's awesome, dude. Congrats! Is that the course record?"

"No, some random dude from the 70s has it. It's like 15:02. Ames thinks mine is the real record though. Says they re-measured the course and found out it was short sometime in the 90s. No one's come within like 20 seconds of the old record since."

"It's alright man. Next year you'll break that."

"Haha, yeah exactly ... What's been up with you? College still treating you well?"

"Eh, it's alright. I still get home sick sometimes, but I've made some new friends from the team and classes and stuff ... You ever heard of Drew Perry?"

"Sounds vaguely familiar."

"He ran for Lower Merion. Pretty solid-like 44th at states last year ... He's probably my best friend on the team. Such a funny kid."

"Oh nice, that's awesome. Are you guys gonna room together next year?"

"I haven't asked him yet, but I hope so. He's like kinda *friends with his current roommate. But I think he would rather live with me, you know? So hopefully it works out."*

"Sweet, I wish you guys luck."

"Thanks man." There was a noticeable pause, the first of the conversation.

"... Well, I should probably get going. My parents and I are grabbing some dinner ..."

"Yeah, of course. Do your thing. We'll talk again soon. Are you gonna be around for Thanksgiving? That's the next time I'll be home"

"Yeah, as far as I know, I'll be in UV."

"Alright sweet, I'll see ya then."

"See ya then."

Jimmy Springer, May, 2015
  Buzz ... buzz ...
  "Hey, Coach, do you mind if I take this real fast? It's Matt Burke."
  "Ah yes! Go for it," Coach Ames said, switching lanes carefully. "Tell him I say 'hey'."
  "Alright, thanks," Jimmy said before sliding his finger across his phone screen. "Hello?"
  "You son of a gun. You're so selfish."
  "Um … why do you say that?"
  "You couldn't just leave one *gold medal for somebody else. You had to take all three."*
  "Haha are results already up?"
  "I'm not sure. I was just following on LetsRace. It was blowing up."
  "Dude, how can you even read that garbage on there? Pretty sure those kids think I'm like 24 years old and on steroids."
  "It's actually EPO that you are on these days. Although the age thing is pretty spot on … But seriously dude, congrats. That is so cool. Don't forget me when you win the Olympics."
  "Haha thanks man I appreciate it … Coach says 'hey' by the way."
  "Oh, are you guys still driving back?"
  "Yeah, we got a bit of a late start and then traffic kinda sucked."
  "Ah, bummer. Well I won't keep you then. I just wanted to check in. I should probably get back to Emily anyway. She still doesn't completely understand 'track nerd Matt'."
  "No worries man-how is she doing by the way?"
  "She is doing well! We're both just excited to be done the first year and have no summer assignments or anything. I'll tell her you asked about her."
  "Sweet sounds good … when do you come back to UV?"
  "I'll be back at the start of June. We'll have to get together and run when I get back so that you can walk me through all these races. Sounded epic."
  "For sure, dude. Sounds great. I guess I'll talk to you again soon then."
  "See ya, Jimmy."

Jimmy Springer, October 3rd, 2015
  "Hello?"
  "Hey Matt, how's it going?"
  "Hey Jimmy, what's up? Everything OK?"

"Yeah … I'm good, just figured I'd call to catch up. You got some time?"

"*For you? Of course I do! Just give me a sec,*" There was a brief pause where Jimmy could hear Matt walking through what sounded like a crowded room. "*OK, I'm good. How you been?*"

"Sorry, am I interrupting something or-"

"*Nah dude, we are just having a little party at our place. It's no big.*"

"I mean I can call back-"

"*Jimmy, it's cool. I promise. So tell me how you've been? How's school and running and everything? I saw you won at Carlisle. That was pretty solid.*"

"Nah it sucked. I had no pop in my legs. That new guy from practice this summer, Coach Thomas, is terrible."

"*He still being a prick?*"

"The prickiest. Like, basically, everybody on our team has either quit or gotten hurt. We aren't even gonna have five guys available to run at leagues. Not that it would matter much: Thomas can't coach worth shit. He's probably never even run a step in his life."

"*Did you ever find out why they made him the coach in the first place?*"

"Yeah, I did." Jimmy's tone changed from melancholy and downtrodden to bitter and vengeful. Mark couldn't decide which tone concerned him more. "Apparently, at Union Valley you get a bonus or something if you have a high performing team. And since Thomas had an in with the AD, he wiggled his way into this spot so he could pick up that extra money. He saw me as his big pay day."

"*That sucks.*"

"Yeah, it does. And he's running me into the effing ground to try and make sure I win everything. Like a lot of power lifting and stupid non-running stuff. Absurd workouts that don't make any sense. I'm stunned I've made it this far without getting injured."

"*You should tell someone, dude. Somebody who can fix this.*"

"Like who? I told you, he's got the AD in his damn pocket-"

"*Other people can do something. I'm sure if you told your parents-*"

"I'm not telling them." He said it with such conviction that Matt didn't press it further. "Look, I should let you get back to your party."

"*Jimmy, I told you already, it's not a big-*"

"I'll talk to you later."

Jimmy Springer, November 3rd, 2015

"Hello?"

"*Hey, congrats champ! Three in a row! That's unbelievable.*"

"Yeah, I guess it's not so bad. Wanted to run a little faster though."

"Well not every race can be a PR, you know? Especially when you're injured. Is it true you have a stress fracture?"

"Stress reaction the doctor said. I'll be skipping all of indoors."

"Shoot. That sucks man."

"Eh, it's not that big of a deal. I was planning to take the winter off anyway."

"Really?"

"Yeah, I just need the time away from running. This year really burned me out, you know? I want to take a step back and look at my goals. I've been running so long … sometimes it's hard to remember why I started."

"Well at least it will give you some time away from Coach Thomas."

"Oh, shoot I didn't tell you, did I?!" He sounded excited for the first time in the conversation.

"No, what happened?!"

"UV fired his ass."

"That makes me so happy. What made them finally decide to do it?"

"I talked to my mom about the training and stuff," Jimmy had a small layer of discomfort in his voice, "and she was *not* happy about what she heard."

"Yeah, I bet. The guy is such an idiot. Glad you finally got rid of him." It was a testament to their friendship that Matt chose to ignore the fact that Jimmy had refused this exact advice a month earlier. *"Who are they gonna get now for track?"*

"No clue. Apparently they got rid of that bonus rule I told you about- makes sense considering how sketchy it was. So I'd bet they'll have a smaller applicant pool to choose from this time around." The bitterness had returned to his tone.

"Well, maybe that means you'll get the right kind of coach this time around."

"We'll see," Jimmy replied skeptically. "But enough about me, how are you doing? Is your season done yet?"

"Nah, I got regionals coming up next weekend."

"What's regionals?"

"It's most similar to districts I guess? Regionals is our NCAA qualifiers. It's actually my first time making the varsity squad for this meet so I'm pretty amped."

"Yeah, that's awesome, man! Do you have a good team? Like any shot at Nationals?"

"Nah, no shot at Nationals or anything like that. We are just going out looking for top ten. That would be a big day for us."

"Sounds good, I'll be on the lookout for any results that come from that … Where do I go for NCAA results anyway?"

"*Just go to TFRRS.*"

"… I'm sorry was that English?"

"*Haha, it's spelled T-F-R-R-S. It's like track and field results something something.*"

"So wouldn't that be tfrss?"

"*Clever, Springer. You've gotten wiser in your old age. How old are you now anyway?*"

"16, but I'll be 17 in a couple months."

"*You've gotta be looking at colleges then.*"

"Yeah, I've gotten a bunch of letters and recruitment crap. Haven't really sorted through it yet … I've still got time."

"*Wow, I'm surprised you're waiting. I feel like it would be so exciting to have everyone coming after me like that. I got a couple letters after I medaled at states and I was super jacked up about it. I was, like, bragging to random people on the street and stuff. For you I figured it would be my letters times a thousand. So who knows what I would have been doing to random people on the street if I was in your shoes.*"

"I won't tell Emily you said that."

"*Haha I appreciate that. You two still need to officially meet, right?*"

"Yeah, still haven't met her yet. You have to bring her back to UV and stop going up to Boston."

"*I do. I want her to see the town and everything. Maybe over the summer. Depends on if I get this internship or not.*"

"Internship?"

"*Yeah, it's just some finance thing up in Boston. Emily's dad put my name in for it, but I doubt I'll get it. It's like super competitive. But if I do, it will be huge for my long term job prospects.*"

"Gosh, now *you* sound old."

"*Haha stay young, Jimmy. Stay young as long as you can. Life is a lot different when you get old.*"

Jimmy Springer, December 19th, 2015

"Hey … it's Jimmy. Looks like we are playing phone tag … Didn't get my tickets for that invitational up in Boston … Apparently Coach never submitted the proper forms. So not only can I not run, but apparently I can't even go watch other people do it … I'm trying to get into this race in New York City though. Should be a pretty awesome event … I'll have to give you the details next time we talk. No need to call back tonight or anything. I'm sure we'll talk soon."

Jimmy Springer, January 8th, 2016

"Hey, what's up?"

"Hey dude, I'm swinging by my house to pick up stuff for school. You gonna be around tonight?"

"Nah, not tonight. I got plans with some of the guys."

"Ah, shoot. I'm supposed to leave tomorrow morning to get back for pre-season week. What are you and the guys doing?"

"Smith is having a house party. You want to come?"

"Wait, Smith? As in Corey Smith? Eric's brother?"

"Yeah,"

"That kid's bad news, Jimmy. I'm not sure a kid like you wants to get mixed up with a kid like him."

"Hey, man, that's my friend. You don't see me talking crap on Drew Perry or someone."

"Right ... Sorry. I was just-well, nevermind it's not any of my business. Would you maybe want to run tomorrow with me before I leave?"

"I don't think that's gonna work either. I'm probably gonna get pretty messed up tonight."

"Too messed up to run the next day? Isn't that like-"

"Shit, bro! What are you my dad? Did you ride your effing high horse down from Boston?"

"I'm sorry, man. I just thought maybe we could catch up. I haven't seen you in forever."

"Yeah? Well whose fault is that? So suddenly you're back in town and I'm supposed to just drop everything for you? Because you're so damn important that you can barely fit me into your loaded itinerary."

"C'mon man that's not fair. I've had a lot going on with work and Emily and ... you'll see when you get to college. Lots of things change really quickly. I'm just trying my best to balance everything."

"Well, I'll give you one less thing to balance-"

"Jimmy-!"

"Good bye, Matt."

Jimmy Springer, May 26th, 2016

"Hey, dude. Figured I might be able to catch you before you left for the meet, but I guess not ... I'm actually here in Union Valley for the weekend before starting this internship up in Boston. Emily's here with me! Hopefully you get this in time so we can all meet up for lunch or something ... Best of luck at states by the way. I'm sure you're gonna kill it like always."

Chapter Eighteen

TrainHard Blog, May 24ᵗʰ 2016
State 3200m Preview
By John Trainor

It's officially state week here on the blog and we are celebrating in style. I'll be breaking down all the important details and names to watch for each of the four major distance events. We'll start with the 3200 meters which will be the first final of the day on Saturday morning.

Key Qualifiers
The top seed and heavy favorite for gold is, unsurprisingly, the defending champion Jimmy Springer. The junior from Union Valley pulled off the unthinkable a year ago: winning the 32, 16 and 800 in the same state meet. It was the first time anyone had won all three events in a championship (the closest before him was Mac Beam back in 1968 who had two firsts and a third).

After an injury this winter, Springer has decided not to chase the triple again, instead opting to focus his attention on not just a win, but also the state record. The mark to beat is 9:00.11, set back in 1992 by Doug Coval of Council Rock. Although the record has survived nearly 24 years, it probably has seen its last full week in the books. Springer has an excellent shot at putting his name atop the all-time list for the first time in his special career after running a personal best of 9:01.82 at the District One Championships. For those of you keeping score at home, that's third fastest in PA history.

"I wasn't really thinking about the record," Jimmy said in a post-race interview, "I didn't even realize how close I was until the last lap. If someone had been willing to take the pace out faster, it would have been mine."

The usually loaded District One had just one other sub 9:20 finisher as Pennridge's Isaac Bryant took the silver medal in 9:16. However, three runners from the cross country state champions, Coatesville, ran together as a pack and took fourth through sixth in the standings. After the race, Raiders' team captain Andrew Rosato said the boys were trying to conserve energy and do just enough to qualify for next weekend's championship.

"Coach Solares really wants us to peak specifically for states. He felt running two hard 3200s back to back would be too much strain. But next weekend, I'll be running all out-and running for the win."

During indoor, Rosato was defeated over the final 400 meters in his bid for his first individual state gold. Jayson Miller of Manheim Township got the upset victory: 8:35 to 8:37.

Speaking of Miller, he won his district meet in the second fastest time in the state this year, trailing only Springer. He opened up a massive lead over Zack

Johnston of Cedar Cliff and Henry Gonzalez of JP McCaskey during the final two laps to clinch the victory.

"I'm feeling pretty good," Miller said after the race, "Looking forward to getting the chance to race everybody at states next week. Definitely going to be a lot of fun."

Out west, the graduation of Pittsburgh Central Catholic duo Scott Zarniack and Robert Runco opened the door for a new star to emerge and lead the district. In a four-way battle, Ben Jacobs of Plum won by less than a second over Chris Cole of Seneca Valley: 9:18.08-9:18.49. To make matters even crazier third and fourth place finishers Noah West and Chase Morgan ran 9:19 and 9:20, making for the tightest finish of the weekend.

Lastly, Bonner's duo of Dan McGee and Tom Seeley cruised to a 1-2 finish in the District 12 Championships and easily punched their state meet tickets while running about 9:30. They won't be among the top seeds, but it's important to remember this pair was third and fourth respectively at the indoor state championships over 3,000 meters.

Analysis

You'd have to be crazy to pick against Jimmy Springer in this race. Even with an injury, he's still managed to win the district title and uncork a big PR. In the past, Springer hasn't really gone all out in the two mile, saving for other events on a busy schedule. But this year, focused and ready to attack, we are finally seeing the true potential for the record many thought he had last year in this event.

Keep in mind that Jimmy Springer has *never* lost an individual state championship race during any season. Even as a freshman, Jimmy went two for two. Many people have speculated he's trending in the wrong direction (over racing, over training), but still no one has been able to beat him when it counts. The kid is just clutch.

However, let's not sleep on Andrew Rosato of Coatesville. The Raiders absolutely dominated during Cross Country season and now seem to be peaking at the right time once again. Rosato looked completely at ease jogging to a 9:22 state qualifying time at the district championships. When he unleashes his full arsenal at states, it's going to be tough for anyone to handle.

The one knock on Rosato has been his speed, but he's taken big steps to improve that so far this spring. He won the mile at the Coatesville Invitational and had a memorable anchor performance on the Raiders' wheel-winning Distance Medley at the Penn Relays. You guys know me. I like to pick the upset. And Rosato may be the perfect candidate.

A lot of the District Three readers have been hyping up Jayson Miller from Manheim Township as the guy who should be my upset pick. I'll admit Miller did run very fast at districts. Plus, he won the indoor state championship over Rosato. That being said, I'd like to see him in a race that's fast from the start. He seems to be good at winding it up and closing, but I'm not sure he will be able to hang at sub nine minute pace. It's worth noting that Miller has outkicked Rosato by one spot the last two times they met at states (in XC they finished fourth and fifth).

I have no idea who the WPIAL's top contender will be. This district always seems to produce a medal contender, but their crop at the top is relatively inexperienced. Jacobs upset win might be a sign of things to come (he was ninth at states in XC), but he still hasn't proven to me that he's healed from his stress fracture. I think it's more likely we have a title contender from the Catholic league than from the WPIAL.

Lastly, keep an eye out for Teddy Crittenton of Wissahickon. He scratched the mile this weekend and is now only running the 3200. He's still pretty inexperienced at this event, but he was a beast in cross country the past few seasons. I think he could make the transition well and use some of that closing speed to make noise at the end of the race.

Prediction

Springer has made it clear he wants the record and will be taking things out hard. Maybe he's healthy enough to do it, but I also wouldn't be surprised if this leaves him vulnerable for an upset. The way the Coatesville guys have been running under Coach Solares it's really hard for me to doubt them. I think Rosato goes after Springer with everything he's got and pulls off the stunner. I'm predicting not just one, but two runners under Coval's state record. Should be one to remember!

1. Rosato 8:58
2. Springer 8:59
3. McGee 9:05
4. Miller 9:07
5. Jacobs 9:11
6. Crittenton 9:12
7. Seeley 9:12
8. Garnett 9:15

Chapter Nineteen

Ben Havleck, May 28ᵗʰ 2016

He pushed the door open to the dining hall, his stomach in knots. He probably wouldn't be able to eat much breakfast, but it was worth a try. The cafeteria was packed with other athletes, up early to grab a bite before a full day of competition. Most of the tables were occupied by teammates, some laughing and joking, others discussing strategy. Even the schools that only had one or two competitors had a coach sitting among them. No one was alone. Well, no one *else* was alone.

Ben walked slowly through the food displays, looking for a suitable meal. After a careful perusal, he decided on a wheat bagel. He lightly toasted it before adding a small layer of peanut butter. With his main course now set, he grabbed a banana and filled his bottle of water. With his morning meal set, he walked out to the tables, looking for a place to sit.

His options were, expectedly, sparse. He paced uncomfortably through the seats, his circumstance oddly reminiscent of his first day at his new high school. Mercifully, he spotted a small table in the far corner that appeared to be unclaimed. He quickened his stride and set off straight toward his target. When he reached the open spot, he slid carefully into the booth. At the same moment, appearing perpendicularly, another boy pulled out the chair opposite him and flopped ungracefully onto it.

"Oh, sorry," Ben said as he realized the newcomer's presence.

"Nah, it's my fault, dude, I didn't see you there." He prepared to return to his feet, looking back over his shoulder. Then, turning around to face Ben, "Actually, do you mind if we just share? Not sure there's much else available."

"No, I don't mind."

"If you're saving this for somebody else, like a coach or teammate-"

"Seriously, it's not a problem. I'm the only one from my team here." Ben cut across glumly.

"Same with me" The stranger leaned back in his chair and ran a hand through his disheveled head of hair. He looked uncomfortable, perhaps even sick. Although he was seated, Ben could tell this runner was significantly taller than he was. The boy stretched his long legs underneath the table, extended his arms above his head and yawned.

His tablemate dipped into his breakfast: a plate full of eggs and a cup of Gatorade. Ben followed suit, taking his first bites of bagel and doing his best to keep it down within his nervous stomach. As they ate, a pair of girls passed by the table. One spotted the boy across from Ben and stared unabashedly, whispering something to her friend, who then copied. This popular stranger was either unaware or ignored this odd behavior as they continued past without a word from their target.

What was that about? he thought, trying to covertly examine the boy's face for any clues about his identity. There was something familiar about the angles of the cheeks, but it was hard to get a good read while his face was down. And he didn't look up much. In between bites, he would diligently check his phone. Not in a rude or standoffish way, but instead as if he was expecting a call.

"Excuse me, Mr. Springer?" A small boy, probably only a freshman or sophomore had approached their table. "Can I touch your leg?"

"Sure, kid," he replied as if this was a perfectly normal question to be asked. While Mr. Springer continued to eat his eggs, the young boy reached out a tentative hand toward his calf. After a brief moment of contact he scurried excitedly away, back to a table of his teammates who were laughing and smiling.

Ben watched in shock, his bagel fixed halfway between table and agape mouth.

"You good, man?" Springer asked nonchalantly, taking a drink from his cup of Gatorade.

"What the heck just happened?" Ben asked unable to control his curiosity. His voice tended loud and high pitched in his angst.

"What-that? Well, I wish I could say that was the first time ..." He removed the long sleeve shirt he was wearing in favor of a cooler option. His top layer was now a blue and orange colored fabric with the name "Union Valley" in bold font across its face. As Ben's eyes flicked across the letters, he finally realized who it was that was sitting across from him.

Jimmy Springer, May 28th 2016

Jimmy picked a little more at his eggs. He could feel the uncomfortable gaze of his tablemate lingering on his chest. Even as he threw down his fork, giving up on any additional food, the boy's stare remained steady.

Jimmy checked down at his phone again. Nothing. *Damn it*, he thought to himself. He checked up again on his shorter compatriot who still remained silent. Lost in thought. For whatever reason, the boy's mind always seemed to be cycling through a complex level of ideas. Feeling uncomfortable, he prodded at conversation.

"So what are you racing today?"

The boy opposite was finally brought back to reality. "I'm running the 3200. How about you?"

Why do these kids insist on calling it a 3200? Jimmy thought to himself as he took yet another drink of Gatorade. *Just call it a two mile. No normal person knows what a 3200 is.*

"Yeah, I'm racing that as well. Should be a fun one. Good luck."

"Thanks. Same to you."

I think you'll need it more than me, Springer thought as he looked the small runner up and down. He took another long drink from his cup. His headache was refusing to subside.

"Well, I should probably get going," Jimmy said finally, pushing creakily up from the table, his meal half eaten. "Won't be long before that warm up jog."

The boy popped up eagerly. "Did you want to warm up together?" He asked hopefully, "Since, you know, you said you were the only one from your team here and-"

Jimmy's head pounded painfully again. "No offense kid," he said clutching at his forehead with one hand and holding his tray in the other, "But I don't think you could keep up with me." And he walked away from the disappointed runner opposite him, hoping to find something else that could cure his hangover.

Ben Havleck, cont.

Feeling rather insulted, Ben slumped back into his chair. For the first time since he woke up, he wasn't nervous. Instead, surprisingly, he was angry. Absentmindedly, he resumed eating, finding room to put away his breakfast. Once more he retreated back into his comfort zone: his own swirling head of thoughts.

He imagined himself racing head to head against Jimmy Springer later that morning. Throwing down a surge at the perfect moment. Leaving a stunned state champ in his wake. Of course, he knew it was an impossible dream. Not necessarily because of a lack of ability, but because their schools were not in the same classification.

To give different sized programs equal opportunity to compete at states, the Pennsylvania Athletic League had split the championships into essentially two separate meets happening under one umbrella. For every event, like the 3200 for example, there would be two different sections contested. The first would be only for schools under a certain enrollment threshold, the next for those schools that were above it. Union Valley was in the large school division while Ben's school, Bloomsburg, was classified as small. So no matter how fast either of the two harriers ran, neither could directly defeat the other.

With a deep sigh, he abandoned his daydream and refocused on the competition he would actually be competing against in less than two hours' time.

McKenzie, Davis and Griffin. Those are the guys you have to worry about, he thought as he gathered up his dishes, *Jimmy Springer should be the furthest thing from your mind.*

"Excuse me." One of the girls who had passed by the table earlier had reappeared at Ben's shoulder. "Can I ask you a question?"

"Sure," He said nervously. Ben could feel his hands getting slightly sweaty against his tray.

"Are you-like-friends with Jimmy Springer?"

"Uh, not really. We just kinda sat down at the same table."

"Oh," She responded disappointedly. The girl looked back over her shoulder. Following her gaze, Ben noticed her friend standing in the corner, mouthing instructions. "Well, if you see him again," She said, relaying the directions. "Can you give him my friend's number?"

"Er-I guess so. But-"

"Awesome! Thanks," she said placing a napkin on his tray. It had a string of numbers jotted neatly across its surface. "He's sooo dreamy, right?"

He gave a fake smile and accepted the paper as the girl turned to walk back over to her comrade. *Yeah*, he thought, *I just can't seem to get him out of my head.*

Chapter Twenty

Ben Havleck, May 28ᵗʰ 2016

He stared up into the stands. Even this early, they were packed with spectators. It was a larger crowd than he had ever raced in front of and that realization sent a shiver down his spine.

Ben entered the stadium tentatively and walked past a race official onto the track. His spike bag hung over his shoulder, bouncing up and down with each step. At about the 20 yard line, he settled into a seated position on the warm turf. He tucked one leg in toward his knee and extended his hamstring. It was a little tight. *You're fine*, he scolded himself, *Don't get psyched out*.

After a few more stretches, he popped up and decided to start his dynamic drills. He cycled through each one, carefully swinging his arms, diligently focusing on proper form. Once complete, he looked round for his water bottle to continue hydrating. A wave of dread crashed over him as he realized he had forgotten it in the cafeteria-distracted by one of Jimmy Springer's adoring fans.

Beginning to feel panicked, he wandered through the check in zone until he found a water jug and some paper cups. He drank some and then splashed more across his face and arms. Still, he was becoming increasingly uncomfortable with these adjustments to his usual routine.

Next, Ben moved onto his strides. He started with a relaxed, long and controlled sprint that covered the length of the football field. He pulled up just before the end zone and gradually eased to a stop. As he stood and recovered, he watched the girls' race right before his own take shape. A familiar runner in dark blue was in the lead, flanked by a trio of pursuers wearing green, red and black.

"Let's go, Quinn!" He cheered and clapped twice as the runners passed. He could feel a slight pull on his throat from his supportive efforts and so he made it a point to grab another cup of water on his return stride.

Finally, it was time to put on his racing spikes. He slipped them from his bag and held their light frame in his hand. His palms beginning to grow sweaty, he laced up his shoes.

"Small School 3200!" A man called from the corner of the check-in tent. Hastily, Ben slapped a pair of number eight stickers on both hips and jogged across to join the gathering beside the track's 100 meter mark. A small cluster amassed quickly as runners emerged from all directions.

He recognized a few of his competitors from the state cross country championships, most notably Terrence Griffin of Wyomissing. Ever since Ben had lost to Griffin at the Muhlenberg Invitational, he had been motivating himself for their inevitable rematch. He flexed his fingers subconsciously as a snow covered track flashed across the surface of his mind.

As they gathered together to jog ahead for the start, some of the runners exchanged a nervous nod or hello, but most were quiet and stoic. In total, Ben counted 21 competitors in the race.

The start will be crowded, he noted to himself as he surveyed his competition. *But once someone strings it out, there's only a few guys who can handle 70 second pace.*

He toed the line. He leaned forward. He let out one last deep breath.

Bang!

The starter's pistol fired into the warm morning air. Ben got off the line well, running with his elbows extended to ward off anyone crashing down on him. He snuck his small frame onto the rail and hugged tight to the first turn.

Through the opening lap, he stayed pinned to the inside, maintaining the shortest distance possible around the oval as planned. He found the pace incredibly easy; and a hurried glance at the clock told him why. They had marched through their initial rotation in just 74 seconds. That was nearly four seconds slower than Ben's pace during his personal best run at Coatesville a month earlier.

It'll pick up, he thought as the pack entered their second lap. *Just be patient.*

He felt a small push in his back as the runners behind him jockeyed wildly for position within the congestion. Fortunately, it wasn't enough to upset his balance, but it did unnerve him.

The pace continued to be pedestrian, allowing a wide range of ability levels to stay in contact with the leaders. All around Ben, runners weaved through traffic, dancing in the crowd, searching for ideal footing. A few tripped in the tangle of legs, but there were no falls.

After three laps of uninspired tempo, things were becoming increasingly physical. Ben could sense danger in his location, trapped against the railing, surrounded by flailing bodies. But he was loath to give up his inside hold and run the extra distance.

C'mon, somebody needs to pick it up, he thought angrily. They were coming up on the mile, the half way point of the race, yet still no one had decided to string out the field with an injection of speed. Ben's mind whirled as he considered his options. He hadn't planned on taking the lead this early. Knowing that it would take more energy to lead than follow, he had been trying to save his surge to the front for the final two laps. But the longer they jogged along conservatively, the more valuable a strong finishing kick would become. And that play just wasn't in his playbook.

After one more lap, I'll mak- But his internal planning was disrupted as a runner in white and black jockeyed with another in red, the former checking the latter toward the inside. Careening off balance, the boy in red ran smack into Ben, knocking him momentarily off the track.

Alright eff this.

He fought his way back onto the oval and surged forward. He broke free from the rail, seizing a small gap in order to swing to the outside. Four quick steps and he was at the front.

Mark Miller, May 28th 2016

"Come on Miller, let's go we're gonna be late!" A tan Honda Pilot was parked outside the Miller residence. Two boys sat in the car, listening to music, while a third scrambled wildly at the front door. After a moment's struggle, Mark came sprinting down the lawn, wearing one sandal and holding the other in his hand. He pulled open the back seat of the car, tossed his drawstring bag across the seat and flung himself inside. "Sorry, I couldn't find my watch. You guys didn't bring running shoes did you?"

"Heck no, I haven't run since leagues. You have to take advantage of the benefits of being slow." Mark's teammate, Ian McPearson, had placed seventh in the 3200 meters at the Lancaster-Lebanon League Championship's but missed the district qualifying standard by one second. "Can you drive a little faster, Tom? We're gonna be late."

"Calm down, Ian, I've gotta be careful. This is my mom's car." The driver was Thomas Winslow, another member of Manheim's Track and Field team. All three runners had just completed their sophomore season on the oval.

"Well you're driving like her so I guess that makes sense … I still don't get why *I* couldn't drive."

"Because Tom doesn't drive straight through the center of a traffic circle," Mark piped in from the back seat. "Yo, turn this song up."

… Word on road is the clique about to blow, you ain't gotta run and tell nobody they already know … We been livin' on the high, they been talkin' on the low …

"This is sick, all Jayson ever plays in the car is country music."

"You know I always keep the Drizzy loaded in the car, homie." Tom and Mark shared a momentary fist bump.

"I don't know how you two listen to this crap. Just another reason I should have driven."

"Sorry Ian, but nobody wants to listen to 'Bleed it Out' on repeat."

"*Guys, seriously, I can't race unless I listen to Bleed it Out first*" Tom made his best effort to mimic Ian's voice while Mark laughed.

It was fantastic weather in Shippensburg. The clouds slightly obscured the morning sun. The air was almost perfectly still with the exception of an occasional cool breeze that was gratefully accepted by the trio of sophomores exiting the parking lot. Even from a distance, Mark could see the bleachers were packed with family, friends and athletes.

"So I guess this meet is like a big deal or something?" Mark chuckled as Ian stepped to his left hip. He too was staring ahead at the stadium.

"It's 9:25 now, so the small school boys are probably just about to start up." Tom stepped to the ground, looking at his watch. "We've got like ten minutes until large schools." He clicked the lock for his car and led the march to the entrance.

At the gate, Mark and Ian chipped in for their driver's entrance fee and, with freshly stamped hands for tickets, they trekked around the outside of the track. The small school race was well underway, with a short, black-haired boy leading the charge. A few runners were hobbling slowly off the back of the pack, unable to handle the pace.

"How fast you think these guys are running?" Ian asked Mark as they passed. "We could totally beat some of these kids if we were in this classification. What a joke."

The trio lined the fence surrounding the track, stopping their meander to catch the conclusion of the race. The smaller boy was fighting hard at the front of the pack. He was opening up a small lead as the pace continued to take its toll on his competition. Only two runners were even within striking distance behind him. Mark kept his eyes on the clock, trying to estimate the runner's pace. "I think that lap was a 67? So they're running like nine minute pace?"

"Yeah-for that lap. But what did they start at? Because total time was 7:06 when he passed by." Ian considered his hand briefly. "That's only 9:28 pace. So they must have started slow."

"Did you just do that math in your head?" Tom asked, sounding impressed.

"Yeah," he reached into his pocket for a pair of sunglasses, "I feel like you guys always treat me like I'm an idiot when actually-" As he tried to raise the shades to his face, the edge of frame caught the top section of the fence in front of him. Knocked from his grip, the glasses soared through the air before landing almost ten feet away on the surface of the track. One of the lenses had popped out of its hold.

"What were you saying, Ian?"

"*ONE LAP TO GO! Havleck, Griffin, McKenzie!*" The announcement came booming over the P.A. system as the lead pack of runners surged by. The dark haired boy at the front was straining to keep his advantage. At the 200 meter mark on the far side, suddenly the runners in second and third sprang into action. They launched into a full sprint, leaving the initial leader fighting through quicksand to keep pace.

Ben Havleck, cont.
   "ONE LAP TO GO! Havleck, Griffin, McKenzie!"
   Ben passed the clock and listened to the bell ring beside him. The crowd was on their feet and cheering, blocking out the noise of his increasingly heavy breathing. He knew he had opened up a gap. But by how much? It probably wasn't significant, yet he was still encouraged by the fact that he struggled to hear the breathing and footsteps of his opposition at the same volume he had a few laps earlier. His adrenaline pulsed as he tried to turn up his sprint another notch, praying he could find the gears to bring the race home. The title on the tip of his tongue.
   When he turned toward the back stretch, a new wave of fans greeted him. Although this crowd was slightly smaller, the cheering still overwhelmed his eardrums. Unable to discern any information by listening, he resisted the overwhelming urge to look over his shoulder at the trailing group. *Just sprint. Sprint as hard as you can.* He was now approaching the last turn. Only half a lap stood between him and the state championship. Ben put his head down slightly and tried to rally his legs for one last surge.
   Then, as he approached a quieter section of the track, he heard it. Footsteps. Turning over quickly. Much quicker than his own. He pumped furiously, his head swinging wildly, desperately trying to float forward. A runner in a white jersey flew by him and blasted into the final straightaway. It was almost as if Ben was standing still.
   Although they never touched, the blow struck Havleck as if he had been punched in the chest. As much as he tried to fight it, the pain in his legs was crippling him and the motivating forces he had been using to retaliate, previously extracted from hope and confidence, were draining from his mind. He hobbled further toward the finish, weakly pumping his arms, his enthusiasm lost. Then, just when he thought his suffering could not be any worse, he felt the anguish of another, final pass. This time, it was his rival Terrence Griffin.
   "It's going to be McKenzie! 9:17! 62 seconds for the last 400 meters!"
   Ben stumbled off the track and onto his back. The cheers from the packed stands continued to roar around his addled mind as he struggled for breath. The last mile was still a blur with few discernable details. He remembered making his surge. Holding the lead tenuously in his hands. And then struggling home. Not much in between. None of his precious numbers or statistics floated to him. Just feelings. Impatience. Excitement. Dejection.

Gradually, other runners came sprinting across the finish. The ground became cluttered with others who were too exhausted to stay on their feet. He sat up and looked around at the droves of competitors he had outperformed. And yet somehow, he had never felt more defeated.

Mark Miller, cont.

"Wow! That was pretty epic!" Tom said as they climbed up the steps, looking for an open seat in the crowded stands. The others murmured their agreement. They had almost walked to the top of the stadium before they slid in next to another group of student-age spectators. "Aren't your parents here somewhere, Mark?"

"Yeah, they got here *way* earlier. Didn't want to be cutting it as close as I was." He perused the section to his lower left. "They probably aren't far from us. Their text said they were sitting with Lauren in the middle of the straight-"

"Wait Lauren's here?" Tom and Ian started frantically scanning the crowd in all directions. Mark smirked, shaking his head in amused frustration. Lauren Johnson was his brother Jayson's girlfriend and, more importantly to his friends, was very good looking.

"Dude, I found her."

"Where?"

"Right there, man."

Tom looked in the direction Ian was pointing. Lauren was sitting attentively with her long blonde hair pulled back into a ponytail, sporting athletic clothing displaying the Manheim Township insignia. She was talking to an older woman whose nose resembled Mark's, but had straw-colored hair to match Jayson's.

"So Mark, is everything still going well with her and your brother? Or like … is she looking for a better looking, more distinguished academic type?" Tom flexed dramatically to underscore his point. Mark stared back, eye brows raised.

"Alright, I take it everything's good, then." He paused as they announced the last call for the large school boys' race. "How 'bout your mom-is everything going well with her and your dad? Or like … is she looking for a better looking, more dis-"

Mark punched him hard in the arm.

At 9:45, they began to line up the competitors for the Boys Large School 3200 Meters. The 3200 (the approximate metric equivalent for two miles) was an eight-lap race around the track, the longest event the PAL offered at their State Meet. This field consisted of 18 runners, including five from District Three, the region of the state in which Manheim

Township resided. Mark recognized a few familiar faces on the starting line, including, most obviously, Jayson Miller.

His brother had won the District Three Championships a week earlier on this same track with a winning time of nine minutes and seven seconds. His margin of victory was nearly 50 yards, most of that coming over the last lap once he really decided to put the hammer down. Here at Shippensburg, Jayson was hoping to become Manheim's first state champion in program history. But one man stood firmly in his way.

"So which one's Springer?" Ian asked as the runners took their marks, anticipating the gun. Mark scanned quickly before spotting a tall figure with an orange singlet and dark blue shorts.

"That one." As if on cue, the gun sounded and Springer sprinted forth, clearing the crowded field and taking up the lead. It was a beautiful, graceful stride, effortlessly gliding to the front. Jayson followed him, running tall and powerful, a look of determination and focus engraved on his face.

"So that's Jayson's nemesis, huh?" Ian said, watching the tall front-runner float along the back straightaway. Jayson was tucked in among the chase pack in about fourth place. "He doesn't seem that impressive."

"Yeah, totally," Mark said sarcastically, "What about seven state championships? Does that impress you at all?"

"Wait, *seven* state championships?" Tom asked incredulously, "Are you serious?"

"Yep. He won the 32, 16 and 800 at states last year. When he was just a sophomore."

"Wow," Ian muttered, watching Springer continue to lead the field. As he came through the first lap, they looked eagerly at the clock. "Did he just split that lap in 61 seconds?! How fast is he trying to run?"

"I think he's trying to go under nine minutes today," Mark replied distractedly as he watched carefully for his brother. Jayson came through in 66 seconds, packed in a crowd of some ten runners, looking slightly uncomfortable. The younger Miller fidgeted nervously with his short pockets.

Springer continued to easily eat up track, rolling past the high jump pit and into the back stretch. His lead was expanding, already approaching six or seven seconds. Meanwhile, the chase pack was thinning. Some of the runners knew the early pace was well over their heads. Others would find out soon enough.

At 800 meters, Springer hit the line with the clocking reading two minutes, six seconds. Next to cross the line, through in 2:14, was a runner sporting a black top with a red "C" on the chest. Jayson ran in sixth place, alongside one racer in green and another in pale blue. He seemed a bit more at ease as the pack around him continued to dissipate. But Mark seemed no less warry than a lap earlier.

"You recognize any of those guys around him?" Ian asked, peering intensely down at the track. "Looks like Gonzalez is in eighth-maybe two or three seconds back-but I don't see Johnston."

"That's gotta be one of those Coatesville dudes," Tom said pointing at the runner in black who was putting in a small surge and drifting ahead of third place. "Those guys are machines."

"I'm pretty sure that's Andrew Rosato," Mark replied, following Tom's outstretched finger. "He's the guy Jayson outkicked indoors in the 3k."

"Oh, *that* kid?" Ian reacted darkly, "He was such a tool." They watched as Rosato set his sights on Springer. "I hate those Coatesville kids. They're so cocky."

"Takes one to know one," Tom muttered quietly.

At the halfway point, Springer held close to a seven second advantage over Rosato. He went through the mile in a blazing fast 4:24, but his pace was noticeably slowing after his ambitious start. Meanwhile, Jayson sat back in fifth place, going through the mile in 4:34. Mark watched as his brother battled for position with a runner in light blue. He looked much more tired than he had the previous week even though he was racing at close to the same pace.

"*C'mon, Jayson. Wake up.*" He muttered under his breath. A second runner in green approached his outside shoulder, but the Manheim Township Blue Streak held his position and forced his trailer in green to go wide. It was the first time since the start that a runner had made to pass him and it appeared to shake him from his slump.

Refocusing, the tall blonde put his head down and put in a small surge. "*Atta boy, Jayson.*" As he battled forward, he gained quickly on third place. His head dipped back slightly as it tended to when he was tired, but he kept his face relaxed and his arms pumping.

"Yo Mark," Tom said suddenly, tapping feverishly on his shoulder, "Look!"

For the first time in minutes, Mark turned his attention back to the front of the race. Jimmy Springer's once insurmountable lead was shrinking quickly as Andrew Rosato continued to eat up ground. Springer looked uncomfortable, his legs not popping off the track with the same bounce they had earlier. Conversely, his pursuant from Coatesville had a wild, fiery hunger in his eyes-with the tempo to match. Gradually, the crowd began to realize a race was developing. A ripple of whispers cut through the previously still air.

The race approached the mile and a half mark, Springer's lead dwindling toward three seconds. The Coatesville Raider was charging forward, making Jimmy look as though he was jogging on a treadmill. Then, as the fans increased in volume, the Union Valley star looked back over his shoulder anxiously.

"He's scared!" Ian called, "He's gonna get caught!"

The spectators around them must have seen things similarly as many were rising to their feet and cheering enthusiastically. Rosato was now within a second or two, but Springer was still holding him off. Every step seemed to cut the distance in half, but, paradoxically, Jimmy held his lead.

Another ripple of whispers whipped through the stadium as the runners approached 500 meters to go. They were passing by the largest section of fans on the home straightaway for the penultimate time. The noise was escalating raucously all around them.

"Let's go, Jayson!" Mark's father's booming voice echoed loudly around the track, causing his youngest son to snap his head around. There, streaking suddenly toward the lead, was Manheim Township's school record holder. Now it was clear to Mark why he had heard that second injection of enthusiasm. It hadn't been for Rosato's pursuit. It was for Jayson's.

Positively jumping with joy, the trio of teammates cheered manically for their captain as he stormed across the finish line, the final-lap-signaling bell ringing loudly in his left ear. As Jayson turned the pace up another notch, Rosato looked mentally defeated. He had worked so hard to catch Springer, only to have another, seemingly fresher, runner take over the lead instead. Remarkably, the exhausted-looking defending champion was the one who managed to latch on to this latest surge, refusing to surrender his state title that easily.

Overflowing with excitement, Mark charged out of the stands and down the stairs toward the near side of the track. He could hear his friends' footsteps echoing loudly in his wake as he kept his eyes pinned to the tall blonde. Frantically, he sprinted forward, wedging himself along the fence between a duo of runners in blue shirts and a girl in white. He craned his neck down the straightaway to watch as the two harriers came storming down it for the final time, racing through a wall of anticipation and exhilaration. They were stride for stride with one another, running shoulder to shoulder as Springer swung wide to try and rally a last ditch effort to steal the gold.

The two passed directly in front of Mark's face. He could see their clenched teeth. Sweat flying from their hair. Their muscles flexed powerfully into attack mode. A second later they were on the opposite side of him. He could only watch their backs as they tore off toward the finish. From this vantage point, unable to see either face, they looked like a pair of robots motoring ahead. They could just as easily been powered by electricity and technology instead of the grit and passion that became evident with one look at the painstaking expressions across the athletes' faces.

Finally, the machines powered down as the crowd gave one final, climatic roar.

"Who won?!" Mark asked to no one in particular, standing on his toes to try and improve his view, but his spot yards down the straightaway was not ideal for determining the victor.

"I don't know."

They watched as the two competitors shook hands. Jayson appeared to be smiling.

Ben Havleck, cont.

"Hey, nice race, man."

"Thanks, you too." *Feel free to lead some next time.* Ben shook the gold medalists hand without taking his eyes off the track. Much more pressing matters than sportsmanship were happening. The invincible Jimmy Springer had just taken the large school race out at a suicidal pace. This was the complete opposite of the race in which Ben had just participated. Of course, it's called suicide pace for a reason.

Currently running in second place, Andrew Rosato of Coatesville was quickly closing down the gap to the leader. Ben whipped out his watch and pressed a button carefully, once when Springer crossed the finish, then again when Rosato did. Thanks to the small school award presentation, he had missed the start of the race, but he was hoping to get a feel for how each harriers' current pacing compared here on the race's sixth lap.

He watched the numbers spring to life on his wrist. *Still about five and half second difference.* Ben looked across the track at the two lead competitors. The chaser looked so much stronger than his prey. *But a lot of time's left.*

As the Union Valley junior passed in front of him, Ben shuffled hurriedly forward, trying to get a better sightline for the finish. He checked down at his watch as each finished their laps. *That's 72 for Springer. Yikes.* He scanned for Rosato and was surprised to see how much he had cut into the lead in just the last half lap. *69 for Rosato. He's closing.*

The enthusiasm in the crowd was intensifying. He had considered his race to be loud, but that roar was little more than a purr compared to the fervor currently building within the Shippensburg stands. Ben looked up at the rows of bleachers and soaked in the grandeur of the moment. It was amazing. Never before had track and field felt so significant.

He turned back to the race just in time to see a blonde streak surging powerfully to the front. *Wait, what just happened?* he thought as he looked hopelessly at his timer for some type of explanation. Another runner, sporting a white and blue uniform with a lightning bolt on the chest, had moved alongside Jimmy Springer's shoulder. He had come seemingly from nowhere and the fans were loving it.

Ben watched the Coatesville runner's expression as he passed. Rosato looked stunned and defeated. Like he had taken a blow to the chest. Ben dwelled on him for another solemn moment before ripping himself from this disconcerting mirror and refocusing on the flurry of feet at the front of the field.

Somehow, Springer had managed to avoid folding up like a lawn chair when he had been passed. In fact, he rallied his energies and fought back. Sitting on the leader's shoulder. Hanging by only a thread, but hanging nonetheless. Together, the duo sprinted off the final turn. Side by side.

The crowd had risen as one to their feet. As best he could in his fatigued state, Ben hustled toward the finish line, hoping to get a view for the tight finish. But even with a massive head start, he couldn't beat them. Wielding furious final sprints, the tall, lanky figures extended their bodies across the finish line.

"Who won?" He asked aloud, slowing his body to a hobbled stop. It seemed the whole stadium was waiting eagerly for the answer to the same question.

Chapter Twenty One

Jimmy Springer, May 28th 2016

Tired and disoriented, Jimmy tried to keep his balance. Raising his head, he forced himself onto the infield, out of the way of the finishers. Here, the man he was looking for was waiting for him.

"Good race, Jayson," He extended a sweaty palm.

The blonde-haired runner grabbed the outstretched hand. Displaying a pallet of surprise, disappointment and fatigue, he smiled. "Great job," he replied. "I really thought I had you." He shook his head in amazement, "But it just wasn't enough."

"It took everything I had, man." Jimmy wobbled unsteadily as he tried to walk forward to the water tent. "Sorry-I gotta sit down for a sec."

"Doesn't sound like too bad an idea." Jayson said, plopping down next to him.

"*And the winner,*" The field announcer's booming voice echoed around the track, "*-by just two tenths of a second-is Jimmy Springer!*" The crowd clapped vigorously as they found out what the two athletes had already known.

"What was our time?"

"Dunno, I stopped paying attention after the mile split." Jayson scratched his head and looked up at the stands in front of him, scanning for someone he would recognize. His eyes stopped ten rows up. Happily, he waved toward a section of the stands. Jimmy watched him enviously, having long since given up his spectator search.

After a brief respite, the large school boys gathered at the medal stand for their award ceremony. Jimmy stood, waiting behind the podium in his orange and blue uniform with Miller on one side and a boy from Bonner High School on his other. They both seemed excited, but he merely felt relieved. Well, relieved and tired.

"*… Third place, with a time of 9 minutes and 8.64 seconds: Tom Seeley …*"

The crowd applauded appreciatively as the boy in white and green stepped up onto the wooden awards podium. He beamed as an official placed the bronze medal around his neck.

"*… Second place, with a time of 9 minutes and 1.47 seconds, the third fastest performer in state history, Jayson Miller from Manheim Township …*"

Jayson stepped up the podium as the fans erupted for their local champion. He looked mildly surprised at the announcement of the time. Pleased, but not quite content. From just behind him, Jimmy cursed himself quietly in his head. Based on the announcement after the race, he was merely two tenths of a second ahead of Jayson's time. That meant he barely missed the state record for a second straight week.

"*... And in first place, with a time of 9 minutes and 1.29 seconds, the second fastest time in Pennsylvania State History, for the third straight year, ladies and gentleman, give it up for Jimmy Springer!*"

Jimmy stepped up onto the podium as the race official strode forward to hang the gold around his neck. The medal felt heavy as it weighed against his chest.

Mark Miller, May 28th 2016

As Jayson trudged off the track, with the silver around his neck, Mark rushed forward, trying to weave through huddled masses of spectators.

"Sorry," He called over his shoulder as he bumped into a passerby wearing a maroon t-shirt. But he didn't stop. He wanted to get to his brother as quickly as possible. Hopefully to celebrate achievement rather than lament failure.

It had been ages since he had even seen Jayson lose a race. Now he was handed defeat on a stage Mark knew he had dreamed about for years. Heck, he'd even hung a picture of Jimmy Springer in his room for extra motivation. So to be edged out of your dream goal by merely two tenths of a second? That had to sting. No-worse than sting. Much worse. It had to hurt too much to even try and describe it with conventional language.

"Jayson!" He called, spotting the tall figure looking around the throng for a familiar face. His brother turned to face him and presented a broad grin.

"Hey bro," He responded extending out his arms. Mark pulled him into a deep embrace. "Thanks for coming out to watch."

"Wouldn't miss it." They released one another. Mark stared into his brother's face, hoping to discern his emotions. A smile was plastered across its surface, but it was covering another emotion. He just couldn't pin point exactly what it was.

"Jayson!"

"There's my boy!"

The Miller parents, accompanied by Jayson's girlfriend Lauren, emerged from the horde to greet their sons. His father looked proud and strong, his mother more sympathetic. Mark could tell she was itching to plant a hug and kiss on her eldest, but she defaulted to Lauren for first dibs.

"Thanks for coming out guys," Jayson said, the same beam on display, "Heck of a race, huh?" He rotated through his hug obligations. After he and his mother broke apart, he pulled out his silver medal from his pocket and hung it around her neck. She wore it with honor, although she looked a tad upset about the amount of sweat on the string.

"You did amazing, Jayson! We were all so impressed!" Mrs. Miller remarked, "Such a great performance."

"I don't know how you do it," Lauren continued, looking up in awe at her boyfriend, "Third fastest runner in state history! That's unbelievable."

"I couldn't have done it without all of you guys' support. It really means a lot." Jayson looked around at each of their faces, the ends of his mouth drifting farther down his own. "I gotta go do a quick cool down before I get too tight," He said, beginning to pry himself from his admirers, "But I'll catch up with you guys soon and we can talk more about everything." He turned to leave.

"You want some company?" Mark asked, removing his draw string bag from his shoulders. "If you give me a sec, I can throw on some shoes."

"Yeah, sure. That'd be great." He waited patiently as Mark hurriedly changed. "It's never as much fun to run alone."

Jimmy Springer, cont.

Jimmy trudged off the track with his spikes hoisted over his shoulder. He spared a brief glance up at the stands. As expected, the person he was looking for was not there. Inwardly, he scolded himself for even getting his hopes up. *You should know better by now.* Head down, he tried to skirt off back toward the dormitories.

"Jimmy!" A voice called back over his shoulder. He turned eagerly around, looking for the source of the shout. To his disappointment, he spotted a tall, bearded man walking toward him, accompanied by a younger boy with a small video camera. It was Dan Richardson, the head administrator for local website VaniaRunning.com. The site covered all of the Pennsylvania Track and Field action, posting results, articles and video interviews. After years of signature victories, Jimmy was no stranger to the last of these items.

"Hey Dan, how's it going?" Jimmy asked, removing himself from the throng of fans and waiting in an open area for the pair of writers.

"Do you mind if we steal you for a quick interview?" Dan asked, having reached his target.

"Nah, go for it." He stared into the camera lens as it stared back unblinkingly. A small light flashed on.

"We're here with Jimmy Springer of Union Valley High School, this year's state champion in the 3200 with the second fastest time in state history. Congrats, Jimmy." The interviewer stuck a small microphone under his nose.

"Thanks, Dan. I appreciate it." He responded lazily, shifting his weight from one leg to the other.

"Now Jimmy, looks like you went out pretty fast in this one-especially compared to last week. Just walk me through the strategy and how you feel the execution went."

"Sure-yeah-I really just wanted to give myself a shot at the state record. You know, unlike last week. And-uh-I guess I got a little too excited." He kept his arms uncomfortably behind his back, unsure what to do with them as he continued to respond to questions.

"Now when Miller went by you on the last lap, what was going through your mind?"

"Well, I think something like 'I'm really tired'," he laughed dryly, but Dan's focused expression did not break. It rattled him slightly, as he wiped the smile from his face. "But-uh-I don't know. I just knew I had to hang on as best I could. Hurt pretty bad, but I really didn't want to lose."

"It was certainly one heck of a race. And, of course, next fall we could see another one since you and Jayson Miller will both be returning as seniors. You think you guys can push each other to that Hershey course record?"

"Um … we'll see, I guess. You know, a lot can happen between now and then." He paused. There was something he felt compelled to say. Something he had been considering for the past month. "Honestly, I'm not positive I'll be racing again next year."

Richardson's jaw dropped. "Wait-not racing?"

"I'm just tired," he pressed on, the words now tumbling forth with ease. "I put a lot of pressure on myself-whether it's practice or competitions-and I'm just sort of burnt out."

"But-but," his interviewer stumbled, trying to regain his professionalism after being blindsided by the news, "You're number two all-time in state history-for two events. Don't you want to take one more-?"

"Yeah, you see, that's the problem. It sounds great to be second all-time. But finishing second sucks. And every time I come up just short like today, it's a real punch in the gut.

"Those records are records for a reason, you know? I may not be good enough to break them. People treat me like-like a super hero or something … but I'm just a normal kid. So when I fall short of the heroic, it just hurts worse. Sometimes the reality of those moments-coming up short like that-I don't know, it's just … heavy. And I'm getting tired of carrying it around."

I've lost a lot away from the track. Losing on it might just be the straw that breaks the camel's back.

"Keep up the good work, Dan." He concluded. And he turned away from the camera's piercing gaze, plunging himself into solitude once more.

Mark Miller, cont.

"OK, it's just you and me now," Mark said as he and his brother strode around an empty baseball diamond. "How are you feeling?"

"I'm actually doing alright."

"C'mon Jay, don't give me that bull sh-"

"No, seriously. I mean, don't get me wrong, I'm miserable. It sucks to be that close and come up short. But, it's weird. I kinda thought it would hurt a lot worse."

"Maybe the reality hasn't sunk in yet? That's happened to you before. Like remember when we lost that basketball tournament in Ephrata? You were fine all the way through pizza dinner and then on the car ride home …"

Jayson chuckled. "I cried like a broken sprinkler. Yeah, that was a rough one." He smiled wryly. They circled past third base and off toward a football field in the opposite direction of the track. Mark felt a rock skip up into his poorly tied shoes.

"Still, I feel like that's not it." The oldest brother continued. "It's more like … remember the time we met Joe Flacco on vacation a couple years ago?"

"Yeah of course. He was actually really nice. Autographed my hat for me."

"Exactly! Yet all this time we were hyping him up as this villain who used to knock the Steelers out of the playoffs. So we just *hated* him. We wanted nothing more than to beat him. But when we met him and he went back to being a normal person, it made the idea of hating him seem pretty silly. It wasn't him we wanted to beat so much as the *idea* of him. What he represents."

The rock continued to bounce around inside Mark's shoe, but he tried his best to ignore it. "So what does the quarterback of the Ravens have to do with the two mile?"

"Last year at states, I reached out my hand to Jimmy Springer-just to say good luck before the race, you know-and he ignored me. So, I thought he was a jerk. Then, watching him win all those races, doing post-race interviews, I got it in my head that he was not just a jerk, but a huge show off too. I wanted nothing more than to go out and put him in his place." They finished the perimeter of the football field. "I trained like a madman with the sole focus of doing just that.

"But today, when I met him … well … he knew my name."

"Knew your name?" Mark responded puzzled.

"Yeah-for whatever reason, that really struck me. Like, he's just another kid. Training, racing … winning. And this whole time, I've been training against the 'idea' of Jimmy Springer. This great, powerful villain. But today, that supervillain was racing some kid. So of course he had the edge." Together the two slowed to a stop as they reached the gate that bordered the track. "Next time, though, I'll be racing some kid, too."

Mark raised his arm and pulled his brother to his side. "Great race out there, bro. I'm really proud of what you've accomplished today."

"Thanks," Jayson said, squeezing Mark's waist slightly before stooping down to the ground and untying his shoes. "I guess second best isn't the worst thing in the world, right?"

The youngest Miller joined the eldest on the pavement. "As long as there's more than two of you," he smirked.

Jayson smiled back before removing his right shoe and shaking it out upside-down. A small rock fell from the heel and danced briefly across the concrete below. Mark watched it move until it came to rest. Then he slipped off his own shoe and copied his brother.

Chapter Twenty Two

Ben Havleck, May 28th 2016

He walked forward distractedly, lost in careful thought as was his default state of mind. It was a bad place to be unaware, within a throng of eager spectators. As the junior sauntered ahead, he bumped shoulders with a tall, black-haired boy, knocking him abruptly back to reality.

"Sorry," he mumbled as the boy hurried off in the opposite direction. Now, more aware of his surroundings, he realized with a sudden rush of excitement that he recognized a pair of boys standing against the chain linked fence some 20 meters in front of him. Eagerly, he rushed forward, opening his mouth and preparing to call out for their attention.

"I hope Sean isn't too bummed." Ben could hear the taller of the two's voice carry to his ears as he approached. "Outside of that top two, doesn't seem like the times were *that* fast."

"He just got sucked out way too fast," said the shorter, "If he had been in that small school race, he would have been way better off." Ben shortened his stride, slowing and keeping out of view. He sensed the direction the conversation was beginning to turn and didn't want to be present for its next stage. Cautiously, he snuck himself along the side of the fence, hiding from view behind a set of wider spectators.

"What did they finish in?"

"Like 9:17, I think. Sean might have been able to win that race."

"Probably. But who would even care? It's not like it's a *real* state title. It's small schools. Nobody any good runs in that division."

"True ... So should we go try and find Quinn?" The shorter boy looked back over his shoulder in the opposite direction of Ben.

"Yeah, I think she was heading toward the tent."

Ben leaned forward to catch sight of his former Downingtown teammates disappearing back into the ocean of spectators. Gradually, the distance between them increased until Ben could no longer see them.

Jimmy Springer, May 28th 2016

"Can I get an Orange Gatorade and a pretzel, please?"

"Four dollars."

He reached into his wallet and put a five dollar bill on the counter. In exchange, an orange bottle and a salted pretzel were handed to him. "Thanks," Without waiting for his change, he turned and left. "Have a good one."

Jimmy walked underneath the stadium steps, enjoying the cool shade it provided. Then, he made a left, pushing open the door to the bathroom. Seeing it was empty, he walked up to the closest urinal. Almost as soon as he reached the stall, he heard the swinging of the door behind him and a pair of boys joined him in the room. In turn, each took a place next to him at the stalls.

"Dude, watching Jayson out there today was unbelievable," the first of the two entrants said brashly, clearly unconcerned about being overheard. "It gets me pumped up to get out this summer and train hard for cross. We could do something special."

"Yep," his friend standing beside him kept his response short and curt. He sounded vaguely uncomfortable.

"Like just think about it. Jayson's our front runner. We have four other experienced seniors. But then after that, it's pretty wide open for the last varsity spots-you know?"

"Yep."

"Honestly, I've never felt as invested as I do right now. I've got a good feeling about-"

"Ian!" The less chatty of the two boys burst out, "Could you chill? *I can't pee while you're talking.*"

"Oh-yeah, for sure." The boy named Ian walked back away from the urinal, his business apparently finished. Jimmy followed shortly thereafter, his bladder equally depleted. "You know, Tom," The boy continued while he and Jimmy washed their hands side by side, "I never thought of you as a shy pee-er. Like Mark? He's got shy pee-er written all over him. You on the other hand? Thought for sure you'd have a stronger stream presence."

"Seriously?"

"Sorry, I'm done. I promise." He moved to the paper towel dispenser, Springer following in his wake. He pulled down on the lever, unleashing a long string of rough, brown paper, then tore it in two and handed some to the man behind him. "Here you go, dude." Ian said, looking up into Jimmy's face for the first time. He looked back at Tom before immediately looking back at the newly crowned state champion.

"Thanks," Jimmy said, taking the towel and drying his hands. He stared awkwardly at Ian whose mouth was hanging slightly agape.

"Holy crap," he said, slowly coming to his senses. "You're Jimmy Springer!" Jimmy fought the urge to reply "I know".

"Can I maybe, like, get a picture with you or something?" Ian asked, taking out his phone excitedly.

"In the bathroom?" Springer asked, looking around uncomfortably.

"Maybe just like-like a selfie or something?" He tried holding his arm out at different angles, inching himself closer to the Union Valley junior's personal space. "Tom, can you take this picture for me real quick?"

"Kinda in the middle of something over here, Ian."

"Here," Jimmy said offering his help. He took the phone from his fan and stretched out his long arms to full extension. Hoping to remove himself from this bizarre situation as quickly as possible, he snapped a picture and passed back the device.

"Awesome. Thank you, man," Ian replied in awe, now looking down at the picture.

"Yeah, no problem," Despite himself, Jimmy smiled slightly at the look on his fan's face. "And, hey, good luck training this summer. I'll keep my eye out for you at states." Without waiting for a reply, he disappeared out of the bathroom back into the consistent throng of traffic. As the door swung shut, he heard a final snippet of conversation behind him.

"Tom, did you hear that?!"

"DAMN IT, IAN! STOP TALKING!"

Ben Havleck, cont.

Ben turned his attention back to the track, trying to brush off the conversation he had just overheard. They were lining up the competitors for the large schools 4x800 meter relay. He looked at the lead off runners, examining each of their faces carefully. *What makes these kids so different from me?* He thought bitterly. *I would have been right with the medalists in large schools.* The gun sounded as the middle distance runners sprinted off the line. *And I wouldn't have had to deal with such a slow early pace either.*

"*Coatesville out well,*" The announcer projected over the speaker, "*With Baldwin, North Penn and Lower Dauphin chasing. Senior Sean Dawson running lead leg for the Raiders.*"

Ben could feel his legs aching as he stood along the fence. The remnants of his previous struggle begged him to get off his feet. He took one last, long glance at the track before turning his back on the relay and looking up into the stands. They looked crowded. Mentally, he prepared himself to trudge through the masses, hoping to find a place among the established relationships that had already assembled. Just like breakfast that morning. Just like his life in general.

"*It's now Cumberland Valley powering ahead! Chris Fuller makes the pass as we head into the exchange. Coatesville will be next, followed by Baldwin and then West Chester North!*"

Despite his fatigued lower body, Ben couldn't resist putting off his quest for seating to watch the teams battling along the home stretch. He turned back around and, as he did, spotted a familiar face.

"Ben?" A taller girl with blonde hair was waving to him. "Ben!"

"Katie?" He replied in shock, walking a little ways up the straightaway to stand beside her. "How are you doing?" To his surprise, when he drew even, Katie reached out and hugged him. He returned the gesture nervously.

Ben had met Katie a few months ago at the Muhlenberg Invitational, an indoor track meet he attended with the hopes of qualifying for the state championship. She had been very friendly, but their interaction had been relatively short and uneventful. So a hug seemed like a rather forward greeting.

"I'm doing well," Katie said, smiling. "I saw your race earlier. You did so awesome!"

"Thanks," Ben tried to sound appreciative, but couldn't completely hide his disappointment. "And Terrence did really well, too. He had a great kick." At the conclusion of his and Katie's first meeting, he had learned his budding rival, Terrence Griffin of Wyomissing, was Katie's boyfriend. He had assumed this was still the case, but when he mentioned Griffin's name, he was surprised to see Katie's previously cheery expression sour.

"Yeah," she replied tartly, "Too bad. I was really rooting for you to beat him."

"Er-Thanks" Although curious to further investigate this odd change of tone, Ben opted instead to change the subject. "I saw you competed yesterday, right? In the high jump? Looked like you did pretty well."

"You saw that?" She perked back up, "I actually jumped a PR by a couple of inches and really got lucky with my misses. I ended up fifth when the tiebreakers were factored in."

"That's great! Congratulations!"

"Thanks!" They looked back at the track as the runners came storming down the straightaway.

"Here comes West Chester North! A huge leg from junior Will Aldrich! He's now powering away from Coatesville and will give his team the lead as we move to the anchor leg!"

"I didn't know you were here yesterday," she continued after the runners had passed, "I would have looked for you to say 'hi'."

"It's OK, I wasn't here that long," Ben said dismissively. "I just came out to jog for a bit, but otherwise tried to stay out of the heat." *Why would she go out of her way to see* me? he thought. *We barely even know each other*.

"Coatesville and North Penn both out very fast on this anchor leg! It's back to a two team race: Kyle King for the Raiders against Bernard Mirun for the Knights!" The announcer's voice incited the crowd as the relay in front of them approached its concluding lap. A runner in a baby blue jersey held a slight lead over another in black.

"So who do you think's gonna win?" Katie asked Ben, watching the two runners fight alongside each other.

"Coatesville," Ben said, slightly more aggressively than intended. "No doubt."

"Why do you say that?" The runner in blue continued to hold an advantage with just half a lap to go in the race. "That guy in first looks pretty comfortable."

"They've got this coach-Albert Solares. He's coached *Olympians*, so imagine the upgrade he is over your typical high school coach." As if in response to Ben's comments, Coatesville's anchor leg sprang to life off the final turn and charged furiously ahead. Pumping his arms, he powered away from his North Penn counterpart and crossed the line first, raising his fist victoriously as he finished.

"Wow," Katie said, her eyes up the track watching the winning teammates regroup and celebrate, "You called that perfectly. How'd you do that?"

"I don't know," Ben shrugged sheepishly, "I'm pretty passionate about this stuff I guess." The gold medal relay was now lining up for a picture. Holding the camera, a man with a navy blue *Ares* sweater directed them into position. "Especially the coaching piece."

"Yeah, I'd be lost without my coach. She's made me a lot better." Ben nodded politely, but remained silent. Katie noticed and correctly interpreted his silence as unhappiness. "Do you not like your coach?"

"I wouldn't say that exactly. I just wish he had a bit more experience."

"Ah, I gotcha. Is he, like, a younger guy? Because sometimes the coaches just out of college are a little more inventive. Not quite so set in their thinking."

"What if they're only 17 years old?"

"17?!" Katie exclaimed. She stared at Ben who raised his eyebrows and smiled. "Wait-are you saying … *you're* your coach?"

"Yep," he nodded again, sporting a wry smile. "Bloomsburg High doesn't technically have a track or cross country team. I lobbied to get club status so I can compete in the PAL and stuff, but we've got no official school funding."

"And that means no money to pay a real coach."

"Ouch," Ben replied in a voice of mock woundedness.

"Oh c'mon!" Katie said defensively, "You know what I mean!"

"I know, I know," he laughed, "I'm just messing with you."

As the conversation slid into silence, they turned back to the track, hoping for something to revive the dialogue. The last team had already come straggling home and the runners were disseminating in their respective quartets, slinking away from the finish and back to the check-in tent. With his colloquial crutch gone, Ben turned back to face Katie, internally debating the next set of words he could piece together into a phrase.

But before he could stumble through a sentence, Katie took the reins. "Did you want to grab some food from the snack bar? I was on my way to get a pretzel when I ran into you."

"Yeah, sure," Ben replied, "I could use a Gatorade or something." And he followed her away from the edge of the fence back toward the stadium's far corner, failing to realize this was the opposite direction that Katie had been headed when they first ran into one another.

Jimmy Springer, cont.

Jimmy wandered out of the bathroom, wiping his hands on his pants. *So what now?* He thought. The 4x800 had to be starting soon. This was one of his favorite events in track. Removing his back pack from his shoulders, he reached inside and rummaged around for his phone to check the time. He shifted through miscellaneous objects, tossing them aside until he landed on his target.

"Yo Springer!"

Jimmy stopped, his hand grasped around his phone, and looked up to determine the source of the voice. A stocky boy with dark hair was walking toward him. He wore a red shirt with cut off sleeves and a pair of black shorts. His physique was muscular and his face was handsome.

"Hey, what's up Devon," Jimmy said releasing his phone and extending his hand for a slap and a shake before precariously replacing his pack on his left shoulder. "How'd the semi-finals go?"

"Not good, dude," Devon replied with a sheepish smile. "I'm really feeling the effects of last night." He ran his hand through the top of his hair. While the top was long enough to properly comb through, the sides were buzzed short. "How'd you do?"

"I did alright," Jimmy brushed off the question, "What time did you go back to your room last night? I didn't even see you leave."

"You don't remember?" Devon asked in amazement, "Bro-*I walked back with you.*" He stared at Jimmy, waiting for some type of acknowledgement.

"Ahh, that's right … I remember now," he lied. Devon looked back at him skeptically.

"Man, I had no clue you were so messed up."

"I was fine. I just needed a little something to take the edge off, you know?"

"Whatever you say," Devon shook his head in disbelief, "You heading back in a couple hours? I heard they are starting up again at three."

"Eh, probably not. Just gonna watch the races. How 'bout you?"

"Nah, I think my coach is trying to get us Boyertown kids out of here after Mary Kate runs the hurdle finals." He paused, pulling out his phone and typing out a text. "Besides, they wouldn't let me in by myself."

"What do you mean? Those guys seemed pretty chill."

"That wasn't just some party, Springer." He looked up from his phone to give Jimmy a proper stare. "That was a goddam recruiting pitch. They're trying to get you to come to Shippensburg."

"Well, I doubt that was all for me. You'd be a good recruit for them too." As he spoke, he shifted his weight and his still open back pack spilled some of its contents onto the ground between them.

"Yeah, but I'm not an effing state champion," Devon said, reaching down for the discarded golden award. "Just alright, huh?" With a twinge of annoyance, he handed the medal to Jimmy, who blushed slightly but otherwise remained silent. He thought further elaborating on his disappointment with his performance would do more harm than good.

"See you around, Springer," Devon finished before disappearing and leaving behind the mess of outstanding fallen items. In the fresh silence, Jimmy heard the stadium announcer's voice reverberate around him.

"Coatesville out well," The voice projected over the speaker, *"With Baldwin, North Penn and Lower Dauphin chasing. Senior Sean Dawson running lead leg for the Raiders."*

Ben Havleck, cont.

After stopping at the snack bar to pick up some refreshments, Katie and Ben set off on a walk around the perimeter of the track. Then they circumvented the stadium itself. And before long, they were exploring the edges of Shippensburg's campus.

Topics bounced freely through their conversation, touching on the obvious, like school and track, to the obscure, like whether the Red Hot Chili Peppers were better than actual chili peppers or if teleportation would be invented during their lifetimes.

"Would you actually use a teleporter if it was invented?" Ben asked as they passed by the same dining hall he had visited that morning, "Or would you be too worried about splinching?"

"What the hell is 'splinching'?"

"You know-like when wizards apparate-"

"Hold on-wizards? How'd we get on wizards?"

"Because they're the ones who-wait … have you not read Harry Potter?"

"No …" Katie replied. Ben stopped and stared at her, his mouth hanging open. "But I saw the movies. Does that count?"

"*No, no, definitely not.*" Ben waited, but was disappointed to see she did not recognize the reference. "I'm not sure we can be friends anymore."

She laughed. "That much of a deal breaker, huh?"

He sighed dramatically. "I'll let it slide this time. But it's going to hurt your creditability as we continue this teleportation conversation."

"Fair enough," she smiled and paused to think of her response. After a moment, "I think I'd do it. It would just open up so many more opportunities. I could travel more … I could go to college anywhere I wanted and still be able to visit home."

"Where would you pick?

"For college?"

"Yeah-like if you were accepted everywhere and distance wasn't an issue. Where would you go?"

"Um … I don't know …" She fidgeted with her hands, "I never really thought about it."

"Never?" Ben responded, sounding surprised.

"Haha no!" She said mildly taken aback. "Sounds like you have though …"

"Yeah," He found himself suddenly feeling sheepish. "For me, it's Georgetown," he spoke more softly than originally intended, "I've wanted to go there for as long as I can remember."

When he fell completely silent, Katie piped up, trying to prod him into continuing. "So are you applying there early decision? Increase your chances of going?"

"No," Ben said, his voice shifting to a mildly darker inflection, "I'm not going there."

"What do you mean? You just said it's your dream school. If you're worried about grades, sometimes the standards they post-"

"I'm not worried about that," he said dismissively. Then, realizing how cocky he sounded, he lamely added, "I mean-I think I have a decent shot to get in based on my application."

"OK, so what's the problem then?"

Now it was Ben's turn to fidget. "If I tell you, do you promise not to laugh?"

"Of course," She nodded.

He paused and looked up into her eyes. Then, he plunged ahead. "I can't run there. I'm not fast enough."

"Not fast enough? How do you know?"

"Well, I went to visit a couple weeks ago and-you may not believe this-but I thought back to our conversation that we had at Muhlenberg. About talking to coaches?" She shook her head to affirm, but otherwise did not interrupt. "So I went to the guy's office and talked to him." He gulped, unexpectedly emotional, "And it was a failure. He had no interest. Barely gave me the time of day."

"I'm sorry, Ben. That sucks."

"It's alright," he lied. They circled around the dorms where the high schoolers were staying during the state championship weekend and started their journey back to the track stadium.

"I wouldn't give up on that dream, though." Katie said firmly when they had finished their about face. "You never know what's going to happen."

"Eh, I guess so. Not sure I could ever bring myself to run for that coach, though."

"Maybe he'll get fired," Katie shrugged, "If he couldn't spot a diamond in the rough like you, he's probably not a very good coach." She smiled and Ben half-heartedly returned the gesture. "I mean, you just finished third in the state!"

"For small schools, though. Did you see those large school guys? They were on a whole other level. If I really want to be considered one of the best, those are the kids I have to beat."

"So why don't you?"

"What do you mean?" He looked at her, his expression shrouded in befuddlement. He explained again, feeling repetitive. "We are in different classifications. Bloomsburg's not just a 'small school' it's microscopic. I mean I don't even have a real coach."

"Or teammates."

"Rub it in." He said sourly.

"No, Ben-*you don't have teammates*. So you can pick your own classification. Without anybody getting hurt by your decision." His unblinking gaze indicated to her that he had yet to catch on. "The classifications weren't put in so the large school kids could *move up*," She pressed, "They were put in to let the small schoolers *move down*. Give them a fair chance to compete." They were almost back at the stadium now, approaching one final crossing before a large parking lot. "But it's just you. Only you would have to deal with the disadvantages. If you want to race the large school kids-race the kids from the best facilities and training programs-no one is going to stop you." She paused briefly to check for traffic at the street corner. "Especially not your small school competition."

Ben let the realization wash over him as they crossed the road. From their heightened proximity, the sounds of the stadium were drifting once more to his ears. The familiar roar of the crowd echoed around his mind, taking him back to the amazing race he had witnessed that morning. Only now it was a shorter, dark haired boy sprinting head to head against the great Jimmy Springer.

"What time is it?" Katie asked, slowing her pace slightly as they neared the stadium's surrounding fence.

"Uh … a little after one o'clock," Ben said looking down at his wrist, "Wow, that was quite the walk! I didn't realize we were out that long."

"Yeah, time flies." She came to a complete stop now, standing and staring at him. Seemingly waiting for something. They stood in increasingly awkward silence. *Is she waiting for me to do something?*

"So … Katie,"

"Yeah?"

"Do you think-um-" He felt a bead of cold sweat drip down under his armpit. She looked at him hopefully. "I-uh-have a haircut appointment tomorrow. What kinda haircut do you think I should get?"

She looked back at him in confusion, completely caught off guard by this random question. *What kind of* haircut *should I get?* He thought, guessing that her surprise was likely mirrored in his own expression. Despite the odd remark, Katie recovered well. She curled her agape mouth into a smile and stepped closer to Ben.

"Your hair is so long and messy," she said, running one of her hands through his hair. "I think it would look a lot better if you just buzzed it all off." She let a particularly long strand flop back onto his head. It dawned on Ben how close their faces now were. He took a deep breath and closed his eyes.

"*And your large school 800 meter champion,*" the announcer's voice echoed around them, "*Kyle King from Coatesville.*

"What?" Ben pulled his head back and whipped it around to face the track. Katie stumbled slightly beside him. "Kyle King?!" He remarked in amazement. Ben looked back at Katie, surprise etched across his face, but she did not echo his enthusiasm. "That's a *huge* upset." He said trying to impart upon her the importance of the moment.

"Yeah … not exactly what I expecting either …" she muttered with a subtle hint of frustration.

"Crazy, right?" Ben replied excitedly, oblivious to her alternative meaning, "Do you think they have the results posted already?" As he stared into her stone-faced expression, the smile at the tips of his lips slowly began to droop. "What?"

"Good luck with those results, Ben." She said, shaking her head and walking away. "I hope they're satisfying."

Jimmy Springer, cont.

Dropping to his knees, he hastily stuffed his spilled items back into his bag as his friend stormed away. Picking up the gold medal last, he tossed it angrily into the sack. As he did so, he heard a small cracking sound.

Damn it.

Diving back into the pack, he pulled out his phone, now with a freshly splintered screen. Jimmy closed his eyes and tried to calm himself. The day was spiraling quickly and he was finding it difficult to keep his composure. Then, suddenly, the object in his hand buzzed and its damaged surface sprang to life. He opened his eyes and looked down to see who was calling.

"Hello?" He answered tentatively.

"Hey, Jimmy?" The voice on the other end said, with a similar note of hesitancy, *"Are you still here? I've been looking for you."*

"What do you mean by 'here'? Are you at Shippensburg?"

"Yeah, man! Didn't you get my texts? I'm in the stands. Top right corner."

"I wouldn't expect you anywhere else," Jimmy replied, his tone rising in excitement. "I'll be right up."

The announcer sounded again as Jimmy hung up the phone and set off at a brisk walk out from under the stadium. *"Chris Fuller makes the pass as we head into the exchange. Coatesville will be next, followed by Baldwin and then West Chester North!"* After a few quick stairs, he spotted the man he was looking for in the corner he had described. Springer rushed forward to greet his old friend.

"Matt!" He said, arms open.

"Hey, great job out there, superstar," Matt greeted him in an embrace. "You really had me on the edge of my seat."

"Nothing easy at states," Jimmy replied simply, taking the spot next to him and turning to watch the track, "Speaking of which, how's this race been going?"

"Eh, nothing too surprising … Looks like Coatesville and North Penn will be battling it out," He gestured ahead at a pair of runners, one in black and one in blue.

"Who led off for Coatesville?" Jimmy asked, leaning forward and watching the two teams come into the second exchange. They were followed closely by a mass of teams in purple, red and white.

"Couldn't tell ya. I barely recognize anyone anymore," Matt responded, scanning the field, "It makes me feel quite old actually."

Jimmy looked away from the race to inspect the runners waiting alongside the track. He recognized one of the stronger runners in black from Coatesville's Cross Country team. "Oh crap, they're anchoring Kyle King!" He remarked in surprise. The junior looked at Matt, but the revelation seemed to go over his head. "What happened to you, man? You used to be good at this stuff!"

"And you had no idea who Steve Prefontaine was."

"Here comes West Chester North! A huge leg from junior Will Aldrich! He's now powering away from Coatesville and will give his team the lead as we move to the anchor leg!" They watched as a powerful close from a runner in white propelled his school to the lead. Just behind was an athlete in blue, followed by the previous leader in black. He was struggling home along the final straightaway, desperately trying to reach the exchange point.

Then, as quickly as West Chester had moved to the lead, the advantage dissipated. The two anchors just behind shot off like fireworks, leaving their opposition in the dust.

"Coatesville and North Penn both out very fast on this anchor leg! It's back to a two team race. Kyle King for the Raiders against Bernard Mirun for the Knights!"

"North Penn's got to win this, right?" Matt asked as he watched the blue runner set the pace, stalked carefully by Kyle King. "The 4x8 is, like, *their thing*. And Coatesville's just an XC power. They usually don't have the horses for mid distance."

"I'm not sure that's the case anymore," Jimmy cautioned, "Coach Solares has turned these guys into super heroes." The crowd rose as one as the two relays came off the final turn, North Penn still holding a lead and seemingly opening the gap. Then, empowered by the crowd, Kyle King turned it up to another level and sprinted forward. Once he hit top gear, there was no stopping the juggernaut.

"Oh my god," Matt muttered, watching the victorious squad celebrate their victory. "What is he feeding these guys?"

"I don't know … but I'd love to get his recipe." He gave the Coatesville relay one last envious glance. "So you came." Jimmy said simply.

"So I came."

The excitement of the previous race having fully died away, the pair sat back down and decompressed. A group of volunteers began moving hurdles onto the track. "I stuck Emily with my mom and my sister for the day. Hopefully, she's not too pissed at me. I just didn't want to miss you race again."

"Well, I appreciate you coming all the way up. It means a lot."

"Of course, bro." He brushed a strand of stray hair off his shorts. "How many state titles is this now?"

"Eight," Jimmy said sheepishly. Feeling awkward, he started stretching his arms.

"No need to feel uncomfortable about it." Matt reached out and pull his closest limb down to its side. "Own it. There's no shame in being the best. There's no shame in being the worst. There's only shame in trying to be something you're not."

The younger nodded, feeling marginally more at ease. "You were always big on speeches. Kinda makes me sad to know you'll be sitting in a cube crunching finance numbers all day."

"Well, when giving speeches starts paying as much finance does, feel free to send in my résumé. Besides, it's a lot more interactive than you think. In fact, just yesterday …"

With the hurdles set up, the gun sounded to start the next set of races. From their top corner of the stands, Jimmy and Matt had an excellent view of the track. In between events, they talked and caught up on life. Then, once a distance race began, they set to work on analyzing it. It reminded Jimmy of his freshman year at the state championships two years earlier when the two had initially discovered this corner. Uncrowded with a direct sightline. The perfect place to properly post up as fans and friends. He missed those days. They felt like a lifetime ago. Or perhaps not his life at all. Was it even possible there was a time that he was so carefree and innocent?

When they eventually reached the final distance event of the meet, the 800 meters, the weather had cooled slightly and the wind had picked up a touch. As the competitors lined up for the race, Jimmy noticed how bulky and muscular many of them looked. He imagined himself, a year smaller and scrawnier, lining up among these giants and smirked. To think that just twelve months ago, he had been able to win this event was astounding to him.

"Who you got in this one?" Matt asked as the athletes jogged down to the start line. "Give me a break down."

"OK," Jimmy said, pointing to the athletes one by one, "That's Andrew Mallon from CB East. He won the 800 indoors and is probably the favorite. We've also got Joseph Rotz from Lower Dauphin. He anchored his 4x8 all the way up to third-"

"That guy? He came from way back! He may have split like a 1:50."

"Yeah, we'll see how much he has left after that. Same goes for Bernard Mirun of North Penn and Kyle King from Coatesville. They both anchored their 4x8s as well."

"So who is fresh that can put some pressure on these guys?"

"Well I'm not sure anybody is going to push the pace quite like last year. Remember Lewis Hadrick?"

"Hell yeah-he used to go out *sooo* fast. By the way, did you see he ran 1:47 this year at NC State?"

"I saw him get his ass handed to him by Lance Andrews at ACCs if that's what you're referring to."

"Geez, you know the NCAA guys too?" Matt replied, sounding impressed. "How do you keep up with all this stuff?"

"I don't know. It's just something I do to keep busy," Jimmy looked down at the track for a moment, the runners on the verge of beginning their race. "Although to be fair, Lance Andrews is my favorite runner right now. He's so tactically sound. So smooth. Plus, he always seems to step up when the pressure is on."

"Well if you like Andrews and those sort of guys, there's this mile race in Boston this summer. It's going to have Andrews, Murphy, Leibowitz, all those guys. You should definitely come up and watch. You can crash with me."

"I don't know," Springer responded tentatively, "I'd have to talk to my parents about it. Just to make sure I get permission."

Matt waited a beat before deciding to press the question. "How are your parents doing? They're not-um-they're not here, are they?"

Jimmy shook his head. "No, they're not. My mom is too afraid of running into my dad … and my dad works so much now that he can never make it anyway." He sighed. "Ironic, right?" Matt nodded his head solemnly but otherwise did not speak. "When I get home, my mom and I will watch the replay of the race on the Pennsylvania Cable Network. My dad … I don't know, honestly. We'll figure something out, I guess. If he cares."

"I'm sure he does."

BANG!

The gun sounded, signaling the start of the 800 meter dash. Any retort that Jimmy may have had was lost in the excitement of the moment. Unlike the race he participated in last year, the pace was relatively tame through the opening 200 meters. As a result, the athletes were packed tightly together. A runner in a red and blue singlet reluctantly took up the lead and worked to keep things honest.

"It's slow," Jimmy muttered under his breath as the competitors approached the first lap split. "Do you have a watch on this?"

"No," Matt replied, "You?" Jimmy raised up a pair of bare wrists as a substitute for a response. "How do you *still* not own a watch?"

"Looks like 56-57," He ignored Matt's question, focused instead on the large scoreboard projecting the time that had elapsed in the race thus far, "This second lap is going to be mayhem."

"The key is to measure it out," Burke explained, rising to his feet as the crowd's enthusiasm increased, "You can't use up all that extra energy in the first 200 or you won't have anything left."

"It's also near impossible to switch gears that fast."

"True."

As the runners careened down the backstretch, elbows and legs became tangled as each competitor felt compelled to pick up the pace as soon as possible. Although no one fell to the ground, it was tricky to build momentum. The runner in blue and red was able to stay clear, maintaining his position at the front with careful surges. Just before 200 meters, a runner in white increased his tempo, trying to rush forth and beat the leader to the turn. However, he was too late in his effort, forced to run wide and cover the extra distance.

"*It's Andrew Mallon and Joseph Rotz with 200 meters to go!*" The announcer boomed over the loudspeaker. The fervor around them intensified as the spectators cheered on the two top athletes. Jimmy watched keenly as the runner in red and blue, Andrew Mallon, got to the home straightaway first. Rotz hung just on his outside shoulder, ready to rally one more time and try to make the pass.

"Rotz has got him!" Jimmy yelled, his voice nearly drowned out by the tumult. He watched as, on que, the runner in white glided a step ahead, pumping his arms furiously. Then, suddenly, Matt grabbed his arm and tugged.

"Look at Coatesville!" He pointed him in the direction of a streaking black jersey. In a repeat of the finish of the 4x800 meters, Coatesville's Kyle King flashed down the final forty, turning over quickly with no signs of tying up. Meanwhile, his nearest competitors had no response for him. With a courageous, ultimate charge, he pushed through the line and crossed in first place.

"Wow," Matt remarked simply, as fans across the bleachers reacted similarly, "That was unreal. Where did this kid come from?"

"That closing speed is unreal. I had no clue he had that in him. Just a junior too." They sat back down in their seats, the excitement starting to dissipate. The last distance event of the school year was officially over.

"Is he any good at cross?" Matt asked, his mind instantly jumping to what was next, "Like are you gonna have to worry about him in the fall?"

"Well, actually," Jimmy said, averting his friends gaze, "I don't think I'm running cross country next year."

He couldn't see his friend's face, but he could hear the shock in his voice when he spoke up. "Wait-really? Why not?"

"I just feel like my heads not in it," Springer replied, still not looking up, "I may just need a break. Take a little time away from it. Then, hopefully, when I come back, I've got something to motivate me." He chanced a glance upward to gauge Matt's reaction. No mouth agape, just a smile.

"OK," he replied, the surprise removed from his tone, "Well I hope you do."

"That's it? You aren't gonna, like, tell me quitters never prosper or some other dad speech like that?"

"Look, running is a brutal sport. It's painful enough when you're having fun." He gestured down at the state champ Kyle King, who was currently bent over a trashcan re-familiarizing himself with his lunch. "Can't imagine it gets any better if you're not."

Jimmy contemplated King as well. He looked absolutely miserable, yet somehow incredibly happy. "Have you ever thrown up after a race before?" He asked.

"Yeah, a few times. Including a couple weeks ago actually. Coach had me do the 4x4 and then-boom. Everywhere." He crinkled his nose.

"What was it like?"

"It was mostly water-but also some eggs. I don't think I should have had those-"

"No, gross," Jimmy said, shaking his head in disgust, "I mean what did it *feel* like?"

"I don't know. It just felt like puking. Haven't you ever puked before?"

"Yeah, but never from a race."

"Trust me, you aren't missing much," Matt leaned back in his position on the stands.

"You don't think it's, like, an effort thing?" Jimmy replied, much less at ease than his compatriot, "Like I haven't been pushing myself enough?"

"I wouldn't read too much into it. I think it's just a tolerance thing. Some people are naturally more prone to it than others." A group of sprinters were now organizing their starting blocks on the track. "Now can we please stop talking about vomit? I'm getting grossed out."

"Sure," Jimmy nodded, not completely reassured, but willing to move on. "What would you prefer?"

"So yesterday, I was in the bathroom, right? And I had just been to Chipotle-"

"You're the worst."

Ben Havleck, cont.

"*You're kidding, right? That's not actually what you said ...*"

"I mean, it was a really big upset. I just got a little excited. I think that's perfectly natural."

"*Yes, it is perfectly natural to get a little excited in that situation. But sounds like you may have went about it the wrong way.*"

Ben smirked. "Honestly, I don't think she was really my type. She's too tall."

"*Have you ever thought maybe you might be too short?*

He rolled his eyes. Although his friend could not see it, he hoped his tone implied it. "Well regardless, it doesn't matter. She wasn't the right girl for me anyway."

"*Whatever you say, champ,*" Neal's voice reverberated in his ear. "*So what time am I picking you up?*"

Ben checked down at his watch. It was almost five o'clock. After an exhausting day, he was riding the bus back from the PAL Track and Field State Championships at Shippensburg University to his adopted hometown of Bloomsburg. Speaking with him on the phone was Neal Simons, his coworker and friend from the local Barnes and Noble bookstore. Since Neal lived just around the corner from the station, he had offered to pick Ben up once the bus arrived.

"Probably another hour or so before I'm there," Ben estimated, "I can text you when I start to recognize some landmarks, but for now just pencil me in for about 6 o'clock."

"*Alright sweet. Did you want to grab dinner afterwards? Bryn and Jared invited us out with them.*"

"Maybe. I have to check something on my email first."

"*Can't you just do that on your phone right now?*"

"No. I've still got a dumb phone, remember?"

"*Oh, right. Well, what is it you have to check? I can do it for you right now if you want.*"

"It's this application thing," Ben hesitated for a brief second, but then decided he was comfortable enough with Neal to share. "I applied to this internship program at Georgetown and I just want to make sure all my references went through."

"*Yo, that's awesome! I didn't know you were applying for one of those.*"

"Yeah, my friend Nicole told me about it actually. During our last study session."

"*Ah yes, I remember your 'friend' Nicole,*" Neal replied playfully.

"What-we *are* just friends."

"*Sure. And I guess I'm 'just friends' with Gal Gadot.*"

"You don't even know Gal Gadot," Ben answered frustrated.

"*When's the next time you're seeing her?*" Neal continued, ignoring his comment.

"I don't know, hopefully sometime next week. We've got to start getting ready for finals."

"*Well, you better make sure you look at all those track results tonight then-*"

"-Good bye, Neal-"

"*Gotta get all that excitement out of your system if you know what I-*" And his voice abruptly disappeared as Ben ended the call.

Mark Miller, May 28th 2016

"Mark, are you coming back home with us?"

"Yeah, one sec," Mark waved goodbye to his family before darting back over to join his friends. The state meet had reached its conclusion, thus officially closing the last athletics season of his sophomore year. Feeling wistful, he climbed into the backseat of the car, as Tom strapped in up front and prepared to drive.

"Well that's it. Another season in the books," Ian remarked. Apparently sharing his sentiment, he looked out at the nearly empty Shippensburg track stadium. Only a few minutes earlier it been packed edge to edge with spectators. "You think we'll ever be good enough to run here?"

"Maybe," Mark said, turning his head forward as the car began its drive, "But I think we have a better chance of making it for cross country at Hershey. We should have a solid team next year."

"Yes! I was just saying the same thing!" Ian exclaimed, hitting Tom in the arm, "Right?"

"Yeah, he was bragging to Jimmy Springer about it." He replied nonchalantly while gingerly rubbing his right arm.

"I wasn't *bragging* to him about it," Ian replied, "Plus, he wished me good luck which was pretty cool-"

"Wait-you were being serious?" Mark asked in amazement, "You guys *actually* met Jimmy Springer? When?"

"Yeah, we didn't tell you?" Tom said, his voice rising now with his own enthusiasm. "We met him in the bathroom."

"How'd it go?"

"Um, it sounded like everything came out fine. He was just peeing-"

"No-not that. Never that. I meant what was he like?"

"Oh, right. Well, he seemed like a pretty normal guy," Tom replied. Now stopped at a red light, he turned around to look at Mark. "I feel like he was super locked in, you know? Very focused. Probably one of those kind of runners."

"But he wasn't a jerk or anything? I've heard he's pretty cocky."

"No, he was nice enough. Maybe confident though. I could see him getting upset if someone tried to step to him or something."

"Oh my God! We barely even talked to him!" Ian interjected loudly. "He's just a fast runner-he's not some celebrity. You guys really need to scale it back."

"Ian … you got a selfie with him."

"Touché."

After a brief spot of traffic, Tom had navigated them back onto the highway with open roads in front of them.

"Anyway," Ian continued, "let's get back to this cross country thing. How good do you think our team could be next year? I mean we've got

Jayson, the Reilly Twins, Pasterano and Delaney all coming back. We lose Hilton and Garraway, but I bet most teams lose a lot more."

"What's Cumberland Valley bringing back?" Tom asked, carefully switching lanes, "That Hartzel kid was a junior right?"

"Yeah, and he's pretty good. He was top 25 last year." Mark responded, "They've also got that kid in our grade. I think his name is Rich something."

"Rich Brown," Ian said venomously. "Hate that kid. He got one of the last spots into districts this year for the two mile."

"So Cumby will still be good, but that's to be expected. Who are the other good schools?"

"I couldn't even begin to tell you," Mark said, shaking his head, "Coatesville I assume? You saw them in the 4x8 today, they were absurd."

"That Kyle King dude is a baller. I hate him, but he's a baller."

"You hate everyone, Ian."

Mark laughed as he took out his phone. "I'll look up last year's state results on VaniaRunning and we can use that as a barometer."

"Ooo good idea," Ian said, unhooking his seat belt and climbing into the back of the car to sit alongside him.

"Seriously?" Tom asked exasperatedly as he watched his friend in the rearview mirror, "Can you at least put your seatbelt back on once you're back there?"

"I'll be fine. You drive too slowly for me to be in any real danger in this thing." He caught sight of Tom's angry glare in the mirror and hastily pulled down the strap. "Ok, there-it's on. Happy?" He shuffled closer to his friend and leaned down to look at the screen. "Now Mark, let's see these results."

"Out of the top three teams from last year," Mark read aloud so that Tom could hear, "Coatesville returns three out of seven-"

"Woah, King is a junior?!" Ian interjected in surprise, "Damn, was hoping he'd be graduating."

"Bonner returns two out of seven," Mark continued unperturbed, "And Horsham brings back three as well."

"But none of those schools had more than two scoring underclassmen. We've got our whole top five back."

"True," Mark scrolled a little further down the page, "Cumberland Valley has four back and then, this team from out near Pittsburgh, North Allegheny, has five. On paper, those two schools are the biggest competition."

"Well, we beat North Albany last year-"

"-North Allegheny-"

"Whatever their name is, it doesn't matter. I'm not afraid of them. Honestly, I think we're the favorites to win states next year." As Ian finished his thought, a hush fell over all of them, the gravity and scope of this realization hitting them. "Us and my good friend Jimmy Springer."

Jimmy Springer, cont.

"Take care of yourself this summer, alright?" Matt patted him gently on the shoulder.

"No guarantees," Jimmy replied with a smile. The final race of the championships, the 4x400 meter relay, had just concluded meaning it was time for the two former teammates to depart in separate directions.

"I'll be back home again in August," Matt said, starting to walk backwards toward the parking lot, "Make sure you save me a night, ok? I may have something big to show you."

"If this is another Chipotle joke, I swear I'll punch you in the stomach."

"Oh, it's much better than that," Matt winked, "You'll have to stay tuned." He turned his back on Jimmy and threw up his hand. "Until next time, superstar."

"Until next time." Jimmy stood and watched his friend disappear among the departing spectators. Then, with a small sigh, he removed the bag from his back and unzipped it, diving in to retrieve his car keys. As he searched, he came across his phone, complete with its freshly cracked screen. He pulled it out and held it carefully in the palm of his hand, trying to assess the damage. He tapped the home screen and was pleased to see he could still read the letters on its surface.

Looking through, he saw he had a few unopened text messages and missed calls, which he assumed had all come from Matt while the two were trying to find one another. He cycled through the notifications, looking to clear the red dot that signaled a missed call. *Matt Burke ... Matt Burke ...* He stopped *Dad?*

Due to an important client presentation, Jimmy had not been expecting his father to get off work until into the night and yet he had a missed a call from him at 11 o'clock in the morning. Slightly concerned, Jimmy scrolled to his father's name in his contacts and pressed call.

"*Hey Jim-bo,*" Mr. Springer's voice floated happily through the speaker, "*How'd the race go?*"

"It was fine," Jimmy said hurriedly, "Dad-what's going on? Why aren't you at work?" To his surprise, his father laughed at his son's anxiety.

"*Goodness, this is how work obsessed I've been, huh? You're nervous when I'm not working all day.*" He sighed deeply, not much differently than his son's bemoaning from a few moments earlier. "*Everything is fine, Jimmy. Or at least, going forward it will be ... I quit my job.*"

"What?!"

"*Sitting there miserable, stuck at work, knowing I was missing my son compete for a state championship ... I just thought-why? And I realized I didn't have an answer.*"

Jimmy stood in surprise, the gentle buzz of white noise in his ear. "So ... what will you do?"

"*I'm not sure. It's a little nerve-wracking. But all that matters is that next fall, when you're running at Hershey for your last cross country meet, I will be there.*"

Jimmy felt his eyes beginning to burn. A single tear shined down his cheek. But unlike so many droplets before it, this was not shed out of sadness. With a smile, he replied excitedly, "I'll make sure it's a good one."

Chapter Twenty Three

In a relatively quiet office, a man sat at his desk, clicking around on his computer. He had an excel spreadsheet open on his desktop. Casually, he flipped through the tabs, nonchalantly checking the charts and numbers that flashed across his screen. He seemed fairly disinterested in his task, almost as if his mind was in another place. Then, as if in response to his boredom, a gentle knock sounded from just outside the office door.

"Come in," The man called, his eyes drifting from the document to watch the entranceway. A short, stocky man with a buzzed hair cut had appeared in place of the door. "Ah, Albert! Please, take a seat."

The man named Albert walked forward and sat in the open chair in front of the desk. He winced slightly as he lowered himself down, his bones and muscles creaking. Reminders of his past sacrifices to the sport of distance running. He sat patient and stoic while the man opposite him fidgeted behind his computer. If he was waiting for Albert to speak first, it was clear he would be waiting awhile. Eventually, he surrendered to this reality.

"So, what did you think of the results today?" He asked excitedly. "The boys looked very strong. You've done an excellent job with them."

"Thank you, Phil," Albert replied softly. He titled his head slightly to show his appreciation. "It was not a perfect day; but, ultimately, I suppose the results were sufficient."

"Are you kidding?" The man replied astonished, "That was utter domination. Multiple state golds and a runaway team victory? What more could you have wanted?"

"The 3200," The Coach responded, "Rosato could have taken that race. We played it incorrectly." His gentle, flat tone was consistent but for a nearly imperceptible twinge of sourness. "Next time we will be ready for Springer."

"Didn't you hear?" Phil typed quickly at his computer, bringing up an article from VaniaRunning. "Springer says he's taking off this fall." He turned the screen to face his comrade. "Says he's done for a while."

The ends of Albert's mouth twitched slightly. Phil guessed it was the coach's best attempt at a smile. "He will be back-I can promise you that."

They sat wordlessly, the man behind the desk tapping impatiently on his desk as if waiting for an elaboration. Again, he found himself in a losing battle. "Why do you say that?"

"He has nowhere else to go," He said simply. Again the length of the answer was unsatisfactory. Unfortunately, over the past year, Phil had found this was all too often the case. *Well, it's a small price to pay for the results he's produced*, he thought to himself.

"So where is the trophy?" He got to his feet and stepped away from the computer. "I have a display case in the new wing that's prepared specifically for it."

"It's at the school."

"The school?" Phil said disgustedly. His eyes flashed angrily. "That *school* would have gladly eliminated the track team years ago if it wasn't for me! Coatesville was nothing before I came along. *Nothing*. Now look at it. State Champions in Cross Country. State Champions in Track. Not only that, but since I moved the *Ares* headquarters into town, the local economy has been booming. Real estate prices are at record highs. I *made* this district." He slammed his fist on his disk. "That award should be in my trophy case."

Albert sat unflinchingly in his seat, apparently unmoved by this impassioned speech. "Pennsylvania sports within the PAL will always be tied to the high school," he said, picking lazily at his right index finger, "But national competitions-those are technically registered by club teams. If you really want a trophy, you'll need a national championship. Not a state one."

Phil stopped his pacing behind the desk, intrigued by this development. "How far away are we from winning nationals?" He asked hungrily.

"It's not impossible, but we do get hit hard by graduation this year. Another guy or two would really help."

"Alright," The pacing recommenced. "There are a few ways that can be arranged. Private school transfers, exchange students … I'll start researching." He sat back down. "In the meantime, I'd like to see the updated training metrics for the end of May-particularly for Kyle King."

"Not a problem," Albert said, preparing to get to his feet. As he reached his full height, another knock came at the door. A younger looking man stood nervously in the entranceway. His face looked slightly sweaty, his expression uncertain.

"Um-Mr. Solinsky? We have some interesting news we thought you should know about."

"Can this wait until Tuesday, Craig?" Phil replied, now reengaged in his computer monitor, "Coach Solares and I are just finishing up our meeting."

"Well, that's sort of why I'm here, sir," Craig said, nervously tugging at his collar, "We just received a job application for our open data analytics department. Georgetown graduate, Class of 1998."

"What the hell does that have to do with anything?"

"The applicant's name was James Springer."

The *Ares* CEO snapped his head away from his desktop and looked excitedly at his head cross country coach. "Albert … I may be able to get you another guy."

Made in the USA
Middletown, DE
08 July 2018